Things Jolie needs to do Before she Bites it

Things Jolie needs to do Before she Bites it

Kerry Winfrey

Feiwel and Friends
New York

A FEIWEL AND FRIENDS BOOK
An imprint of Macmillan Publishing Group, LLC
175 Fifth Avenue, New York, NY 10010

Our books may be purchased in bulk for promotional, educational, or business use.
Please contact your local bookseller or the Macmillan Corporate and
Premium Sales Department at (800) 221-7945 ext. 5442 or by e-mail
at MacmillanSpecialMarkets@macmillan.com.

Library of Congress Cataloging-in-Publication Data is available.

ISBN 978-1-250-11954-4 (hardcover) / ISBN 978-1-250-11955-1 (ebook)

Book design by April Ward

Feiwel and Friends logo designed by Filomena Tuosto

First edition, 2018

1 3 5 7 9 10 8 6 4 2

fiercereads.com

To Hollis and Harry, my favorite guys

Things Jolie needs to do Before she Bites it

Chapter One

$\mathcal{S}$ ometimes I think my parents named me Jolie as a joke. It means "pretty" in French, although that's not why they chose it—I'm named after some long-dead great-aunt. But they had to know as soon as I exited my mom's birth canal, when I was still all purple and covered in amniotic fluid, that Jolie Peterson was not going to be pretty. *Très* not *jolie*, if you will.

I'm a lot of things—the smart one. The reliable one. The one who can binge-watch an entire season of any drama on Netflix, no problem. But the pretty one? Well, that's never been me. My older sister, Abbi, has always worn that crown—and also the prom queen sash and the Miss Brentley tiara. On the mantel in our living room there's a framed photo of her smiling on the football field as she's being crowned at the homecoming game, showing off her perfectly white, straight teeth that never even needed braces, let alone braces and a palate expander and a retainer and surgery and *more* braces.

Abbi's looks have been cooed over and awarded forever; people simply avoid mentioning mine. I mean, no one insults me. No one says, *Whoa, get a look at the jaw on that one!* But when our relatives tell Abbi how lovely she is, they inevitably pause when they get to me, then ask vague questions about where I'm going to college.

I know I'm not hideous. I don't terrify children, and dogs don't bark at me. No one's forcing me to live in the Notre-Dame Cathedral.

But I do have mandibular prognathism, which in non-oral-surgeon terms means I have an underbite—my lower jaw sticks out farther than my upper jaw. My teeth only meet in one tiny spot, which makes chewing difficult and means eating takes forever. I get headaches all the time, especially if I chew gum or talk too much. And it means that the oral surgeon's office is my home away from home, if "home" is a place where someone constantly takes pictures of you in profile and then measures the distance between your upper and lower jaws.

But what matters to me most right now is that my underbite makes my chin stick out past the rest of my face, it makes my smile look weird, and it makes my face look awkward. It makes me anything but *jolie*.

But on June 2, two weeks after junior year ends and the day after my seventeenth birthday, I'm getting fixed. I'm having surgery to move my unruly jaw into place, and after a summer spent letting the swelling go down, it'll all be over. Goodbye, jaw pain. Goodbye, being the last person at the table to finish every meal because it takes me forever to chew. Goodbye, headaches.

Then I'll be normal. I'll be like Abbi.

I'll be pretty.

I've known I need surgery for years. Ever since my dentist recommended that I see Dr. Kelley, it's been pretty clear that my problems aren't exactly of the "totally fixed with one round of braces" variety. Dr. Kelley started me on a years-long plan that involved multiple rounds of braces and the dreaded palate expander. Seriously, a device that a doctor puts in the roof of your mouth and then slowly expands? It sounds like a medieval torture device, but it's just something I had to have because my upper jaw was narrower than my lower jaw.

And then, of course, comes the surgery. My parents never pushed it; they were clear about it ultimately being my decision. But Dr. Kelley was honest about what would happen if I didn't get the surgery. My jaws being "misaligned," as she put it, basically means that my teeth rub against each other and years of that could lead to all sorts of complications. Plus, it turns out it's kinda stressful on your joints when things are constantly out of alignment. I already have a hard time biting into food, and that would only get worse. Plus, I would have to deal with way more jaw pain as I got older, and possibly even problems speaking if my jaw continued to shift and grow. And when she put it like that . . . well, who's like, *Oh, sure, a lifetime of pain and difficulty eating? Sign me up.*

But I can't lie; the bonus effect it will have on my appearance, the normal silhouette I'll have, the smile with my teeth lined up exactly where they're supposed to be . . . that's what I think about most of all.

Of course, when we first started talking about surgery I was barely a teenager—it was easy to say yes to something that seemed like a lifetime away. Now that I'm almost seventeen, it's starting to hit me that this is really going to happen. Dr. Kelley is going to break my jaw, move it into place, and put in metal screws to keep it where it's supposed to be. When I think about it too much, I get a little woozy and wonder what made me think this was a good idea. That's when I reread the list in the back of my journal:

THINGS TO DO AFTER MY SURGERY

1. EAT AN APPLE WITHOUT CUTTING IT UP FIRST.
2. KISS A GUY.
3. WEAR GLOW-IN-THE-DARK VAMPIRE TEETH.
4. SMILE.

Eating a piece of fruit might seem like no big thing to most people, but when your teeth don't meet in the front, biting into an apple is pretty much impossible. If I were ever in an emergency bobbing-for-apples situation, I would be screwed.

As for the second item on the list: I, in news that will shock absolutely no one, have never been kissed (unless you count a playground kiss, which I emphatically do not). The only boy I even talk to on a regular basis is Derek, and we've known each other since we were in kindergarten. I still see him as the awkward, bony-kneed kid I grew up with who used to burp the alphabet, even though now he rarely burps in front of me, and Abbi swears he got "way hot" over the past year and now looks "all sophisticated and suave like he's James Bond or something." I told Abbi that doesn't even make sense because we still live in a world that's incapable of having a black James Bond even though Idris Elba and David Oyelowo are *right there*, but she told me that wasn't the point.

But *my* point is that dudes aren't exactly lining up around the block to kiss me.

As for number three, those glow-in-the dark vampire teeth . . . they just aren't made for people with underbites. Every Halloween I stare at them longingly, thinking of the Dracula costume that can never be.

And fourth? Smile. I mean, I smile now, but I never smile without thinking about how my teeth look. I'm always conscious of who's seeing me in profile and wondering why my face looks so weird. It's like I'm always looking at myself from the outside, always imagining how other people see me, always looking at myself through the lens of judgment. I smile with no teeth so no one will see the gap between my lower and upper jaws. I keep my lips slightly parted to make the place where my teeth don't quite meet less obvious. And if I can't avoid being photographed, I'll do whatever I can to make sure it's not from the side.

Since I know my face will never be perfect (not until after my surgery, anyway), I have to compensate. I keep my hair in a wavy bob, making sure my bangs are always straightened and sprayed into submission. I've perfected my eyeliner, even though it took me, like, three weeks and no fewer than five YouTube video tutorials to get it right. I use a sheer pink lip gloss, one that makes my lips look nice without drawing too much attention to my mouth. And I always wear clothes that are cute but not flashy—I need to be trendy enough to keep up, but not so much that I stand out. If H&M had a section called "Dresses to Help You Blend in and Make Sure Eyes Pass Right Over You," I would buy all my clothes there. As it is, I wear a lot of neutrals, no wacky patterns, and definitely no bold colors.

I hope that by making sure every other part of me looks good, people won't notice my face. If I can keep everything else perfect, maybe my jaw won't matter. I'll never be one of those girls who can wear a T-shirt, running shorts, and a ponytail and make it look cute and effortless. Evelyn, Derek, and my family are the only ones who ever see me in sweatpants.

It's exhausting, constantly feeling like you're on display. Trying to be as small as possible. Trying to make yourself invisible.

But after my surgery, I won't have to worry about that. I'll be able to wear bright colors or pick out a bold lipstick. When my teeth meet in the front and I have a normal profile, no one will be able to get me to stop smiling—and by then, I'll have a lot to smile about.

The most important thing to know about my sister, Abbi, other than the whole "she rolls out of bed looking like a beauty queen" thing, is that she's pregnant.

We were all surprised when Abbi came home one day to tell us that she was two months along. She's in her second year at a nearby community college, but she still lives at home, so we see her all the time. And she's never, ever brought a guy home, not since her senior year high school homecoming date, Anthony, who was definitely gay and definitely not going to impregnate her. I just assumed she didn't think any of the men of Brentley were worthy of her, which is probably true.

She told us at dinner one night like it was no big deal. "Pass the broccoli, and by the way, I'm pregnant." My dad contorted his brows in confusion, but that's the look he wears ninety percent of the time; honestly, he looked so shocked that I was a little worried I would have to explain to him how babies are made. A look of wide-eyed surprise passed over my mom's face, but soon her calm demeanor was back, like the sun popping out from behind a momentary cloud. She's never really been a yelling-and-pointing-fingers type of mom, so it wasn't that weird that she immediately switched into "get shit done" mode and started planning out where the baby would sleep and how she'd be able to babysit and basically making plans for its first eighteen years. She was just being her usual "I accept your choices" school counselor self.

With Mom taking care of the conversation, I didn't have a chance to say anything, even though I had one million questions. Questions like, *Are you serious?* and *How could this happen to you?* and *Who's the father?*

Now it's April and Abbi is a little over two months away from pushing out her baby (and pooping on the delivery table, from what I saw in a birth documentary on Netflix). She spends most of her time waddling into the living room, waddling into the kitchen, and studying with her books propped up on her gigantic belly. Oh, and watching television with my mom.

They're obsessed with what I call Worst-Case Scenario TV. Their favorite thing to do is to park themselves on the sofa and turn on any true-life show about murder, catastrophe, or disease. A *Dateline* episode about a bunch of missing or murdered prostitutes? They're into it. A special report about a woman who was terrorized by her stalker because the police wouldn't intervene? They've watched it twice. An episode of *Sex Sent Me to the ER* about a man who broke his penis? Unfortunately, they've seen that one, and so have I. It was traumatic, and I wish I still lived in the state of blissful ignorance I had before I learned that genitals are capable of breaking. It all used to stress me out, but I've become used to it at this point.

Tonight, they're glued in front of an episode of some show about medical mishaps.

"I just can't believe this," Abbi whispers, lying on the couch and shoveling another barbecue potato chip into her mouth. "Can you imagine a doctor leaving a pair of scissors inside of you?"

My mom shakes her head. "What a nightmare."

"Did you see that episode of *Grey's Anatomy*?" Abbi asks. "The one where a surgeon left a towel inside someone? Imagine! Living with a towel inside of you and not even knowing it!"

Dad walks by, holding a book. "Going to bed," he says, and each of us turns up a cheek for a quick kiss. My dad has zero interest in Worst-Case Scenario TV. Besides teaching shop class at a neighboring high school, his main interests are (a) watching TV shows and movies that have happy endings and zero botched surgeries, (b) building furniture in the garage, (c) cooking, and (d) being confused by pretty much everything the women in this house do. But a few years ago he finally got strong enough to stay in the room whenever one of us mentions the word "tampon," so I have hope for his future.

Once he's upstairs, the show switches its focus to a doctor who was supposed to amputate a patient's right leg and instead amputated the left.

"I woke up and thought, 'Wait, this can't be true . . . ,'" the woman on the television says.

"I'm never going to a hospital," Abbi says with a full mouth.

"Aren't you having a baby in two months?" I ask.

"Shut up," Abbi says, waving me off. "It's just that hospitals are scary, you know? You go in for some basic surgery and the next thing you know, you're dead."

She shrugs and goes back to the woman who lost the wrong

leg, but her words bounce around in my mind. *You go in for some basic surgery and the next thing you know, you're dead.*

Because, hello, I'm going in for not-all-that-basic surgery soon. I mean, a doctor will be breaking my jaw and moving it into place.

What if the surgeon leaves scissors inside my body? What if she gets the wrong instructions and amputates my leg? What if I end up with a towel inside my body and I don't even know it? What if I *die*?

"Oh my God," I mutter.

"I know," my mom says, nodding along as a man on TV talks about waking up in the middle of surgery.

I jump out of the recliner and walk into the kitchen, where I send a quick text to Derek and Evelyn. Derek is my forever best friend, but the best friend I actually talk to the most is Evelyn. I can't have *one* best friend any more than I can have one favorite TV show or one favorite flavor of ice cream.

SOS. Emergency meeting needed ASAP.

Evelyn responds immediately. *Applebee's?*

Of course, I type. And then, *Derek, if you aren't there, I'll never speak to you again.*

I was talking to my mom, chill, Derek responds after a long twenty seconds. He's not a big texter, so he doesn't place nearly enough importance on a quick response time. *I'll be there.*

I grab my keys off the hook by the door and call out, "I'm going to Applebee's. I'll be back soon!"

I look into the living room to see Mom raise her hand in a wave, not taking her eyes off the television. Mom pretty much gives me free rein to go where I want because she's "trying to foster independence" and "letting me find my own consequences," but secretly I think it's because she knows I'm such a dork that I'm never really going to get in trouble.

So why do Evelyn, Derek, and I hang out at a chain restaurant instead of, like, some hip bar that doesn't card?

(a) There *are* no hip bars in Brentley, just the American Legion and this place called Happy Endings where middle-aged people hang out.

(b) Derek doesn't drink because he's never broken a rule in his life, and Evelyn says she's only going to drink when she's old enough to afford the good stuff.

(c) Appetizers are half off after eight p.m., duh. Have you even had those Chicken Wonton Tacos?

When I get there, Evelyn and Derek are already sitting at a booth in the corner, talking earnestly about something. Derek is wearing his usual uniform of a red hoodie and jeans, twirling a fork in his hands while he talks. Evelyn has her messy dyed-gray curls shoved into a bun on the top of her head and is patiently listening to Derek. Wearing her purple cat-eye glasses, she manages to be the most glamorous person in this Applebee's. Which isn't exactly some huge feat, but still. Evelyn has major plans to become a fashion designer, a dream she got when she had a hard time finding stylish plus-size clothing she actually wanted to wear. So now she makes all her own clothing and always looks amazing.

She immediately stops talking to Derek when she sees me and slams her hands down on the table so hard that the water glasses shake. "What is it? Tell me now!"

I slide into the booth, appreciating that Evelyn has never been able to stand a secret.

"This had better be important. I was in the middle of recording," Derek says. He has a podcast called *Deep Dive* that he records in his bedroom closet (where he swears the sound is better, or at least it's quieter because his twin seven-year-old brothers can't find him in there). Whenever he has a break from his one million extracurriculars, he records an episode about something that he's obsessed with, and since Derek is interested in basically everything, this has included topics from Charles Manson's music career, to the early films of David Lynch, to moon-landing conspiracy theories. Unsurprisingly, this helps him pretty much kill it on the Brentley Academic Challenge team. I don't think anyone at our school listens to *Deep Dive* other than me (even Evelyn can't handle it; she says she's not going to listen to Derek's nerd rants in her free time), but he has a surprisingly big following in Denmark.

"What's your next episode about?" I ask.

"Landfills," he says. "Did you know there are over twenty billion disposable diapers dumped in landfills every year?"

I wrinkle my nose in disgust as Evelyn sighs.

"I can't believe I have to say this to you two, but can we please not talk about diapers at a time like this? Jolie, what's your emergency?"

I turn to face her. "I'm dying."

Derek drops the fork and it clatters to the table.

"Ohmigod!" Evelyn says. "Are you sick? Do you have black lung?"

"Why would I have black lung?" I ask. "Isn't that something coal miners get?"

"We learned about it in history class last week and it's been stuck in my head."

"So you failed your last pop quiz but you *do* remember what black lung is?" I ask.

She shrugs. "Diseases are easier to remember than dates and names."

"Coal mining," Derek says, his fork back in his hand as he fidgets. "That would be a good topic for *Deep Dive*."

"Do they have coal mining in Denmark?" I ask.

"The people of Denmark aren't my only listeners," he counters.

"Right." I smile. "There's me. And your mom."

Evelyn snaps her fingers. "Uh, hello? Are you just going to drop that you're dying and then not finish the thought?"

Derek grabs my hands and inspects my fingernails. "No coal dust. I think you're good."

I pull my hands out of his. This isn't going like I'd planned. "I'm not dying, like, right now. But I could die. In the hospital."

Evelyn and Derek stare at me in silence for a minute. Then Derek says, "Have you been watching Worst-Case Scenario Television again?"

I squirm a little bit. "Yes, but . . ."

Derek gives me a serious look, then firmly says, "You're not dying. Evie, tell her she's not dying."

She reaches up to adjust her glasses. "It's not like you're *certainly* going to die. But . . . well, it could happen. Sometimes people go under anesthesia and never wake up."

"See!" I point triumphantly to Evelyn.

"My uncle had to have jaw surgery when he got hit in the face during a softball game," Derek says. "And all that happened was that part of his bottom lip went a little numb. Literally the worst thing about it is that sometimes when he's eating dinner he doesn't realize that a piece of corn is stuck to his mouth until we laugh at him."

I throw up my hands. "So you think I should be totally chill about facing a life of having unnoticed corn stuck to my face?"

"All I'm saying is that you're not going to die in surgery."

I turn to Evelyn. "You know my 'Things to Do After Surgery' list?"

She nods encouragingly. "Vampire teeth, apple eating. Yes, I know it."

"Well," I say, "I need to make another list. 'Things to Do Before My Surgery.' You know, in case I die on the operating table."

Evelyn leans forward. "What's on your list?"

"I'm going to the bathroom," Derek says, sliding out of the booth before heading toward the back of the restaurant.

"I don't know yet," I tell Evie.

Evelyn leans back. "Just think about what you would regret not doing if you died."

"I guess . . . I want to finish *Jane Eyre*."

Evelyn notes this in her phone. She has a list for everything ("Things I Need to Do This Afternoon," "Films I Need to Watch Before I Turn Twenty"), and I know she's just started another one: "Things Jolie Needs to Do Before She Bites It (Which Is Super Unlikely, but Still, It Could Happen)."

"Let me get this straight," Evelyn says. "You have two months left on this Earth, and you're going to spend it reading? I mean, no offense to whatever Brontë wrote that, but . . ."

Evelyn doesn't understand because she's never been a huge fiction reader. Her shelves are filled with, like, weird German art books and other stuff she uses for inspiration. She says she doesn't see the point in reading a book that's been around for hundreds of years when she could be making something new . . . which

I guess is a good point, but I *like* those books that have been around for hundreds of years.

"I wish I had time to read the entire literary canon, but I don't," I say. "So I'm going to focus on *Jane Eyre*. I don't want to end up in the afterlife wondering if she ever gets together with Mr. Rochester. Oh! Okay, I have another one. You know that cliff that hangs over Brentley River?"

"You mean the one with the sign that says 'No Jumping'?" Evelyn asks.

"Yeah, I want to jump off that. And," I say, ticking things off on my fingers as I really get rolling, "I want to eat every appetizer on the menu at Applebee's. We always get the Chicken Wonton Tacos and mozzarella sticks, but now that I'm staring death in the face, maybe we should branch out, you know? And I want to go to a real bar. And . . ."

I trail off as I think about my list of things to do after my surgery. Sure, I'm looking forward to biting into an apple, but what I'm really concerned about is kissing a guy. What if I die before I get the chance? Maybe I need to bump that one up, just to make sure I don't turn into a sad ghost who can't move on to the afterlife because she keeps floating around haunting cute boys she never had the chance to kiss.

"And I want to kiss Noah Reed," I say, folding my hands in front of me on the table.

Evelyn's eyes widen as she types in what I said. "Damn, girl. Aiming high. On that last one, anyway. The first one should be easy to accomplish."

Derek sits down again, and we fill him in on the list we've just compiled.

"You know there are literally two bars in Brentley, right? And we're sixteen?" Derek asks.

"And I might never get the chance to turn twenty-one!" I practically shout. A drunk dude at the bar sits up, scowls at me, and slumps over the bar again.

"You're not going to die," Evelyn and Derek say at the same time.

"And Noah Reed?" Derek asks. "Really?"

"Do you have something against Noah Reed?" I bristle.

Derek shrugs. "I just don't see what the big deal is. You could choose to kiss any dude in school and that's who you pick?"

Okay, well, I can't really choose *any* guy to kiss, and finding a way to kiss Noah Reed is going to be a challenge, but whatever. I'm not going to argue that point right now. It's not like Derek would even understand that Noah Reed's hair is so fluffy and perfect that it's basically sonnet worthy.

"I get that you guys don't understand why I want to become more literate or kiss someone before my surgery," I say. "But this isn't your list. If it were, it would include, like, competing on *Project Runway*—"

"Please." Evelyn sniffs. "I would blow them all out of the water."

"Or getting syndicated on NPR—"

"No thanks," Derek says. "Independent media is the future."

"Whatever!" I shout. "That's not the point! The point is that I want to do these things. I could die, and if I do, I want to be more well-read, and to have kissed somebody, and to at least know what the inside of a bar looks like. Even if it is Happy Endings. And even if I have to sneak in the back door or get a fake ID."

"My cousin could help you with that," Evelyn says, just as Derek says, "That's super illegal."

Evelyn puts her phone down as a waitress lays two plates on our table.

"Chicken Wonton Tacos and fried mozzarella sticks," she announces before walking away.

"Here's to branching out—next time," Evelyn says, toasting me with a mozzarella stick.

Chapter Two

After about another half hour of talking about my list, Derek's phone buzzes.

"It's Melody," he says, meaning his girlfriend, whom neither Evelyn nor I have met. "I'm telling her we're wrapping this up so I can call her when I get home."

"All right," I say, even though I would gladly hang out until we shut down this Applebee's. "Let's roll. I wouldn't want to keep Melody waiting."

I try not to let sarcasm seep into my voice, but there it is anyway. It's not that I don't like Melody—I mean, I don't even know her—but it's just annoying that we have to cut our hangout short so she and Derek can, like, make kissy noises at each other on the phone. Or whatever it is that people in relationships do.

Derek doesn't seem to notice my annoyance, though. He's busily, if begrudgingly, tapping out a message.

In the parking lot, we say our goodbyes as Derek gets into

his rusted-out truck. After we watch him drive away, Evelyn turns to me and asks, "Do you think Melody is real?"

I choke out a laugh. "What?"

She puts her hands out. "I don't know, think about it! We've never met her. She lives in North Dakota, a place Derek has never been. And he brings her up when he wants to get out of things or go home. It all just seems too convenient."

I fix her with a skeptical stare. "He met her at an Academic Challenge meet last year. You know that. And he's a terrible liar. Also, what motivation would he have for making up a girlfriend?"

She shrugs. "I don't know. So he could spend more time alone without people bothering him about it?"

"That *does* sound like Derek," I say. "I'm still pretty sure Melody's real. But he didn't seem to be in a very good mood when he left, did he?"

"Uh, no shit, Jolie," Evelyn says. "No offense, but you don't exactly have to be Benedict Cumberbatch to figure out why our conversation bothered him."

"That's an actor *playing* a detective, but sure," I say. "What are you talking about?"

She widens her eyes and gives me a pitying look. "His *dad*, Jolie. It's been four years today, and you just spent an entire evening talking about your possible upcoming death."

"Oh, shit," I say.

Derek's dad died four years ago, when we were twelve and the twins were only three. He was a surgeon, just like Derek's mom, and he had a heart attack when he was at work—sudden, unexpected. They said he was dead before he hit the floor, which I think was supposed to be comforting but really wasn't. It would've been more comforting if he were still alive.

No one was one hundred percent sure what had caused Dr. Jones to have a heart attack in his forties. It could've been his high-stress job. It could've been genetics. It could've been his love for eating huge steaks every Sunday, which he said he deserved because "a life without red meat isn't worth living."

Or it could've just been plain old shitty luck.

But in the end, it didn't really matter what caused his heart attack, because figuring it out wasn't going to bring him back.

The funeral remains the one and only time I've ever seen Derek cry. Evelyn and I went with my parents, both of us dressed in whatever black clothing we could scrounge together from our twelve-year-olds' wardrobes. Seeing Derek there felt like a punch in the gut, like there was no air left in my lungs. His arms hung limp at his sides as he stared off into space. I still remember the awful music, a tinny version of "Amazing Grace" that Derek's dad would for sure have hated. Why couldn't they have played music he liked, like one of the records that was always spinning at Derek's house whenever I went over?

I couldn't help myself when we walked in and saw Derek standing there by the coffin—he just looked so small, staring off into space as his mom hugged some adults I didn't recognize. I ran to him and threw my arms around him and he sobbed into my neck. We didn't say anything. We just cried.

And the next day, when he came over, I guess I expected more of the same. Crying, hugging, maybe some talking about feelings this time.

But instead, when I opened the door, I found him there with Boggle. "Do you think Abbi wants to play with us?" he asked, because everyone knows basically all games kind of suck with just two people.

And then we played Boggle all afternoon, him finding words

like "fart" and "poop" and ignoring the fact that when he went home, his dad wouldn't be there.

That's how it's been for the past four years. There are times when it comes up, but we always move right past it, dancing around the topic with a joke or talking about something— anything—else. Mom says everyone deals with trauma differently, but I can't help but think that totally ignoring it is maybe not the best tactic.

But I guess I can't really make him handle his dad's death in a certain way. All I can do is be his friend.

I realize that bringing up my potential death considering Derek's relationship to the subject makes me sound like a monster. But in my defense, we literally never talk about it. Like, ever. If I didn't have such visceral memories of him letting me hug him at the funeral, I might forget it even happened.

But I know it did, and it was stupid of me to forget about it, especially on today of all days—the four-year anniversary of his death.

Dad made me promise not to text or talk on the phone while I'm driving, not even if I'm using the Bluetooth, because he's worried about me being distracted. So instead I call Derek the second I pull into the driveway and park my car behind Mom's Subaru.

"I'm sorry," I say as soon as he picks up.

"For what?" he asks. I can picture his bedroom perfectly: the crate of his dad's records in the corner, the ones that haven't been played in four years. His laptop set up on his desk so he can edit his latest episode. The airplane quilt that's been on his bed since we were kids, which should probably seem childish but actually just seems kind of sweet.

"For . . ." I trail off. I need to bring this up delicately, but I don't really know how to be delicate. Derek and I have a long history of not talking about this subject.

"For bringing up death," I say finally.

"It's okay," he says with studied ease.

"Because I wasn't even thinking about your dad when I—"

"Hey, have you ever heard about the world's loneliest whale?"

I pause for a second. "What?"

"There's this blue whale who's been making whale sounds for, like, twenty years, but his whale voice sounds so weird that no one else can understand him. So he's just wandering around the ocean, making sad whale sounds, looking for someone to love him."

"Huh," I say thoughtfully. "Not to turn this back to me, but I can relate."

"Jolie," he says, and I can hear the smile in his voice. "You aren't a lonely, sexless whale."

"Not in so many words."

"I'm gonna talk about this on an upcoming *Deep Dive*. Bonus: I'm learning so much about whales, I'm gonna kill it if there are any whale questions in the next Academic Challenge meet."

I can't help laughing. Only Derek would think knowing a bunch of random stuff about whales was in any way a bonus.

"Okay, but can you at least accept my apology before you go down a lonely whale rabbit hole and emerge knowing way too much about ambergris?"

"How do you know about ambergris?"

"You're not the only super-nerd who read *Moby-Dick* for extra credit last year, bro."

"Well, I accept your apology, even as I maintain that it was wholly unnecessary," he says. "And Jolie?"

"Yeah?" I ask, turning off the car.

"It's okay. Really. It was four years ago."

I run my tongue over my braces. "Yeah, I know, but . . ."

"I've gotta get back to editing, okay? Talk later."

"Yeah," I say, suppressing a sigh. "Talk later."

I hang up and lean back against the headrest. I know Derek's free to handle his own problems any way he wants to, but I can't help but feel like he's holding back. I know he says it's totally fine, but I'm still worried he's hurting, and it's among my official job duties as his best friend to help him deal with it.

So, okay, sure, I'm still afraid I'm going to die and I still have my list of things I need to do before surgery. But maybe from now on I won't refer to it as my death plan in front of Derek. From now on it's "Jolie Peterson's List of Things She Has to Do Before She Gets Surgery and Can't Tell If She Has Corn on Her Face Anymore."

When I go inside, Mom and Abbi have gone to bed. No doubt visions of serial killers and stalkers are dancing in their heads as they slumber.

I know I should feel lucky that I actually get along with my parents. My dad's worst crime is that he's kind of goofy, and I can't really complain about that. Likewise, my mom's always been more weird than irritating, even though all the television shows about high school tell me that I'm supposed to hate her and yell things like *"I'm not like you, Mom! And I never will be!"* before speeding off to make reckless and dramatic decisions.

But I don't hate her. Sometimes I'm like, "Seriously, why are you whistling Christmas carols even though it's nowhere near Christmas and everyone knows whistling is so annoying that it should be punishable by jail time?" but it's no big deal. Mostly I think of my parents as comforting, like an old but soft blanket or a plate of meat loaf and mashed potatoes. As weird as it sounds, and as much as I love hanging out with Derek and Evelyn, some of my favorite nights are the ones I spend with my family. They're the ones who've known me forever, the ones who don't even register my jaw, the ones who just see *me*.

Derek gets along just fine with his mom, but it's in that typical boy way where he barely talks to her unless she asks him a question, and even then it's a one-word answer. He's obsessed with the twins, Jayson and Justin, though. He spends most of his evenings (the ones he hasn't crammed with Academic Challenge meets and track practices and volunteer work at an animal shelter or one of the other million extracurriculars he's picked up) playing basketball with them in the driveway or helping them with their homework.

And at Evelyn's house, it's just her and her mom. There's nothing *wrong* with her mom—I mean, I know she loves Evelyn, in her own way—but she one hundred percent does not understand anything Evelyn's doing with her life. As Evelyn puts it, "She's always like, 'Evelyn, why aren't you getting better grades? Why aren't you studying more?' and I'm like, 'Do you think Christian Siriano spent time studying for biology tests? I need to make a new A-line skirt! Stop breaking my balls, Patricia!'"

I've tried to get Evelyn to stop using the phrase "breaking my balls" on account of it being extremely inaccurate and also just gross, but she persists. Either way, I can tell it bothers Evelyn that her mom doesn't get her, but I keep telling her she can use this feeling of alienation in her art. Evelyn ends up spending a lot of time at our house, which is more than fine by me—sometimes I come home and find Evelyn already there, sitting at the kitchen island with my mom as the two of them enjoy a cup of tea, Evelyn saying, "Oh, Rebecca, you're a card."

In my room, I turn on my bedside lamp and reach under my

bed, where my fingers close around a notebook. I slide it out, sit on the floor, and lean back against the bed.

Most people who keep scrapbooks probably fill them with photos of loved ones and cherished mementos. Mine's more of a vision board, I guess you could say. But it's not about traveling or my love life or fancy possessions I want to "manifest" or whatever. It's about one thing: beauty.

On these pages are picture after picture of girls' faces. Girls of all skin tones, hair colors, ages. The one thing they have in common is that they're beautiful. They're smiling in a way that says, *Yes, I know I look good. No, I never worry that no one will love me. Yes, I do feel happy when I look in a mirror. No, I've never had a problem chewing my food.*

Because the one thing these girls have in common, besides being beautiful, is that none of them have an underbite. None of them have a facial deformity that's immediately visible to everyone who meets them.

When Abbi's done reading all the cheesy fashion magazines she subscribes to each month, I take them and cut out the pictures of the most beautiful women. It doesn't matter whether they're in advertisements, fashion spreads, or celebrity profiles. I know it sounds weird, but there's nothing in my life that I find as soothing or as hopeful. *This will be me someday,* I think. *Someday I won't have braces, or frequent trips to an orthodontist's office, or a jaw that's going rogue.*

I approach my scrapbooking as carefully and methodically as Evelyn approaches a hair-dyeing job. But tonight, I'm not pasting in any more pictures. I'm just looking, completing my nightly ritual, running my fingers over the faces of all these perfect smiles and symmetrical faces and normal jaws and thinking, *Someday.*

In two months.

Chapter Three

The next morning, Abbi waddles into my room. "Hey, loser, wake up."

I groan and put my pillow over my head. "I'm pretty sure your baby can hear what you're saying. She's going to come out of the womb with your bad attitude."

Abbi pulls the pillow off my head. "I don't care. I'm cranky and I have to pee twenty-four/seven."

"Charming," I say, and she hits me with the pillow.

"Mom's busy, so you have to drive me to my doctor's appointment," she says.

I groan. I had plans for my Saturday. Like, I don't know, going to Applebee's to get some appetizers for brunch, or reading a chapter of *Jane Eyre*. I'm never going to complete every item on my list if I don't apply myself.

I know Abbi doesn't like going to her appointments by

herself, and only a real jerk would refuse to drive her pregnant sister to the doctor's office, so I begrudgingly drag myself out of bed and pull on dark jeans and a long, beige sweater that's basically the same color as my skin. I take the time to curl my hair into waves and brush on some mascara, even though Abbi is (slowly) pacing the hallway and grumbling about how we're going to be late.

Between Abbi and me, our family basically spends our entire lives at doctors' offices these days. I have my oral surgeon consults with Dr. Kelley, and Abbi always has to get something checked out by the obstetrician.

By the time we get there, Abbi's already moaning about being starving and having to pee, which are, like, her two favorite topics of conversation these days. We hang out in the waiting room, during which I get more than enough time to watch a highly inappropriate round of *Family Feud* and flip through a women's magazine that's ninety-five percent ads for menopause-related products. When the nurse calls Abbi's name, I'm surprised when she grabs my hand and pulls me along with her.

"I'll be okay out here," I say as I drop the magazine.

"I hate going in here alone," she hisses. "Just come with me."

Abbi situates herself on the examination table, and I grab a seat in a chair shoved in the corner. The nurse takes Abbi's blood pressure, then promises that the doctor will be in shortly. Abbi doesn't seem interested in conversation, so I keep myself occupied by reading a pamphlet about breastfeeding until the doctor walks in.

"So," the doctor says, checking her clipboard, "thirty-two weeks along?"

Abbi nods quickly, looking more nervous than I usually see her.

"And are you feeling okay?" the doctor asks.

Abbi just nods again. I'm trying, as usual, to stay quiet and out of the way, but the oppressively strong scent of hand sanitizer makes me cough.

The doctor turns to look at me, startled, as if this is the first time she's noticed I'm in the room. "And you are . . . ?"

"My sister," Abbi says, finally getting her voice back.

There's a moment when a flash of shock rolls across the doctor's face. She recovers quickly, but I know I saw it. It's like in one of those old-fashioned horror movies, when a skull flashes over a person's face. It's barely there, but you can see it.

And I'm used to it—to people being surprised I'm Abbi's sister. I mean, why should this objectively beautiful woman have a sister with an underbite? It seems like a joke. Like, we can't possibly be from the same family tree.

"It was nice of you to come along since Dad can't make it," the doctor says, and I'm too shocked to say anything back. And even if I could, the warning look Abbi shoots me would convince me otherwise. This must be a new doctor if she doesn't know that the father of Abbi's baby has never even been inside our house, let alone the examination room.

The doctor lubes everything up and rubs some device over Abbi's belly. And then, there she is—Abbi's baby. We already know it's a girl, so there aren't any surprises at this point, but this is the first time I've actually seen her on the screen.

"That's her hand!" I say, and the doctor gives me a smile.

"That's right. She's growing perfectly. It looks like she's going to be a big baby."

Abbi beams like she just got an A on an exam. *Growing a Big, Healthy Baby: A+, excellent work.*

After Abbi gets all that goo off her stomach, goes through

the rest of the exam, and we're back in the car, there's only one thing I want to ask her. And it's not "Is it really cold when they put that goo on you?"

She pulls on her seat belt and sighs. Before I can even say a word, she turns to me and says, "Listen, I have my reasons for not talking about things, okay?"

I just nod because I don't know what else to do.

Abbi looks straight ahead and nods once, resolutely. "Okay. Good."

I'm so distracted by baby hands and ultrasounds that I forget to check my phone until I get home. The text that's waiting for me is, in true Evelyn fashion, mysterious and exciting.

I may have found a way for you to be in v. close contact with Noah Reed. Details later.

I almost squeal in frustration. "Details later?" Who does Evelyn think she is, a news anchor going to a commercial break?

I text back, *??????*

When that leads to no response, I decide to try *!!!!!!!*

Then I pick out a few choice emojis, mostly that angry red face.

Still nothing. I call Derek, because he's an eighty-year-old man trapped in the body of a sixteen-year-old and actually prefers phone calls.

"Derek," I start before he can even say hello, "do you have any idea what Evelyn's plan is?"

He sighs heavily, sounding even more like an old man. "Which plan are we talking about?"

"Something about a way to get me into close contact with Noah Reed."

"Oh no," Derek says with a sardonic chuckle. "I know exactly what she's doing."

I perk up. My previous plan to get near Noah Reed involved waiting for a tornado or other natural disaster and then getting trapped in the school together, forced to subsist on cafeteria food, after which, eventually, we would end up making out. But a lot of factors have to fall into place for that one to work.

"It's the musical," Derek says. "He's in it every year, and tryouts are on Monday and Tuesday."

"What?!" I screech. "First off, how do you even know this—"

"Because I'm in charge of set design."

Of course Derek, king of extracurriculars, would be in charge of set design.

"And second off, how does Evelyn expect me to be in the musical? She knows I can't stand being in front of people!"

I let out one of my own grumpy-old-man sighs. Honestly, I kind of liked my plan to get close to Noah better, and that one involved waiting for a natural disaster and eating canned pudding.

"It's not that big a deal," Derek says. "It's Brentley. Half the school is in the musical because there's nothing else to do."

Derek may think this is no big deal, but I'm starting to feel sick. Being under a spotlight, with everyone staring at me? That's almost literally my worst nightmare (except for that one where I have to give a report on *The Great Gatsby* while wearing the SpongeBob SquarePants nightshirt I've had since seventh grade). Evelyn knows I can't do that—all those people looking at me as I forget all my lines and possibly faint and/or barf and/or spontaneously combust into embarrassed confetti right there onstage.

"But you said you're in charge of set design, right?" I ask.

"Yes. But you can't help," Derek says firmly.

"Why not?"

"Because you have the artistic talent of a five-year-old and the coordination of a three-year-old."

"That's not exactly accurate . . ."

"You're right. It's insulting to toddlers and their crayon skills."

I scowl into my phone. "Thanks for telling me about Evelyn's plan. No thanks for the insult."

"You're welcome. Hey, real quick: What do you know about lemurs?"

"Nothing, but I'm sure I'll find out plenty on *Deep Dive*."

"See you Monday."

"See you."

I fire off a quick text to Evelyn—*I know what you're doing and I don't like it*—before crashing in my room. I flop onto my bed and flip through the scrapbook as I run my tongue over the bumps of my braces. One of the biggest bummers about this surgery is that I have to wear braces before and after. When everything's said and done and my chin looks normal, I'll have had braces for almost five years, including part of my senior year.

I still remember how excited I was to get braces at first. They made me feel grown up, and I loved to get rubber bands in different color combos—pink and purple, black and yellow, red and green for the holidays.

But then I started to get older, and fewer and fewer people had braces. And no one had an underbite, or a palate expander that stretched out the roof of their mouth and gave them a speech impediment, or frequent appointments with oral surgeons and orthodontists.

And now, the only people I see with braces are some freshmen roaming the halls. I know I was the one who set the goal to kiss Noah Reed, but I was drunk on the promise of Chicken Wonton Tacos and under the influence of Worst-Case Scenario

Television. I couldn't be trusted to make serious decisions. There's just no way Noah would want to kiss someone who could charitably be described as Brace Face.

On Monday, Evelyn is waiting for me at my locker, clad in a bright blue Evelyn-original dress that's covered in appliquéd flowers.

"Good morning," she says, wiggling her eyebrows. "Get my text this weekend?"

I open my locker, and she moves out of the way of the swinging door. "Um, yeah. And I responded. About a million times."

"Huh. Must've missed those," Evelyn says, but I know she just wanted to tell me in person for maximum drama. "So, are you curious about my plan?"

I stack my trig and Bio II textbooks in my arms and turn to face her. "You think I should try out for the musical."

Evelyn widens her eyes. "How did you know that?"

"I talked to Derek."

"Ugh," she says, sighing. "Well, this isn't fair. You two always gang up on me and outsmart me."

"We don't do that," I say, swinging my locker door shut.

She nods. "You definitely do. It's always, 'No way, Evelyn, a hot dog is not a sandwich. We're right and you're wrong.'"

"That doesn't have anything to do with us ganging up on you," I say as we start to make our way down the hallway, pushing through the throngs of students. "That's just a factually correct statement."

"All I'm saying is that a hot dog is surrounded by bread, like any other sandwich!" Evelyn shouts to be heard over the locker-door slams and sneaker squeaks just as Noah Reed himself walks by.

I'm struck by how he's tall and lanky, but not in an awkward way. Every part of him moves gracefully, like his limbs all know they're working toward one purpose, and that purpose is Making Noah Reed Look Great. He looks like the lead on a CW show— you know, those guys who are supposed to be teenagers but look like they're twenty-five and are perfectly styled and don't have zits all over their chin like the rest of us do? That's what Noah Reed looks like.

And that's what I'm thinking about as he turns around in what feels like slow motion and looks straight at me.

And smiles.

"Whoa," Evelyn says. She reaches out to grab my shoulders and move me out of the path of an oncoming football player. "You almost had a head-on collision with Jockpants McBiceps back there."

"Oh my God," I breathe.

"I know! I would've been wiping you off the floor. That dude's like four hundred pounds of muscle."

"No, Noah Reed," I whisper-hiss. "He smiled at me."

Evelyn stops, causing three people to run into each other behind her in a pileup.

"I'm sorry, what?" she asks.

"Noah. Reed. Smiled. At. Me."

We start walking again, and she's talking so quickly that I can barely keep up. "I can't believe this. Noah Reed is already smiling at you! My plan is so brilliant that you haven't even started it yet and it's already working!"

"Okay," I say as I start to duck into trig, which Evelyn's not in because she hates math with the fire of a thousand particularly math-averse suns. "I have class. You know, that thing where we learn stuff?"

Evelyn shakes her head, feigning confusion. "Never heard of it."

"Hey!" I grab her arm as someone pushes past me into the classroom. "You're not going to ditch class again to go research Edith Head in the library, are you?"

"Only time will tell!" she sings, scooting out of my grasp and disappearing into the crowd.

I take my seat in trig, right behind Derek, and pull out my textbook.

"So," he says, turning around. "Noah Reed smiled at you, huh?"

I freeze. "How did you know that?"

He raises his eyebrows. "Uh, you guys were basically shouting in the hallway."

"Yeah," says Sean Morrison, the super-genius who sits beside me and usually only speaks when he's correcting someone in our class. "And a hot dog is not a sandwich."

"Thank you," I mutter, but I can feel my face turning red.

"Hey, it looks like you have a little something here." Derek reaches out to touch my face, then pulls his hand back as if I've burned him. "Oh, sorry, that's just your cheeks."

"Shut up," I grumble.

I try to focus on my assignment as our teacher starts talking. And while on most days I would be super into cofunctions, the only thing going through my head right now is *Noah Reed smiled at me.*

Evelyn and I are both weirdos, don't get me wrong, but she's always been the more glamorous weirdo. She's the one who has hair that's often streaked with the colors of the rainbow. She's the one who does themed manicures. She's the one with the purple-rimmed glasses, the outfits that look like costumes, and the sewing skills to make every outfit she's ever dreamed of. That's why she's head of the costume department for the school musical.

"What is it this year?" I ask her, stealing a french fry off her lunch tray.

"*To the Moon and Back*," she says, holding her hands in front of her and staring off into space as if she's looking at a marquee.

I shake my head. "I've never heard of that one."

"That's because it's never been performed," Evelyn says. "One of Mrs. Mulaney's former students wrote it, and she wants to stage the premiere performance."

"You mean our school can't even get a real musical?" I ask.

Evelyn shrugs. "We don't have the budget to pay for the rights for something famous. And, honestly, there's a lot to do costume-wise, so I'm not complaining. I mean, I have to make space suits because part of it takes place on the moon."

I narrow my eyes. "The moon?"

Evelyn nods and starts describing the plot. "So it's about little Bobby, who grows up on a farm . . ."

While she's talking, I let myself zone out a little bit. Is it ridiculous to think I could maybe try out for a chorus part in the musical? I mean, I'm not naïve enough to think I could be the star even if I wanted to, but a background player, maybe? Just enough to get close to Noah?

I snap out of my reverie when I hear Evelyn talking about a scene involving grown-up Bobby. "And who's going to play Bobby?"

"It hasn't been cast yet," Evelyn says. "But probably Noah. He always gets the lead."

I nod. Right. So now all I have to do is sidle my way into a background part, and I'll have a ticket to staring at Noah from a respectable distance at every single practice. I could think of worse ways to spend my evenings and weekends.

"Oh no," Evie says, squinting at me. "You've got it again— that Noah Reed look in your eyes."

I focus on my lunch tray. "I have no such look in my eyes."

"You're absolutely, truly, completely full of shit," Evelyn says. "I'm all about helping you achieve your goals, but I *do* wish they were cooler goals. Like, things that don't just revolve around a dude or a book."

"That's easy for you to say," I grumble. "You've kissed half the guys in this school."

She shrugs.

I may be exaggerating a bit. I'm not saying Evelyn's kissed her way through Brentley's male population, but she has kissed upwards of five guys. (Okay, six . . . she's kissed six guys.) And that's six more than I've kissed, playground kiss excluded.

"Noah Reed," I say, lowering my voice, "is a worthy goal."

Evelyn shrugs. "He's not really my type. But at least he's better than your last fantasy crush."

I *may* have a tendency to choose boys I don't know all that well and then imagine our perfect lives together. Like the time I was convinced that the guy who worked the counter at the QuikStop was my soul mate, but then he ended up getting arrested for stealing massive amounts of money and a year's supply of Monster energy drinks. Or that time I was so sure that if Zayn Malik and I could only meet, he would realize I was the girl for him (I just think he needs someone to talk to!). And then there was my massive crush on Johnson Bennett, a guy in my study hall. We never spoke, but I could always see him doodling in his notebook and I knew, just *knew*, that he was secretly a brilliant artist.

My crush on Johnson ended when I finally saw his notebook

and discovered that it was entirely full of cartoon animal heads that had nude human bodies. And then I realized he always carried around an empty Mountain Dew bottle so he could spit his chew into it.

"I know Noah's not your type," I tell Evelyn. "The point is, I want to do this. I want to kiss Noah Reed before I get surgery."

Evelyn takes a bite of her yogurt. "Well, whatever. I certainly can't stop you. At least he doesn't carry around a spit jug."

I fix her with my most withering scowl, which isn't really all that withering. "Fine. I'll try out for the musical. But I'm already nervous."

"Don't be. This is Brentley, not Broadway, remember? It's not like you're competing against Lin-Manuel Miranda."

Maybe for Evie the stakes are low. But for me, they couldn't be higher. Yes, I want to kiss Noah Reed until my knees buckle, but I have never, ever harbored dreams of stardom. More like dreams of hiding in the background and praying no one can see me as I lip-synch along. I don't even sing in the shower because Abbi overheard me once, then spent the rest of the week making fun of my rendition of the *Unbreakable Kimmy Schmidt* theme song (whatever, it's *extremely* catchy). The idea of actually really doing this, of willingly standing up on a stage and asking people to look at me, is terrifying.

Then again, so is dying before I get the chance to meet my goals.

"What do I have to do, Evie? Lay it on me." I slam my hands on the table, and a freshman sitting down the table from us jumps. "Sorry," I whisper.

"It's no big deal," Evelyn says in a sugary-sweet voice that lets me know it's going to be at least sort of a big deal for me. "You just need to read the monologue they give you."

I slump in my seat, already starting to feel sick. I guess I'd been hoping the audition would involve someone psychically intuiting that I should be in the choir.

"But there's one more thing you need to do, and it's the most important."

"Oh God," I groan. "I don't have to dance, do I?"

Evelyn shakes her head. "There are a couple choreographed numbers, but it's not like you have to be one of Beyoncé's backup dancers or anything. You'll be fine."

I sigh with relief.

"What you need to do is take up space," Evelyn says, and I stare at her as I try to make sense of her words.

"What?" I finally ask.

"I'm saying you need to own it, Jolie! Stop selling yourself short. Get up there on that stage and *be seen*. Stop whispering. Stop apologizing to some random freshman," she says, gesturing at the kid down the table from us. When he looks at her indignantly, she says, "No offense. We don't even know you."

I roll my eyes. "You don't get it."

"No, actually, I do, and that's why I'm telling you this. If you want to try for this, you need to give it your best shot. No one's going to believe you can do it if *you* don't believe you can do it."

I blink. "I think I read that on a magnet once."

"It's hanging on a sign in the guidance counselor's office," says the freshman.

We turn to stare at him.

"Kindly stop listening to our conversation, young man," Evelyn says.

He picks up his tray and walks away.

She waves a hand in the air dismissively. "Wherever it comes from, it's good advice. I'll help you prepare your audition, but there's absolutely no reason you can't do this. You're Jolie Peterson. You've got it."

"Sure, Ev." None of this seems hard to her. Evelyn, who loves creating outfits based on the record covers she picks up at Goodwill. Who loves dyeing her hair to fit her mood. Who doesn't mind knowing that every pair of eyes in the room is fixed on her. Who, in fact, *loves* knowing that they are. Who knows that everyone isn't wondering what's wrong with her face or thinking about why she looks so weird. Of course she wouldn't understand why it makes me bone-deep nervous to even think about being on a stage.

Just then, Noah walks by our table, all long-limbed, big-haired ease. He walks like he has somewhere to be, like he knows where he's going, like he's already a star. Evelyn and I stop talking and watch him walk by. I swallow, hard.

"Okay," I say. "Teach me your ways, master."

Chapter Four

"Wait, you're doing what?" Abbi asks, pausing with her fork in the air.

"Don't talk with your mouth full, Abs," I say, and she shoots me a snotty look.

"I think it's great that you're trying something new," Mom says in a calm tone. She's very good at reacting to things in a measured, nonjudgmental manner. This is annoying when it comes to Abbi's pregnancy because I just want someone to pepper her with questions until she spills everything, but I appreciate it right now.

Although you wouldn't know it if you looked at her, my mom used to play music. She actually dropped out of college to tour with her all-female punk band, Sister Wives. She met my dad in some no-name bar in Ohio and even though, as she put it, "nothing about him was remotely cool," she fell in love with him and they got married. Eventually she went back to college to become a school counselor so she could work with kids who are, in her words, as screwed up as she was. When I see pictures of her wearing a nose ring and a T-shirt with no bra, I wonder how she ended up here, married with two kids and a house and a Subaru in the driveway. The only way you'd even know about her past is because she has framed concert posters instead of framed paintings, and she listens to Sonic Youth in the car instead of the country station, like Evelyn's mom does. It's not that she seems unhappy, but I guess part of me wonders if she regrets it. If she wishes she were still crammed into a dirty van, headed to some town she's never been to in Pennsylvania, playing the drums night after night. I wonder if she looks at her kids—one of them pregnant, the other not even able to get kissed—and wonders where she went wrong.

"Thanks for the encouragement, Mom," I say sweetly, keeping my eyes on Abbi.

"But you hate being in front of people," Abbi continues. "Remember when Mom said you had to be in the fourth-grade musical and you cried for days?"

Ugh. I wish she hadn't reminded me. I was so nervous about it that the only thing that calmed me down was when Derek came over and performed stand-up comedy routines he'd memorized by secretly staying up late watching Comedy Central. Let me tell you, Patton Oswalt routines lose a lot of their punch when they're recited by a fourth-grade boy, but they were still funny enough that I was able to stop freaking out.

"We had to sing Disney songs. It was beneath me."

"I just wanted you to have a new experience," Mom says, spooning more roasted carrots onto her plate. "But you've always been a little hesitant to try new things."

I'd be offended, but she's right. For my fifth-birthday party, they bought me a tricycle, but instead of trying to ride it, I hid in the garage and cried until everyone went home.

"So you actually *want* to be on a stage? Like, with people looking at you?" Abbi asks.

The thing is, she's not trying to be mean. She's way too obvious for that. She's genuinely confused about what I'm doing, and I wish she'd just shut her mouth (both figuratively and literally, because I don't need to see the half-chewed pork tenderloin that's in there).

"I hope you teach your child better manners," I say, and Abbi closes her mouth and chews deliberately while staring at me.

"Anyway, Evelyn's coming over tonight to help me prepare," I say, polishing off the last bite of my carrots. I stand up and give my dad a quick kiss on the head. "Thanks for dinner, Dad."

"Thank Giada De Laurentiis," he says. "The woman knows her way around a pork roast."

Abbi screws up her face. "Gross, Dad."

He shrugs. "What? I like watching Food Network."

Mom raises her eyebrows. "Really? Then why aren't you waxing rhapsodic about Bobby Flay?"

I'm walking into the kitchen to escape their conversation when I hear the doorbell ring. "I'll get it!" I yell.

It's Evelyn, as expected, and she has Derek in tow.

"Why are you here?" I ask.

"Oh, I'm fine, thanks for asking, how are you?" he asks as he brushes past me into the house.

Evelyn smiles wide as she steps inside. "I figured you could use a practice audience. And what better audience than your best friends?"

Derek rubs his hands together. "I hope you're ready for some serious heckling."

I sigh as we walk back to my room (but not before Derek stops by the dining room to say hello to my family; annoyingly, they seem to like him more than they like me). Evelyn's right—having an audience will be nice, and the great thing about her and Derek is that they're well aware of all my weaknesses, so they can zero in on them and beat them out of me. You know, musical theater–style.

Evelyn sits down on my bed and brandishes a sheet of paper. "Guess what I have?"

We stare at her blankly.

"A . . . piece of paper?" I ask.

"Yes," Evelyn says. "But what's on the piece of paper?"

I open my mouth, but before I can speak she says, "Please don't say words and sentences."

I shut my mouth.

"This is a list I wrote for you. 'Jolie Peterson's No-Fail Guide to Taking Up Space and Projecting Onstage.'"

Derek and I keep staring at her.

"Okay, so it's a long name, but it's accurate," she says. "Since you're trying out for a background part, you don't have to do much—just read the part Mrs. Mulaney gives you."

I nod.

"But," she continues, pointing at me, "you do have to prepare. Because if you go up there looking like you do right now, you're not going to get even the smallest part."

"What's wrong with how I look right now?" I self-consciously touch my face. "Do I have pork tenderloin in my teeth?"

"Nothing's wrong with how you look," Evelyn says. "This is about presence."

"Presence?" I repeat.

"You can't just stand there with your shoulders hunched and a frown on your face. You've gotta earn that spotlight."

"Right," I say, unconvinced.

Evelyn claps her hands. "Okay, stand up!"

Reluctantly, I stand up.

"Shoulders back," Evelyn says, standing in front of me and physically pushing my shoulders down. "No, Jolie, not up by your ears. Back."

"Got it."

"Chin up," she says, pushing my chin up from its permanently tucked-in position. "Arms uncrossed. And eye contact!" She points at her own eyes.

I widen mine at her dramatically. "Are you happy now?"

"Almost," she says, sitting back down on the bed beside Derek. "Now, tell us who you are."

I look back and forth between them. "Um . . . Jolie?"

"No!" she shouts with such ferocity that Derek jumps.

"Good Lord, Evie!" he says. "Do you really think going full-on *Whiplash* is the best tactic here?"

"Oh, I'm sorry," Evelyn says sweetly. "I wasn't aware that holding hands and singing 'Kumbaya' would get Jolie the lead in the musical."

Derek shrugs at me like he's saying, *Sorry, I tried.*

I shrug back, like I'm saying, *Yeah, well, Evelyn's an unstoppable force of nature.*

"Stop using your secret eye language!" Evelyn says, pointing to both of us. "Just remember: No 'ums.' That's public speaking 101. If you don't know what to say, don't use a filler. Just pause. A powerful pause."

"A powerful pause," I repeat slowly.

"Okay," Evelyn says. "Now tell us who you are again. And make eye contact."

I clear my throat. "I'm Jolie Peterson," I say, looking back and forth between Derek and Evie. Derek crosses his eyes and I try not to laugh. "And I'm auditioning for a background part."

"Louder!" Evelyn shouts with glee.

We spend the better part of an hour this way, with Evie adjusting my posture and my voice to mold me into someone who appears to have confidence. Or talent. Or presence.

They finally leave when Derek says he has to have his nightly phone chat with Melody ("Right, your girlfriend," Evie says, doing air quotes behind his back).

"You'll be fine tomorrow," Derek says on his way toward the door.

I roll my eyes, and I don't know if I'm just really obvious or if we have some sort of psychic best-friend bond from having known each other for so long, but he stops, comes back, and looks me straight in the eye. "I mean it, Peterson," he says, putting his hands on my shoulders. "Go kick some musical-theater ass."

"Make out with Noah Reed until he can't see straight!" Evelyn shouts.

"I'm not attempting to blind anyone with my make-out prowess, but okay, thanks," I say, giving her a hug.

Then I'm left alone in my room. I flop back onto my bed, my nest of fluffy pillows catching me as my stomach churns with dread and anticipation. For maybe one tiny moment when Evelyn was shouting at me, I felt like this was achievable, that I could actually get a part, however small, in the musical.

But can I? I stand up and cross the room to stare at myself in the mirror. I lift my chin and put my shoulders back like Evelyn taught me. I'm so used to keeping my chin down, my eyes down, my shoulders up. Anything to hide what I don't want people to see—*me*. After all, this face isn't the final product. And in the power pose Evelyn taught me, my imperfections are on full display. It's like I'm daring people to notice me, and it feels all wrong.

I'm tilting my face back and forth, inspecting my jaw in profile, when Abbi knocks and then walks in without waiting for my response. "Hey, weirdo. Your friends leave?"

"Yep," I say, meeting her eyes in the mirror.

She stands beside me, and I'm forced to take in our reflections, side by side. We're like one of those games I used to play in *Highlights* magazine where you had to inspect two similar pictures and point out the differences. This sister has a jaw defect; this one doesn't. This sister has never even made out with anyone; this one's pregnant.

"So you're seriously trying out for the musical, huh?" Abbi asks, grabbing one of my bottles of lotion and squeezing some on her hands.

"Yep," I say again. I'm waiting for her to say something else— to express more confusion, to point out that I threw up in the kitchen sink the last time I had to give a speech in history class, to tell me I should save myself the embarrassment.

But instead she focuses on rubbing the lotion into her hands and says, "Good for you, Jolie. I'm glad you're doing something new. You've got to take life by the balls while you still can. Or by"—she squints—"the ovaries. Or something less gendered, I don't know. The point is, you always think you have all the time in the world, but you don't, you know?"

She meets my eyes in the mirror and all of a sudden I get the feeling that we're not really talking about me at all.

"Yeah, I know," I say, even though I don't. I give her a smile and watch my jaw in the mirror.

I can't sleep. I just keep imagining myself onstage, people looking at me, people judging me. People saying, *Why did that girl think she could do this? Why did she think people wanted to look at her? Why did she just run offstage crying, muttering something about how this was just like the tricycle at her fifth-birthday party?*

Plus, spending so much time talking (sorry, "projecting") today has given me a jaw ache that's morphed into a headache. The thing about having a jaw that's out of alignment is that it's basically normal for it to hurt, and Dr. Kelley says that if I don't get the surgery, it will only get worse. After I run to the medicine cabinet to pop a Tylenol, I grab my laptop and get back into bed.

Reddit has a pretty bad reputation as a place where gross trolls congregate and share hacked photos of female celebrities, but there's a whole other side of it, too. No matter what sort of niche you're interested in reading about (horror stories, skin care, or pictures of old people doing ridiculous things on Facebook), there's an entire community of people asking questions and sharing their personal experiences. So it comes as no surprise that there are tons of people writing frantic posts about their upcoming jaw surgeries and lots of threads with titles like "I Had Surgery to Correct My Severe Underbite: Ask Me Anything."

Sometimes, scrolling through these can help me. I like the before-and-afters, seeing exactly how people's faces changed. Most of the time, I even like reading their recovery stories, even though they're usually full of pain pills and Ensure nutrition drinks and massive swelling. Tonight, I click on a thread I've read a million times before from a guy in Australia who had underbite surgery two years ago. But right now, even reading the normally reassuring details of someone else's transformation doesn't make me feel better. All I can think about is the harsh glare of the spotlight on me as I stand onstage, my voice squeaking out of my mouth and floating up toward the rafters as everyone in the audience laughs at me or feels sorry for me.

I pull out my phone and call Derek.

"Hello?" he asks.

"Sorry," I say. "Did I wake you up?"

He chuckles. "Yeah, no. I'm on the Wikipedia page for lemurs. Did you know that lemur means 'spirit of the night' in Latin?"

"I did not," I say. "And I can't imagine many people do."

"Well, now we both know, so you're welcome."

"I'm sure this will come in very handy during the 'Lemur Facts' portion of my audition tomorrow."

We're both silent for a moment, and then he says, "So what's up?"

I sigh. "I'm nervous. Why am I doing this?"

"Honestly, I'm not super clear on that."

"Not helpful!"

"Okay, okay." For a few moments, he doesn't say anything, and I start to think the call got dropped. I'm just about to ask if he's still there when he says, "You're doing this because you want to try something. You feel like taking a risk. You're ready to let people really see you."

Oh. Derek can always do this—easily figure out exactly what's really going on in my head, even if I can't. I guess that's what happens when you've known someone almost your whole life.

"And because I want to kiss Noah Reed," I say lightly.

"Hey," Derek says, "did you know lemurs have something called a toilet claw?"

"Hanging up now!" I laugh.

"Night, Jolie."

"Good night."

I sit my phone back on my nightstand, rest my head against the pillow, and stare at the ceiling. Yeah, so I tried to play it off like I'm only doing this to kiss Noah. And I *do* want to kiss him.

But Derek's right—there's a pretty big part of me that's actually curious about whether or not I can do this. Can I, the same Jolie Peterson who's spent years doing everything she can to make sure people don't see her, actually get up onstage and demand attention?

My phone buzzes.

A text from Derek: *Seriously, stop stressing out and get some sleep.*

I smile and close my eyes.

I wake up feeling queasy about the audition after school, but first I have to get through an appointment with Dr. Kelley. Getting out of my morning classes is the only good part of going to my appointment, where Dr. Kelley will inevitably study my X-rays while making a serious face and muttering to herself. In my experience, you never want someone to mutter while they're looking at an X-ray of your face. It just doesn't bode well for you.

There are fewer menopause-related magazine ads in Dr. Kelley's waiting room, which is probably because I'm surrounded by twelve-year-olds. The TV is playing a compilation of Disney songs, and the small children surrounding me are rapt. I feel like leaning over to the girl next to me and asking, "What are you in for?" but she's busy texting. And anyway, I can tell by looking at her that she doesn't have an underbite. She probably just has a gap between her front teeth or crowded molars or some other minor issue that's easy to correct. I involuntarily sneer at her at the exact moment she looks up at me, and I have to glance away quickly.

The TV has just started playing "Let It Go" for the third time when the receptionist calls my name and both Mom and I stand up.

"Seriously, Mom. You don't have to go in there with me."

"Of course I have to go with you," Mom says, striding ahead of me as I sigh, feeling even more like one of the twelve-year-olds in the waiting room.

Dr. Kelley has tight curls that are always perfectly maintained and she wears heels that look at least five inches tall, which seem like they would be difficult to stand on all day. But she always looks calm, comfortable, and in control, which is exactly how I want the person who's going to break my jaw to look.

We all look at the printouts of my jaw. Sometimes, it's easy for me to forget how different my face is from everyone else's, but looking at it in front of me in black and white, it's impossible not to see.

Dr. Kelley points out the place where my jaw will be broken, how much of it she'll take out, and how she'll slide it back into place to approximate a more "typical bite." Referring to my teeth as a "bite" will never stop being funny to me, but I've learned not to laugh or make too many vampire references.

"So," I say, "I was reading on WebMD—"

"Don't do that," Dr. Kelley says.

"Well, it's too late, and I read that sometimes surgery can cause permanent facial numbness. Is that true?"

Dr. Kelley nods slowly. "It's possible, but I urge you not

to take that too seriously. Any numbness is typically not that noticeable."

After a second of silence, I ask, "So could I die during surgery?"

"Jolie!" my mom scolds.

Dr. Kelley stifles a laugh. "There's always a risk involved in any surgery. But, no, I can say with almost certainty that you're not going to die."

"But I could," I say, raising my eyebrows.

"And a rogue asteroid could hit our building right now and kill us all," Dr. Kelley says.

Great. Another thing to add to my list of worries: a giant asteroid.

"Which is not to say that there aren't risks," she continues.

I lean forward again. "Like?"

"The aforementioned numbness. Nerve damage."

"What about leaving a towel inside my body?" I ask.

Dr. Kelley tilts her head. "I'm pretty sure I would notice if there was a towel in your jaw."

"Right." I nod. "That would probably be more of an issue if we were operating on my stomach or something."

Dr. Kelley opens her mouth, then closes it again. "Let's get back to your X-ray," she says finally.

I half listen as she goes through the details of the surgery, the ones that I've already heard a million times. All I'm thinking about is numbness. It could happen—my lips could become numb. I've never even had a full-blown, mind-melting, hot and heavy make-out sesh, and now I could get saddled with numb lips? Life is unfair. I start to understand what Abbi was telling me last night, about how you think you have all the time in the world when you really don't.

I know I should be relieved that Dr. Kelley said I'm not likely to die, but she didn't say it was impossible. It's not like Derek's dad knew he was going to die when he went to work that day—it just happened, and he wasn't even going under anesthesia.

When we leave the appointment, I'm only thinking about one thing, and it's not the weird sugar-free lollipops they give out at the reception desk or the trig test I have to take.

I'm thinking of Noah Reed's lips, and how if I want to get anywhere near them, I have to ace this audition.

Chapter Five

I pace back and forth backstage, my flats sliding across the floor. "I am Jolie Peterson, I am Jolie Peterson," I mutter to myself. I stop, throw my shoulders back, and announce to a fake tree that must be left over from musicals past, "I am Jolie Peterson!"

"Did that tree forget your name again?"

I turn around to see Derek.

"Thank God you're here." I rush toward him. "I need a pep talk."

"Go get 'em, tiger," he says, deadpan.

I give him my most wild-eyed look. "That's supposed to help?"

"I'm not Evie!" Derek says, holding up his hands. "I'm not ready to give a motivational TED Talk at a moment's notice."

"Then how am I supposed to calm down?!" I practically screech, and Derek holds a finger up to his lips.

"People are auditioning out there. Just take a few deep breaths."

I wring my hands. "I think I'm hyperventilating or something."

"You're not." I look up and realize that Derek's staring into my eyes with an almost unnerving intensity, which causes me to spend more time looking at him than I normally do. It's not like Abbi's wrong; he *is* good-looking. Much better looking than he was when he used to burp the alphabet. And the way he's looking me right in the eyes is kind of making me wonder why I haven't noticed that before.

"What's that look all about?" he asks, widening his eyes.

I look away quickly, but before I can worry about translating my thoughts into words, Marla Martinez walks backstage.

"You're up," she says, raising her eyebrows. "Thanks for yelling through my audition. It really added a certain je ne sais quoi to the whole thing."

"Sorry," I whisper, even though it's too late to whisper at this point.

"Whatever." She rolls her eyes and breezes past me, leaving the scent of fancy shampoo in her wake. Marla is probably the prettiest girl in school, and her dark hair is tied into a ponytail that somehow manages to look effortlessly glamorous instead of how my ponytails always look, which is sort of weird and lumpy and not something I would ever in a million years wear in front of other people. She's not only beautiful, but also the cocaptain of the Academic Challenge team (along with Derek), and she has an amazing singing voice, which everyone knows because she was the lead in last year's musical—pretty much unheard of for a sophomore. I'm sure she killed it this time, too, even with me screeching in the background. Basically she's perfect, but she's not even mean about it, so I can't really hate her. She *is* remarkably aloof, but I guess that's what happens when you have a single-minded determination to master every high school extracurricular so you can get into a good college.

"Hey," she says as she gives Derek a quick high five. I bristle with annoyance, part of me wanting to yell at her, "Hey, he's *my* best friend! You never watched *Blue's Clues* with him when you were five-year-olds!"

But I don't. Because that would be inappropriate, and anyway, it's not like I'm the boss of Derek. If anyone should be upset about him talking to Marla, it should be Possibly Fictitious Melody. I wonder if made-up girlfriends get jealous?

I snap out of my daydream when Peter Turturro, Mrs. Mulaney's student assistant, pokes his head behind the curtain.

"Jolie?" he asks, so impatient he practically snaps his fingers. "Are you coming out? You're the last audition of the day, and I want to get home to watch *Dr. Phil*."

"I'm coming!" My stomach flips a few times and I start to run out onto the stage, but Derek grabs my arm.

"Hey," he says. "Break a leg out there. Or a jaw, or something."

I laugh, even though my legs feel like the gross cafeteria Jell-O no one ever eats. I also feel a little bit satisfied because Marla looks confused. "Thanks."

Peter clears his throat. "Jolie, today Dr. Phil's having former reality TV contestants on to explain to them what's wrong with their sad, sad hearts, and if I miss even one of their fake tears—"

"I'm coming, Peter!" I'm so perplexed by Peter's love of late-afternoon television that I forget where I'm going.

That is, until I step onto the stage and into a spotlight that shines right into my eyes. I now understand the phrase "deer in the headlights," because that's how I feel as I come to a stop, unable to move left or right as a potentially very awful situation barrels toward me.

"Hello?" asks a disembodied voice, one that I assume belongs to Mrs. Mulaney.

"Um, hi," I say, stepping toward the center of the stage. I hear Evie's voice in my head reminding me to avoid fillers and have a presence. I put my shoulders back and say, "I'm Jolie Peterson."

"I know," says Mrs. Mulaney, who comes into focus as my eyes adjust to the light. "You were in my freshman English class, remember?"

"Oh. Right." So much for presence.

"Okay, so you'll be reading the part of Prudie," Mrs. Mulaney continues, and Peter runs up onstage to hand me my lines.

"Make it quick," he whispers, tapping an imaginary watch on his wrist.

"But I . . ." I pause. Powerfully. "I'm just auditioning for a background part."

Mrs. Mulaney waves a hand. "That's fine. Everyone's reading this part so I can get a feel for your strengths."

I'm fairly certain my strengths don't include being the lead, but whatever. I just nod.

"Noah? Can you take it from the top?" Mrs. Mulaney asks.

What? I look to my right and see him. Noah Reed. Standing there this entire time. He looks up from his paper and even though I know time doesn't work like this, I swear he moves in slow motion. His eyes meet mine and he smiles, confident and calm.

"Hey, Jolie," he says.

He knows my name?

HE KNOWS MY NAME.

"Noah!" I say, then have to stop myself from smacking my palm across my face. "I mean . . . hey. Noah. What's up?"

He points to the paper in his hand. "Just, you know . . . auditions."

"Sometime today, please," Peter says as Mrs. Mulaney waits patiently.

Noah clears his throat. "Prudie, I know I'm just a simple farm boy, but I have a chance to do something more. To *be* something more."

I stare at the paper in my hands, the words blurring together. I try to focus on my line, but the light is so bright, so hot. I feel exposed.

"But what about . . . ?" Noah mutters, prompting me to read the next line.

I'm Jolie Peterson, I remind myself (but silently, not out loud . . . I don't need a repeat of the last time I said it). Shoulders back. Chin up.

"But what about our life together? The farm? The pigs?"

My brow furrows before I can stop it. Okay, well, Evelyn did warn me that this wasn't exactly Tony Award–winning stuff.

"Prudie, you know I'll miss you, but this may be my only chance to colonize the moon."

"The moon can wait!" I shout with passion that surprises even me. "What about our wedding?"

"We have our whole lives to spend together," Noah says, looking into my eyes, and for a moment I just stare at the artfully styled swoop of his hair and the urgency in his face and pretend that he's really feeling it for me instead of the character. That we're actually engaged and he's considering space travel.

"If you go to the moon, we're over," I say, my heart breaking just a little as I deliver the line. "When you come back to Earth, you can't come back here and expect me and the pigs to be waiting for you."

Wow. A surprising amount of pig talk in here.

"But I love you," Noah says, and just for one more moment, I let myself believe that someone like Noah could really love someone like me. It takes all I have not to go off script and tell him that the pigs and I will wait for him forever.

"I—I—" I stammer, willing the words on the paper to make sense to me. Beads of sweat pop up on my forehead and my mouth goes dry. The paper shakes in my hands.

Noah coughs quietly, the only sound to punctuate the silence of the auditorium.

"I know you do," I say with as much force as I can muster, looking right at him. "But you love the moon more."

"Aaaaand, scene!" shouts Peter. "Are we done here, Mrs. M.?"

"Jolie? Could you wait just a minute?" Mrs. Mulaney asks as I attempt to flee the stage.

Oh God. She's not going to tell me what a terrible job I did in front of Noah, is she? Am I going to get a verbal smackdown while Peter Turturro misses precious seconds of *Dr. Phil*?

"Would you mind singing a little bit for me?"

"But I . . . I'm just trying out for a background part," I remind her, my hands folding and refolding the piece of paper in my hands. "I didn't prepare a song."

Mrs. Mulaney leans forward. "I know. But I'd like to hear you sing."

I have to stop myself from scowling. What sort of weirdo is Mrs. Mulaney that she gets her kicks by torturing innocent bad actors? This is like that part on televised talent shows where the judges focus on all the awful contestants, and then someone's terrible rendition of an Adele song gets remixed into a catchy jingle that everyone makes fun of.

"I don't really know any songs from musicals," I say, racking my brain. Presumably Mrs. Mulaney doesn't want to listen to me screech my way through the Ariana Grande song I heard on the drive to school, and right now I've forgotten every other song I've ever heard.

"It doesn't matter what you sing," Mrs. Mulaney says, clearly trying to hide her impatience. " 'Happy Birthday.' 'Twinkle, Twinkle.' Just sing."

I look at Noah, as if he can help me out. He shrugs (it's a very cute shrug, but still).

"All right," I say, fighting the urge to use fillers and instead employing another pause that may or may not be powerful. "Here goes."

I avoid looking at Mrs. Mulaney or Peter. I definitely don't look at Noah. Instead, I focus on all the empty seats in the darkened auditorium as I open my mouth and slowly start to sing "Twinkle, Twinkle," my voice echoing through the room.

When I woke up this morning, I never would have thought that I'd end my school day by singing a popular children's lullaby in front of the cutest guy in school. But sometimes life's just unpredictable, I guess.

When the last few notes leave my mouth, the room goes silent. I watch dust particles float through the stage lighting as I wait for someone to say something.

"Thank you, Jolie," Mrs. Mulaney finally says. "You're our very last audition, so I'll be making decisions tonight and posting them outside my classroom tomorrow."

I wait for her to say something else, but she starts gathering her papers and putting them in her bag. She and Peter aren't giving me a standing ovation for my heartwarming take on a classic . . . but they also aren't clutching their bleeding ears and calling for an ambulance.

"Okay . . . bye," I mumble, then practically run offstage. I find my backpack shoved behind the fake tree, but Derek is nowhere to be found, thank God. I'm definitely glad he didn't hear that nightmare of an audition.

"Hey, Jolie?" I hear as I'm hoisting my backpack onto my shoulder.

"Every second you spend complaining to me is a second you don't spend watching Dr. Phil's bald, bulbous head," I say without turning around as I head toward the backstage door that leads to the hallway.

"Technically that's true of every conversation, but I've never really thought about it that way."

I whip my head toward the sound of that distinctly non-Peter voice and see Noah Reed smiling at me, one hand on his hip.

"Sorry, I thought you were Peter," I say, gripping my backpack strap so hard I'm afraid my fingers might break.

Noah nods. "I get that a lot."

"Really?"

"No." He laughs.

I feel my chin drifting toward my chest as I wait for him to say whatever it is he chased me back here to say. Was I that awful onstage? But then, like a particularly well-dressed hallucination, I see Evelyn in my head. *Presence.*

I lift my chin, put my shoulders back, and ask the most casual question I can think of. "What's up?"

"I just wanted to say that you were great out there."

I involuntarily narrow my eyes. "Wait, what?"

He nods enthusiastically and his hair bobs. "Seriously. I don't know what part Mrs. Mulaney is looking at for you, but I hope it's a big one."

I shake my head. I don't know why Noah's being so nice to me, but he doesn't get it. "I'm only trying out for a background part. She's probably going to cast me as one of the pigs."

"The pigs are actually one of the most important parts," Noah says. "But there's no way you're going to be in the background."

Suddenly, I feel too queasy to even answer him. Mrs. Mulaney won't give me a bigger part, will she? Can she even do that?

"Anyway, there's no such thing as a small part. Only small actors. And you," Noah says as he walks backward away from me, pointing at me with his rolled-up script, "are definitely not a small actor."

He disappears onto the stage, and I'm left staring at the swaying curtain. I'm pretty sure Noah was speaking figuratively, not literally, because I'm only, like, five foot five on a good day. But even then, I don't know what that means. I've never acted before, unless you count that fourth-grade Disney musical Abbi reminded me of, and even in that one I only mumbled through "Be Our Guest" in the chorus while dressed as a mop.

I walk out into the hallway, then push the door open into the parking lot. The April sunshine is brighter than I expected, and I blink a few times as my eyes adjust. The stress of the afternoon eases a little bit, and as I walk to my car, I can't help but smile.

Chapter Six

*T*hat night, I text Evelyn and Derek.

Emergency Applebee's meeting. SOS SOS SOS.

Evelyn texts back immediately. *I'll be there in ten. I'll put in an order of spinach and artichoke dip for you.*

Derek texts back too, although I can practically feel his hatred for the medium radiating from my phone. *Is it possible you and I have different definitions of the word 'emergency'?*

Just be there, I tap.

I'll be there. Obvi. Just have to finish up this game of Candyland.

I smile at the abbreviation. I'm pretty sure "obvi" would've never snuck into Derek's vocabulary if it weren't for me and Evie. I wonder for a moment how he talks to his super-genius girlfriend, if Melody's the type of person who would roll her eyes at a cutesy shortened word. They probably communicate in, like, theorems or equations or some sort of code only the two of them know.

Not that I *care* how Derek talks to his girlfriend. I just, you know . . . wonder.

And anyway, I have more important things to think about than the abbreviations, or lack thereof, that Derek and his mystery girlfriend use. I've called tonight's emergency meeting because now that I've had hours to obsessively mull over my audition, my characteristic self-doubt has started seeping in. Even though Noah was strangely complimentary about my performance, that doesn't mean anything. It's possible he was just being nice because he felt sorry for me, sort of like he would if I were a small child who had struck out in a softball game: *You did soooo good, and we're so proud of you, slugger!*

Chances are pretty good that I screwed up royally and Mrs. Mulaney is currently eating dinner while wondering how she can avoid giving me even a background part. Probably my mere presence onstage would ruin the entire musical. I wonder how I'd thought this was a good idea; if I don't even like people looking at me in class, what made me think I wanted people to look at me onstage, when I'm under a spotlight and heavily made up and possibly dressed as a pig?

True to her word, Evelyn greets me in our usual booth with a steaming bowl of spinach and artichoke dip as the Applebee's speakers play their reliably tired mix of songs from ten years ago. Derek slides into the booth beside her shortly after I sit down.

"So how did the audition go?" Evelyn asks as Derek grabs a chip.

"Not great . . . I think." I wrinkle my nose, mentally discounting Noah's comments.

"Oh no!" Evelyn wails so dramatically that you'd think she was the one who tried out. "But you were so prepared!"

I shrug. "It turns out all the preparation in the world doesn't make up for a total lack of talent. Who knew?"

Derek shakes his head. "But you're not untalented. I mean, listen . . . I'm not saying you're Beyoncé. Or Taylor Swift. Or even Meghan Trainor. Or—"

I hold up my hands. "I get the picture. I'm not a famous, successful singer."

"But"—Derek points at me with half a chip—"you're not terrible."

I dramatically put my hands over my heart. "Me? Not terrible? Oh, Derek, you shouldn't have."

Evelyn looks back and forth between us with irritation shining in her eyes. She always says that the two of us spend too much time doing bits, and we leave her out. Which is sort of true, but still. "Okay, this has been another great episode of the Derek and Jolie Variety Hour, but it's over now. What happened out there?"

"Mrs. Mulaney made me sing."

Evelyn widens her eyes.

"I know! And I thought she might give me some sort of feedback, but she was just like, 'Okay, see you, Jolie. Don't let the door hit you on the way out.'"

"That's not really what happened," Derek says.

"And how would you know? Did you stick around to watch?"

He double-dips his chip, giving the spinach and artichoke dip way more attention than any appetizer merits.

"You watched my performance?" I screech, and a couple at the table next to us looks at me in alarm.

He shrugs. "Maybe I hung around in the back of the auditorium," he says with his mouth full.

Evelyn turns to him. "And? How was she?"

Derek gives a thumbs-up as he chews.

"Oh, don't condescend to me." I scowl. "First Noah, then you."

"Noah said you did a good job?" Derek asks.

I sigh. This is ridiculous. I did a *terrible* job today, and that's the entire reason I called this meeting.

"Listen." I wave my hands in the air like I'm wiping the slate clean of this entire conversation. "The point is, I sucked. I bombed. I bit the big one. And I need to regroup. I need you guys to help me with my list."

Evelyn nods and grabs her phone. "On it."

"If I'm not going to be in the musical, that means I'm not going to kiss Noah. Which, sure, is a disappointment. But there are other things I want to do. And we've already eaten almost every appetizer here, so we need to dig a little deeper."

I think about what Dr. Kelley said—that I probably won't die—but guess what? "Probably" isn't good enough for me right now. There's still a chance, however small, that I won't make it through surgery, and although I won't say it in front of Derek, my possible impending death is all I'm thinking about.

"So far we have jumping off the Cliff and sneaking into a bar. And reading a book," Evelyn reads.

"I'm definitely waiting until it's warmer to jump off the Cliff." I turn to Derek. "Do you want to go with me?"

He looks at me like I've just suggested robbing a bank. "No, Jolie."

"Why not?" I whine.

"Uh, let me think. Maybe because that's considered trespassing, and I'm not super psyched to potentially get arrested?"

"Oh," I say. "Right."

Derek leans across the table, tugs on my shirt, and says, "Sorry, your white privilege is showing."

"Okay, okay." I wince, properly chastised. "But maybe you

can help me run a mile, since you're a cross-country champ and all."

"Run a mile?" Evelyn sounds skeptical, but she types it into her phone. "But you hate exercise."

"I do," I admit. "But I've always wanted to be a runner. You know, like, tossing on a pair of sneakers and being like, 'See you guys later, I'm going for a run.'"

"You know running is a lot more involved than that, right?" Derek asks.

"What else?" Evelyn asks.

I pause. What if I really do die on the operating table? What would I be upset about never having done? What would make me turn into an angry ghost haunting this world until I found closure?

"I've always wanted to drive a convertible," I offer.

Evelyn puts down her phone. "Jolie. Have you become a middle-aged man? What's next, having an affair with your secretary?"

I just shrug. The truth is, it would be too hard to explain to Evelyn and Derek that whenever I see myself post-surgery, I imagine being totally, completely happy. I'm smiling, I'm laughing, and I'm speeding down the highway in a red convertible, not worrying at all about how my jaw looks or where I'm going. There's a guy sitting in the passenger seat, and he's ridiculously in love with me—and why wouldn't he be? I'm beautiful. I'm normal.

But since there's a chance I won't be able to do that after surgery, I can't really afford to wait.

"Well, it's your list," Evelyn says diplomatically as she types it into her phone. "But, frankly, I think you could use some more exciting stuff. I mean, you're literally reading a book."

"It's a classic, and I don't know if there are books in the after-life," I say in my defense.

She widens her eyes and nods. "I'm just saying, why don't you want to, like, skydive? Or travel to Paris?"

"Ev." I shake my head at her. "Do you think my parents are going to fork over the cash to send me to Paris? I'm pretty sure they spent all their retirement savings on cute wall hangings for the nursery. I'm working with what I have, dammit!"

I slam my fist on the table and the silverware clangs.

"I'll see if my uncle has a convertible hookup," Derek says, and I smile in gratitude. His uncle owns a used-car dealership, which is where Derek got his barely drivable pickup truck.

"This is the list of a nerd, Jolie," Evelyn says delicately. "And I'm saying that because I'm your friend."

"Well, then"—I fold my hands on my lap—"I guess I'm a nerd."

Evelyn sighs, surely wishing she had more daring friends, but Derek smiles at me conspiratorially. I smile back with my lips closed (because there's a ninety-five percent chance I have spin-ach stuck in my braces). Sure, I may have less than two months left on this earth, but you know what? At least I have a plan.

That night, I listen to Derek's podcast, just like I (and countless Danes) do whenever he posts an episode. He usually posts them in the middle of the night so they go up at an ideal time for his primary audience, which is about six hours ahead of us. I try to listen to them as soon as I can, but this is the first chance I've had all day. I get into my pajamas (which are covered in adorable tiny dachshunds), crawl into bed, and push play.

Listening to Derek's voice in the dark feels intimate, even though he's not here. But it's calming, and I have to stop myself from falling asleep as his radio-perfect voice floats into my ears.

"*The Princess Diaries. She's All That. Cinderella. Pretty Woman.* What do all of these movies have in common?"

"You hate them," I say out loud, even though Derek's not here to hear me.

"The women all have makeovers. And on today's episode of *Deep Dive*, I'm exploring this trope by watching all of these movies—"

"You watched *The Princess Diaries* without me?" I almost yell before remembering that everyone else is asleep.

"And I've got some questions. Mostly: Why does this trope exist? I mean, yeah, it's fun, but what's it really saying? That you only deserve good things if your hair looks perfect? That you can't find love if you wear glasses? That a guy is only gonna fall in love with a girl if she undergoes some ridiculous transformation, even if she was smart and funny and great before she went through a montage set to a terrible pop song?"

I roll my eyes. Derek's doing it again—this thing where he tries to convince me that there's nothing wrong with me and I'm perfect the way I am. Motivational Speech 101, blah blah blah. It all started when I accidentally left my scrapbook out, and Derek and Evelyn came over. Evelyn just raised her eyebrows, and now makes occasional references to my "weird lady notebook," but Derek wouldn't let it go for a while. I tried to explain what my scrapbook does for me—that it gives me hope that someday I'll be okay—but he just kept talking about how he couldn't believe I didn't know how great I was. It was all very Sitcom Dad and he was seriously about one step away from telling me I'm *beautiful on the inside and that's what counts* as an emotional piano soundtrack played.

The thing is, he doesn't get it. Derek couldn't possibly understand the appeal of a makeover, because he doesn't *need* a makeover. He doesn't know what it's like to look in the mirror every day and hate what you see, to know that everyone else is wondering what's wrong with you, to be impatiently waiting for the day when you'll be fixed. And honestly, I don't really appreciate him hashing this whole thing out on the air when really it's up to me (not Denmark) how I feel about the way I look.

I listen to the rest of the episode until he signs off with "This has been Derek Jones. Stay deep."

I text Derek. *Stop talking about me on your show.*

Derek responds immediately. *Who said I was talking about you? Maybe I'm just inspired by Anne Hathaway's joyful spirit.*

I text him again. *Stop watching movies without me.*

He doesn't text back right away, so I assume he's reached his limit of nightly texting. Until another message pops up: *You were great today. I'm not kidding.*

This is all very nice of him, but it's not like he has an objective opinion.

I put my phone on my nightstand and sigh. If only my transformation would involve a simple montage and a fun soundtrack instead of surgery and swelling and recovery time. But Princess Mia already looked like Anne Hathaway. All Rachael Leigh Cook needed to do was take off her glasses. Julia Roberts just had to become a fancier prostitute. I can't take off my glasses and change my hair; I have to get major surgery.

Derek might not get it, but a makeover sounds pretty good to me right now.

I somehow make it through the next school day: Dissecting a sad, gelatinous frog corpse in Bio II. Partnering with Derek in trig.

Spending lunchtime listening to Evelyn alternate between complaining about the C+ (still pretty good) she got on her English essay about *Our Town* and giving me pep talks when I bemoan my terrible performance after school yesterday.

When the last bell rings, Evelyn heads home to study, but instructs me to let her know the moment I find out anything. The cast list is posted in the hallway outside Mrs. Mulaney's classroom, but because of the crowd I would've been able to find it even if I hadn't known that. The hum of voices and excitement makes me feel like I'm part of a giant swarm of musical-theater-loving bees. I don't know if musicals are a big deal at other schools, but there's very little going on at Brentley. We have to make do with what we have.

"Congrats, Jolie."

I look up from my constant chin-down position to see Donny Jackson, a senior I had a study hall with last semester, giving me a thumbs-up.

"Thanks?" I say.

He doesn't stop to talk to me. But then a girl from trig tells me congratulations. And a few freshmen I don't recognize, too.

I pick up my pace, my flats slapping against the tile as I speed walk down the hallway. I careen around a group of kids huddled at their lockers and narrowly miss the volleyball coach pushing a cart of equipment toward the gym.

I see the cluster of people around the sheet and dart toward it. Some kids high-five each other, someone starts crying and gets a hug from someone else. But I can barely focus on the drama in other people's lives right now—I have to get to that sheet.

I push my way past the crying girl (as gently as I can) and scan the sheet, my eyes racing and my lips parted. I start at the bottom, waiting for my name to jump out at me from the jumble of letters, like a familiar phrase in a word search puzzle.

Farmers. Pigs. Astronauts. Senators. I'm not any of these. Where am I?

And then, there's my name, the letters arranged the same way they always are but somehow looking completely different in this context. Right under Noah's name, there's mine: Jolie Peterson—Prudie.

I'm the lead.

Chapter Seven

I whip around in a panic, looking for someone to explain this to me, but I just come face-to-face with a crowd of well-wishers. Their congratulations barely register with me, and I mumble my thanks as I try to make sense of this.

That's when I see Marla Martinez standing at the back of the crowd, her arms crossed as she casts a narrow-eyed stare at me. If looks could kill, I would be one of those homicide victims they find during the first few minutes of an episode of *Law & Order*.

I try to walk past her without making eye contact, but she steps in front of me. "Congratulations," she says, not sounding entirely sincere.

"Thanks," I say to my shoes. "I wasn't trying for this, you know. I mean, I wasn't trying to steal your part."

She sighs and I can practically hear her eyes rolling. I look up to see her bored expression.

"At least own it, okay, Jolie? The 'poor little me' act gets old fast."

She spins around and walks away, the scent of her hair lingering as I fight the urge to rub my face like I just got slapped.

I shake my head. There's no time to worry about Marla right now; I just need someone to help me figure out what the hell is going on. Was there a mistake? Did Mrs. Mulaney mean to type Jordan Paterson and autocorrect filled in my name? Is Peter Turturro holding a grudge because he missed *Dr. Phil*'s opening credits and now he's playing a practical joke?

I pull out my phone and text Evie. *I'm coming over.*

Evelyn's biggest obsession is *The Golden Girls*—you know, that old sitcom about four elderly women who live together in Florida. It's super weird for a sixteen-year-old to be so into it, but Evelyn can relate pretty much any situation back to that show. "This is just like that time Rose got fired from the pet store for being too old," she'll say, shaking her head, even when I fail to see how my personal problems relate in any way to a fictional elderly woman's.

When I show up at her house she is, as usual, watching the show while drinking a mug of tea. "Come on in," she says, answering the door. "Sophia's just about to lay down another sick burn on Dorothy."

"I thought you were studying for history," I say.

"Perhaps you could say I'm studying the history of sitcom fashion," she says as we nestle into the couch.

"Perhaps I could say you're procrastinating. You do know there are shows about people our age on TV, right?" I ask.

She waves a hand. "Yeah, but I don't relate to those."

She has a point. Evelyn is kind of like one of the brash,

no-nonsense characters on *The Golden Girls*, and not just because she currently has dyed-gray hair. Evelyn just doesn't care what people say, and she cares even less about what people think. *Will anyone else like this outfit?* is a sentence that has probably never even run through her head. Right now, she's wearing a denim vest over a floral button-down with a suede skirt and black tights. It's an outfit that would make me look like an overgrown toddler allowed to dress herself for the first time, but on Evelyn, it some-how makes sense. Life just isn't fair. She was born knowing she'd look awesome in anything, whereas I wouldn't even dare stray from my palette of neutrals.

She reaches out and grabs my arm. "So what happened? Did you get your part in the chorus?!"

I can't even be mad that she's changing the subject from her (lack of) studying because her enthusiasm is very sweet . . . even if I am internally freaking out right now.

"I'm Prudie. I'm the *lead*."

She pauses the TV and stares at me, mouth open. "Seriously? This is fantastic! I told you that you could do it!"

I scowl. "What happened? Did you put a curse on Mrs. Mulaney or something? How did I get the lead? And why aren't you surprised?"

Evelyn shakes her head. "Despite that time I tried to put a curse on Mr. Kader so he would get food poisoning and be unable to administer our algebra test, I don't actually possess mystical powers. Even if I wanted to, there's no way I could convince Mrs. Mulaney to cast anyone. She must've just liked you."

I pick at my cuticles. "I don't know if I can do this, Ev."

She tilts her head, encouraging me to go on.

"Like, I know excitement was riding high before my audi-tion, but this isn't what I thought would happen. I thought I'd be in the background if I got cast at all. But the lead? The one everyone's looking at? The part with the most lines and, oh yeah, solos? I don't think I can do this."

"Are you going to start talking about all your barf-related performance stories again?" she says, and takes a sip of her tea.

"I get nervous! I just don't like people looking at me," I say, burrowing farther into the couch. "You know that. It makes my hands get sweaty and my face get red and my stomach feel like it's staging a revolt against the rest of my organs."

Evelyn raises her eyebrows. "But you can't just spend all your time hiding from things that are scary, even if you are trying to become one with my couch right now."

I don't point out that she's also kind of hiding from studying, but I don't have to, because from behind her mug she says, "Patricia blew a gasket when she found out I failed last week's history quiz."

"You failed it?" I wail, then try to rein in my despair when I see how upset Evelyn looks. "But we studied together! I thought you knew everything there was to know about the Revolutionary War."

She shrugs, but the gesture seems forced. "All of those dates. It's like they go into my head and then shoot back out again to make room for something more practical. Anyway, now Patricia's threatening to take away my sewing machine unless I get my grade up, and I was like, 'Uh, do you expect me to sew denim by hand, lady?'"

I wince. "Sorry. Are you sure you don't want to study right now for this week's quiz? I could help you—ooh! We could make flash cards!"

She shakes her head. "I'm trying to drown my sorrows in tea and television."

"Okay." I prop my feet up on the coffee table, all too eager to forget about my musical-related nerves.

Evelyn presses play. "So, I'll fill you in on what's happening. Blanche is about to go on a date with this guy . . ."

As she describes a plot that I don't really care too much about, I let myself space out and think about the musical. The biggest part of me doesn't think I can do this—memorize these lines, somehow learn to sing entire songs, act next to Noah Reed without freaking out or passing out. But I'll admit it: Evelyn's confidence in me has boosted mine a bit, and there's another, smaller part of me that's standing up straight and getting ready to go. The part of me that says, *I did it. I tried out and I got the part.* The part of me that actually wants people to look at me, that actually wants to be a star.

Chapter Eight

When I get home, Abbi greets me at the door. Well, "greets" might be too kind a word for it; she basically assaults me, grabbing me by the shoulders and pushing me right back out the door.

"Where have you been?" she yells. "We're going to be late!"

"For what?" I ask as she directs me to the driver's seat of my car.

She gives me a look that's equal parts pouting and frustration. "My first childbirth class!"

She lowers herself into the passenger seat as I ask, "What are you talking about? Why am I coming to your class?"

She shoots me a look. "Do you really not remember? We had an entire conversation about this. I need a support partner, none of my friends would take this seriously, and the thought of Mom or Dad coming along makes me break out in hives. So you have to come with me."

I back out of the driveway as I consider this. Did we have a conversation about this and I just blocked it out?

"You've been too distracted by your musical thing to pay attention, but we talked about it," Abbi says, rifling through her bag. She pulls out a lip balm and swipes it on her lips.

Oh. I guess that's actually pretty plausible.

"Well, what are sisters for?"

She snorts. "Come on. I know you don't want to come to this. You're going to learn *way* more than you want to know about the miracle of birth."

When we arrive, we walk into what looks like a meeting room in the hospital, and I see that she's right. There's a giant diagram of a pregnant woman on the wall, and I can't help noticing that the baby is pretty big. The place it's coming out of? Not so much.

A woman with cropped white hair stands in front of the room and gives us a smile as we walk in and sit down at a table. She has the air of a kindly grandma. There are only four other couples here, and they're all just that . . . couples. As in, no one else conned their little sister into being their "support person." It's all women sitting next to the men who presumably impregnated them.

"Okay!" The woman at the front of the class claps her hands as Abbi and I sit down. "I think everyone's here, so let's go ahead and get started. My name's Kathy, and I've been a labor and delivery nurse for thirty-five years. I've seen it all, so you can ask me anything. No question's too weird."

Kathy's about to continue speaking when one of the guys raises his hand.

Kathy points to him and gives an encouraging smile. "Yes?"

"Is it true that women, you know . . ." He leans forward and stage-whispers, as if all of us can't hear him. "Poop? While they're giving birth?"

Kathy smiles sympathetically at the guy's partner, who looks mortified. "It happens. But the nurses have seen their share of poop. And when you're focusing on getting that precious baby out, you won't even notice a little poop. Trust me."

I turn to Abbi and widen my eyes. "A little poop!" I mouth. She gives me a threatening look.

"But we'll get to the rest of your questions later," Kathy continues. "For now, let's start by going through the stages of labor."

Poop talk aside, Kathy proves to be a pretty engaging speaker. In fact, I find out that most of what I thought I knew about giving birth is wrong. It turns out that it isn't usually like in the movies, where a woman's water breaks dramatically and then a frantic husband speeds down the highway to get to the hospital on time but she ends up having the baby in the car because of course she does. Kathy says that ninety percent of the time, a first-time mom's water breaks when she's been at the hospital laboring for hours.

"Hollywood is full of lies," I whisper to Abbi, but she's staring at Kathy's PowerPoint and scribbling down notes.

I've just started to relax and think about how I'm going to share the particularly descriptive details with Derek and Evelyn later when Kathy says, "Are you guys ready to take a little break and hang out on the floor?"

"Wait, do I have to do this part?" I lean toward Abbi as we watch all the women and their partners set up camp on the floor.

Abbi looks at me like I was the one who asked the poop question. "Yes, you have to *do this part*. That's why you're here."

Kathy hands out pillows and blankets as we sit down cross-legged. "I'm not saying anything will take away the pain of childbirth completely—there's a reason it's called 'labor,'" she says as she takes her place again at the front of the room. "But there are some tricks you can use if you want to alleviate the pain. Distractions like music, aromatherapy, massage. And of course, there are drugs." She smiles widely. "But whether or not you go for the meds, the techniques we learn today will help you be more calm and present on one of the biggest days of your life."

I glance sideways at Abbi to see if she thinks this is as unbelievable as I do—I mean, aromatherapy? Is an air freshener really going to help dull the pain of pushing a human being out of your body? But she's making eye contact with Kathy, nodding along to everything she says.

"Support people, this is where you come in," Kathy continues. "It's your job to do everything you can to help Mom out in there. Does she need ice chips? Get them. Does she want a massage? Go for it. You can remind her to keep breathing . . ."

Is Abbi actually going to forget to breathe? I wonder. But then, as Kathy starts demonstrating, I realize she means breathing in a certain way—that exaggerated "hee-hooooo" type of breathing you see on TV. I thought that was just another thing that TV lied to me about, but apparently I was wrong.

"Support people, I want you to sit behind your partners and let them lean against you, okay?"

Everyone scoots into position. "Um . . . this is . . . kind of difficult . . . ," I mutter as Abbi attempts to relax against me. All of these support-partner bros are significantly bigger than their wives or girlfriends, while Abbi is a couple inches taller than me.

"Just . . . stop moving!" Abbi snaps as she leans against me. I sigh.

"Now, what I want you to do is reach around your partner and place your hand on her thigh, right above her knee."

I do it. It's kind of hard to reach, but I remember that I'm here for Abbi.

"Now squeeze. As hard as you can."

"Is she serious?" I whisper to Abbi. "I don't want to hurt you—"

"Just squeeze!" Abbi hisses.

"Okay, okay!" I squeeze with all the strength I can muster, my fingers pressing into her leg.

"Not with your fingernails!" Abbi practically shouts.

I notice that none of the other women are having this conversation with their support partners. In fact, they're all staring at us. Maybe we could volunteer to come to their delivery rooms and the distraction we'd cause with our scene would be another effective pain reliever.

"And now, ladies, I want you to try your breathing. 'Heeeeee. Hooooooo. Heeeeeee. Hooooooo.'"

The room is filled with the sounds of very loud breathing. It would be funny if it weren't sort of creepy.

"Support people, try squeezing again, okay?"

This time I barely squeeze Abbi's leg. I don't want to get yelled at again.

"Now," Kathy says, "that was better, right? It hurt a lot less?"

"Whoa," Abbi says, her eyes wide as she turns around to look at me. "I barely felt that. The breathing really worked."

"Um," I say, not eager to tell her that I was barely touching her. "Wow. Pretty cool."

The rest of the class requires much less participation from me, thank God. And it proves to be extremely entertaining when Kathy puts on a video that shows a real birth and one of the support-partner dudes faints. Kathy dismisses us with a homework assignment to "practice our breathing," which I have zero intention of doing.

Neither Abbi nor I say anything to each other until we're in the car and buckling our seat belts.

"Don't even say it," she groans finally.

"What?" I ask as I start the car.

"That this is all totally ridiculous and you'd rather be, like, hanging out with Derek and making fun of everyone or whatever it is that you guys do."

I snort. "Since when do you care if I'd rather be doing something else?"

But when she doesn't say anything, I start to feel a little bad. I steal a glance at her out of the corner of my eye (I mean, I'm driving a car so I can't just, like, full-on stare at her) and see that she's looking out the window, and she doesn't look happy. I don't know how a woman's supposed to look after she gets out of a childbirth class, but probably not forlorn.

"Hey," I say when we stop at a red light. "I had a good time today. It was fun."

Abbi turns to me and gives me a smile that can only be described as sarcastic. "Right. Because your idea of a good time is getting an up-close look at a baby being born."

I shrug as the light turns green. "Remember how that one support-partner bro looked like he was going to cry?" I imitate his face.

"Things could be worse, I guess," Abbi says. "That guy could be my birth partner."

I know I'm not going to get any answers, but this seems like a window and I can't help flinging myself toward it. "Did you . . . ask the father if he wanted to come with you?"

"Nope," Abbi says firmly, not offering me even the smallest bit of information.

The window slams shut. Well, I had to try.

Chapter Nine

*E*very pair of best friends has their "thing," the activity that holds them together and makes them remember why they're still BFFs after all these years. For me and Derek, it's watching bad movies.

We used to invite Evie to our Terrible Movie Nights, but she pretty quickly realized they weren't for her. "I just don't get why you want to spend your time watching something *bad* when you could be watching something *good*," she said, and I guess that explains the difference between Evie and me. Evie prefers something that's perfectly art directed, with beautiful costumes and poetic dialogue. I find a satisfying sense of comfort in watching something that's full of flaws, like any given Nicolas Cage movie. And Derek enjoys doing things like watching the entire Nicolas Cage oeuvre so he can talk about him on an episode of *Deep Dive*.

The thing about Terrible Movie Night is that the movies

can't be *intentionally* terrible. We're not watching *Sharknado*, a movie that is completely aware it's awful and revels in that fact by including scenes like a man cutting his way out of a shark with a chain saw. We like to watch movies with zero self-awareness, where everyone involved is trying their best but still somehow failing. I mean, sometimes you can try your hardest to make a great work of art, and instead you end up making something that two people will make fun of thirty years later. It's all oddly reassuring, in an existential way.

The movies Derek and I like to watch have titles like *The Satanic Rites of Dracula* and *Manos: The Hands of Fate*. On Thursday evening after the twins go to sleep, we decide to watch *Staying Alive*, the not-at-all-loved sequel to the much-loved *Saturday Night Fever*. We're halfway through an opening sequence that's full of John Travolta wearing spandex and dancing when Derek finally says, "So, are we just not going to talk about you being the lead in the musical?"

I groan. I'd thought that maybe we were just avoiding talking about my starring role the same way we avoid talking about Derek's dad. It's uncomfortable, so let's talk about lemurs and pretend everything's fine!

"Ugh. Whatever." I put my feet up on Derek's lap, not even caring that I'm wearing old socks that have a hole over my left big toe. "I'm just trying to pretend it's not happening. Do you even remember what happened in the fourth-grade musical?"

"You threw up. I know. But you can't keep trotting out one vomit-related childhood memory as a reason why you can't do something." He rests his hands on my feet.

I scoff. On-screen, John Travolta is twirling around wearing a leotard. I settle into the couch and Derek mutters something about how he doesn't understand why my feet have to be in his lap, but this is our thing, the same position we've always watched movies in, and I don't intend to change it just because my feet are "gross" or "I need to buy new socks" or whatever.

"That's a point—write it down," I say, and Derek grabs his notebook. We have an elaborate rating system for our terrible movies. They get points for having gratuitous nudity (which terrible movies reliably have), an unexpected celebrity cameo, a grisly-but-fake-looking death, bad wigs, a continuity error, or, in this case, a dance sequence. There are about a million other ways to get points because at this stage, Derek and I are basically terrible-movie experts.

After he writes down the point, neither of us says anything as we watch the movie. That's the great thing about being around Derek. I mean, I love Evie so much that I would probably murder someone for her (not that I can imagine a situation in which that would happen, since Evie takes self-defense classes and could kill a grown man with her bare hands), but when we're together it's nonstop talking. And that's great sometimes. But Derek and I can carry on a conversation without even saying anything.

"I just don't really understand what's going on," I finally say.

"John Travolta's trying out for a part in some show and he's wearing a bonkers headband," Derek says.

"No, I mean with the musical."

Derek doesn't pause the movie as he turns away from the screen to look at me. That's part of the allure of bad movies; it's not like you're going to miss some important plot point.

"Like, I keep thinking this is all some elaborate prank, and someone's going to post a video of my terrible audition online and then the ensuing bullying will get so bad that *Good Morning America* will do a story all about how teens these days don't have empathy or something." I take a breath.

Derek nods slowly. "That's a possibility. Or—and hear me out—you could've just done a good job in your audition."

I roll my eyes.

"So," Derek says, and this time he actually does grab the remote and pause the movie. "You said Noah thought you were good?"

"When did I say that?"

"At Applebee's." He watches the screen, even though it's just paused on a blur of pink and purple spandex.

"Uh, yeah." I shift slightly on the couch. "He was actually really nice about it. I didn't think he even knew who I was."

"Wow," Derek says sarcastically. "The great Noah Reed deigned to know your name."

"Very funny," I say. "It's just . . . nice to hear a compliment."

"I compliment you all the time," Derek says.

I roll my eyes. "Yeah, but you have to, because you're my best friend. It's kind of a given that you think I'm okay-ish at most things."

He looks at me. *"Okay-ish at Most Things: The Jolie Peterson Story."* Then he runs a finger slowly down the bottom of my foot, sending me into convulsions of giggles.

"Ugh, stop!" I squeal, pulling my foot back and then kicking him in the leg. "You are the literal worst. You know I'm super ticklish."

"Then maybe stop putting your most ticklish body part directly on my leg. Just a thought."

I lunge at him—this is normal for us, goofing off and forcing each other to endure tickling. But I guess I've forgotten how much stronger he's become, because he easily pulls me into a headlock, and when I squeal and he releases me, I end up falling right into his lap.

"Hey," he says with a small smile as I look up at him, and I can't help noticing how impressively solid he is now. I open my mouth to say something, but all that comes out is an exhale.

Okay, so it's not like I've never thought about what it would be like to date Derek. I like boys and he *is* a boy, so of course it's popped into my mind before. And there was this one time last year when I thought that maybe there was something between us.

It was during Brentley's Movies on the Lawn thing at the park last summer, and they were showing *The Wizard of Oz.* I guess I fell asleep, because one minute there were flying monkeys on the screen and the next thing I knew I was waking up with my head in Derek's lap as everyone was picking up their blankets. I blinked a few times as I yawned, then looked up and saw that he was looking down at me and smiling. "You fell asleep," he said, and he brushed my hair out of my face. I don't know what it was—the way he said those three words, the way his touch felt different than it normally did, the way he was looking at me—but I felt something, some inkling that *maybe* there was *just possibly* something between us.

But then Evelyn was like, "You guys, if I don't get home by ten p.m. Patricia is going to call the police and report me missing," and the moment was gone. And a few weeks later Derek started dating Melody, so I figured it had been all in my head. It was a relief, honestly, because Derek and I have spent our entire lives being best friends, and I didn't want to ruin that, but at the same time, it stung a little. Because part of me does wonder: If I were prettier, would Derek have a crush on me?

But right now, I'm wondering if maybe I was right during that movie at the park, if maybe, just maybe . . .

Derek's phone buzzes, and he shifts to pull it out of his pocket, spilling me off his lap and back onto the couch.

"It's Melody," he says, waving the phone at me. "I'm gonna take this."

And then he walks into the kitchen, talking in a low voice. I wonder if he tells Melody when I'm here, or if he tells Melody about Terrible Movie Night, or if he tells her that I was just sitting on his lap. I mean, it's not like anything happened—obviously—but still. I just wonder if that's the type of thing a girlfriend gets mad about.

I pull out my phone and scroll through the IMDB page for *Staying Alive* for a few minutes until Derek comes back into the room and tosses me a half-full bag of jelly beans. "I found this in the kitchen—I think Mom's been holding out on us."

Derek's mom is all about a low-sugar lifestyle, so this is a real find. I pull the bag open and shove a handful in my mouth.

He sits down. "Ready?"

I put my feet back in his lap and with a mouth full of jelly beans I say, "Ready."

"You're disgusting, you know that?" he says, but he's giving me one of his wide Derek smiles, so I know he doesn't really mean it. I lean back against a pillow and make a face at him, thinking about how I'm glad this is how things are: We're best friends, I can count on him, we have our spots here on the couch, and that will never change. He presses play and rests his hands on my feet, and just for that moment, it's like everything in the entire world makes sense.

Chapter Ten

I still can't believe this is happening.

I tap Evelyn on the shoulder and pass her the note. We're in study hall, which is ruled by Mrs. Wise's iron hall pass. She used to be an algebra teacher, then she retired, then she came back to be a study hall monitor. All of which means she's approximately one million years old and is prone to telling us, disapprovingly, about how kids acted in "her day." She usually says this when she sees a story about a new app on the *Today* show, which she watches every morning on mute. I'm relatively sure teachers aren't supposed to be openly watching daytime television, but no one tells Mrs. Wise what to do.

I watch Evelyn read my note and then start writing. This would be so much easier if we could just covertly text like normal people, but the last time Mrs. Wise saw Sam Grady playing *Candy Crush* she took his phone away and then gave us all a lecture on how mobile gaming destroys our attention spans, and then I didn't even have time to finish my trig homework. She doesn't care if we're actually studying or if we're just asleep, like Oliver Norton, who's currently drooling on the desk next to me, just as long as we don't interrupt her TV viewing.

Evelyn keeps her eyes on Mrs. Wise, who keeps her eyes on Al Roker, as she slides the note behind her back.

Well, believe it. It's all happening/baby you're a star/etc., etc. Are you ready for practice tonight?

Beside that, she drew a big pair of lips, presumably mine.

Absolutely not, I write. I don't even know how to act, in case you forgot. And I hate the first days of stuff. What if we have to do icebreaker activities? I don't want to tell everyone one interesting fact about myself. There are no interesting facts about me. I wish I was Lana Meyerhoff. Her parents own a llama farm, and every time she has to tell an interesting fact about herself she just says, 'I live on a llama farm.' She can coast on that one forever.

I slide the note to Evie and she reads it, smirks, and starts writing. Al Roker's still talking about the weather and Mrs. Wise is rapt. All the while, Oliver Norton lightly snores.

She passes it back.

Why in the name of Mrs. Wise's turtleneck would there be an icebreaker activity? This is Brentley. We've all known each other since kindergarten. You'll probably just get your scripts and go over the schedule. The musical's so soon, you're going to have to practice constantly. God forbid BHS actually, like, not half-ass something.

PS: Do you think Lana's parents just really love llamas and wanted to name her Llama? But they were like, "No, that's too weird" and decided Lana was the next best thing?

I'm barely even a part of the musical yet and I'm already kind of offended at Evelyn's suggestion that it will be half-assed.

Although, yes, the reluctance to spend any money and the one month to rehearse it would lead one to assume that this is, at best, partially assed.

I'm still not 100% convinced that I'm going to stay in the musical, I write. *I think maybe this was all a mistake. Like, maybe Mrs. Mulaney meant to write Marla's name on the cast sheet but got distracted by Peter's constant whining and wrote my name instead?*

Evelyn audibly snorts when she reads the note and Mrs. Wise looks up, her eagle eye roaming the room. Evelyn makes a big show of coughing, then primly says, "Excuse me." Mrs. Wise doesn't look happy (maybe in her day kids never coughed), but she turns back to the television. Evelyn slides the note back.

JOLIE. Get it together. I'm getting so tired of telling you how great you are that I'd rather be doing my algebra homework. PS—I need help with my algebra homework. Mr. Kader keeps talking about the quadratic equation, but he still hasn't explained why I should actually care. Also, did you realize that there's a kiss in the musical?

I have to stop myself from shouting *What?* which would surely get Mrs. Wise's attention. Somehow I completely missed this information, probably because my brain was playing a song called "I'm Totally Freaking Out, I Can't Possibly Do This" on loop.

Um, no. I most certainly did NOT realize this, I write.

I'm so distracted by this kiss information that I don't notice Mrs. Wise looking right at us when I pass Evelyn the note. Mrs. Wise slaps her palms on her desk and crosses the room toward us. With a snort, Oliver Norton wakes up.

"Do you ladies have something you'd like to share with the class?" she asks.

"No, we don't, ma'am," Evelyn says politely, folding her hands over our note.

Mrs. Wise holds out her hand.

Uggggh. Everyone in the class is looking at us, and the only thing worse than feeling awkward in front of people is everyone *knowing* how awkward you feel.

Evelyn hands something to Mrs. Wise, but I can tell right away that it's not our note.

"*The ABCs of Abstinence?*" Mrs. Wise reads, confused.

Oh, geez. That's the pamphlet we got in health class earlier this year, and Evelyn keeps it in her notebook so we can read it when we need a laugh. It's so cheesy and poorly written, and even though I'm clearly not considering having sex with anyone, it's a thoroughly unconvincing document. E stands for "Everybody's not doing it!" and X is for "X-Cuse Me: Hands Off!"

"I would actually love to share this with the class," Evelyn explains. "I think it's a super important message."

Mrs. Wise considers it skeptically, then takes it back to her desk.

"That was close," Evelyn mutters as she turns around. "But I'm really going to miss that pamphlet."

"Ladies!" Mrs. Wise barks.

I lean back in my chair and spend the rest of study hall worrying about practice.

I walk into the auditorium after school and see everyone onstage, talking to each other in clumps. These are the types of situations I hate: showing up somewhere alone and knowing that everyone else knows each other, but *you* don't know anyone. And then you're forced to either sit there by yourself and look super awkward or elbow your way into a conversation and look even *more* awkward. Basically you're awkward if you do, awkward if you don't.

It's not that I don't know these people at all—after all, BHS isn't that big. But other than study partners in some of my classes, I don't really hang out with anyone other than Evelyn and Derek. That would involve actually, like, putting myself out there.

I walk up the stairs to the stage, trying to look casual while I scope out the groups of people and figure out who I can talk to, when Peter Turturro steps in front of me.

"Uh, hey, Peter," I say, craning my neck around him to see if I can spot Noah.

"Jolie." He nods. "I just wanted to apologize for my behavior at auditions. I may have been a bit . . . overzealous."

I look at him and take in his ensemble: a black turtleneck and a scarf. Not a winter scarf, but a *fashion* scarf. He looks sort of like a caricature of what someone thought a serious stage actor looked like.

"You were oddly obsessed with a TV shrink," I say, trying to edge past him. "But thanks for the apology. I appreciate it."

"I just didn't think you'd be any good," Peter says.

I stop walking.

"I mean, before you did your audition, I just assumed you were going to be terrible."

I tilt my head. "Thanks?"

Peter puffs out his cheeks and blows the air out forcefully. "Oh, man, I'm really screwing this up. What I'm trying to say is: I didn't think you were serious. You kind of shuffled out onstage with your head down, looking all mousy—"

"Not helping, Peter."

"Right. Well, I thought you were just wasting our time, and Mrs. Mulaney and I are taking this musical really seriously."

"I can see that." I gesture to his scarf, and he nods in thanks.

"I just didn't want anyone to come in here and treat it like a joke. But then when you read with Noah . . . well, you blew us away."

"I . . . what?" I ask, but right then Mrs. Mulaney walks into the room and claps her hands.

"All right, everyone!" she calls. "Take a seat on the stage, please. You'll have to get used to being up there eventually."

I sit down next to Peter—at least that problem is solved. I look around the stage as discreetly as possible and see Marla (glaring at me, yikes), plenty of people I only sort of recognize, and Noah. To say he stands out from the crowd would be an understatement. It's like his head is surrounded by little hearts, like he has his own real-life Snapchat filter.

Next to him sits Toby Lewis. You know how some people are known more for being sidekicks than for being themselves? Like, you don't have Robin without Batman, or Donkey without Shrek, or that weird scary purple guy without Ronald McDonald. That's what Toby is to Noah.

And yet Toby is nothing like Noah—where Noah is tall, Toby's short. Where Noah has hair like a member of One Direction (may they rest in peace), Toby's is short and nondescript. Where Noah walks through his life like he's the star of every scene, Toby's more like the side character that's just there to make dick jokes.

As I'm staring at the two of them and composing my mental list of all the ways that Noah is far superior, Noah looks over at me, smiles, then lifts his hand in a wave.

I freeze. Noah waved at me. *Noah waved at me.* What should I do? What would Evelyn do?

Before I can stop myself, I give him a thumbs-up, then feel my insides try to make a break for it by leaping out through my throat.

Peter leans over. "Did you just give Noah Reed a thumbs-up?" he whispers.

"Shut up, Peter!" I hiss.

Mrs. Mulaney pauses to give us a stern look, then keeps talking.

"As you all know, this year we're lucky enough to be performing onstage for the first time *To the Moon and Back* by BHS's own Johnny McElroy."

Out of the corner of my eye, I catch Marla rolling her eyes.

"Most of you probably aren't familiar with this musical, but let me assure you: Although it may not be as famous or well-known as, say, *Oklahoma!* or *The Music Man*, it provides just as many opportunities for you all to shine."

It also features many more songs about space travel.

"And speaking of shining," Mrs. Mulaney continues. "You've all seen the cast list and you all know who's playing who. I'm sure some of you may be disappointed"—and here I think I see her look pointedly at Marla—"but please remember: Every single part is essential to this musical. We can never pull this off if each and every one of you isn't doing your best."

An audible snort. Marla again.

"That being said, this musical is primarily about two people: Bobby and Prudie. Noah and Jolie, would you please stand up?"

"My boy!" Toby lets out a whoop as Noah stands up.

I didn't know I was going to be put on display this early. I stand up, thanking the musical-theater gods that I decided to dress in a very cute ensemble today: a black flared mini, black tights, and a black sweater with little cat faces on it. Sure, it's a lot of black (the better to blend in), but the cat faces are light pink! I'm branching out!

Either way, I'm sure the stage lights make me appear

translucent as I stand up, shaking in my very cute yet nondescript flats. Every head swivels to look at Noah and me, and I can feel my face getting red under the glare of the lights and eyeballs. I imagine what each person is thinking: *What's wrong with her face?* Every part of my body yearns to sit back down, but that would only draw more attention, so I focus on Mrs. Mulaney and pretend that she's speaking to only me.

"When you look at Noah and Jolie, I don't want you to see Noah and Jolie. Instead, see Bobby and Prudie. This is the story we're telling—two people who love each other through obstacles most of us will never have to deal with, like political campaigns and space travel. Just remember that that's what this musical is about: love. I'm sure you've all heard the saying 'There are no small parts, only small actors.' Every action each of you takes on this stage is in service to our greater story. Whether you're in the chorus or one of our leads, you have an important role."

I can't help but feel like Mrs. Mulaney has a lot riding on a musical that features a chorus of pigs. I wonder what's going on in her personal life.

"That being said," she continues, "most of the heavy lifting will be done by Noah and Jolie. You two are onstage in almost every scene, and you have the most lines to memorize. Most of the time, the audience's eyes and ears will be on you."

I gulp.

"I know that you're both talented enough to do this, but I want to make sure that you're committed. I have full confidence in your abilities, but I want to make sure you do, too. This is going to be your life over the next month. Daily rehearsals, learning songs, learning lines, even some choreography. If you're not in, let me know right away."

She stares at us expectantly.

"I'm in," Noah says. Toby fist-pumps.

She turns to me. I swallow, my throat constricting all of a sudden.

"I . . . uh . . . ," I stammer.

I look around the stage in a panic. Peter looks like he's afraid I might pass out. Marla couldn't look any more bored. And Noah . . .

Subtly, so that only I notice it, he gives me a tiny thumbs-up.

"Me too," I squeak, nodding.

"Good," says Mrs. Mulaney. "Peter, can you pass out the scripts so we can go over some things?"

The next hour passes in a blur. I can barely concentrate on anything Mrs. Mulaney is saying, and Peter has to elbow me to respond two times. All I can think about is what she said earlier: *The audience's eyes and ears will be on you.* As in, everyone will be staring at me. As in, everyone will be thinking, *What's wrong with that girl? Why did she trip over a hay bale and forget all her lines? Why didn't Mrs. Mulaney cast that shiny-haired girl in the pig costume instead?*

I can't do this. That's all there is to it. As soon as practice is over, I'll wait for everyone else to leave and I'll talk to Mrs. Mulaney. I'll tell her I'm sorry, that this was all a big mis-understanding, that I would much rather be hiding inside a pig costume, that I don't actually care if I never kiss anyone before a surgeon breaks my jaw while I'm under anesthesia . . .

I glance at Noah and think about that little thumbs-up, how silly and cute it was. Now we have a joke, me and Noah. Our thing. Someday I can be like, "Remember that time you gave me the thumbs-up?" and he'll be like, "Yeah, that was the moment I knew you were the one for me and—"

"Jolie."

I sit up straight. Mrs. Mulaney is staring at me. "It's your line."

I press my lips together. "Right, right. Sorry."

As soon as we move on to a monologue from Toby, who's playing the narrator, I mentally chastise myself. Not for not paying attention . . . after all, I'm not even going to be in this musical, so who cares? No, I berate myself for pretending I even have a chance at kissing Noah. Breaking him down with my sparkling wit and wonderful personality was the whole point of this thing. Now that it won't be my name on those playbills, I'll be back to my original plan of waiting around for a natural disaster. That's pretty much my only shot, because it's not like Noah is going to be charmed by my flawless looks.

I'm startled out of my thoughts when Peter nudges me again. "Are you okay? You're really sweaty and you look disoriented."

"I'm not disoriented. I promise," I say, standing up when I notice that everyone is heading off the stage and practice is over.

"Did you have a hot dog lately?" Peter grabs my arm.

I pause. "I'm not sure that's an appropriate question to ask a girl, Peter."

"I only ask because Molly Weber got food poisoning from eating the cafeteria hot dogs. If you got sick, it would really screw up the musical."

"Thank you for the concern." I push past him. "But I have to talk to Mrs. Mulaney now."

"Just promise me you won't eat a hot dog!" Peter shouts at me as Noah and Toby walk by.

"Heh," Toby chuckles to himself. When he notices me looking at him, he says, "See, it's funny because it sounds like he's talking to you about penises. You know, because hot dogs are—"

"Yeah, I get the joke, Toby," I mutter, brushing past him.

"You should really take your act on the college circuit," I mutter, brushing past them.

"Hey," Noah says as Toby starts talking to Peter about God knows what. Probably more metaphors for penises.

I spin around.

"Sorry," Noah says quietly, gesturing toward Toby. "For him. He's, well . . . we've . . ."

After struggling for a bit, he finishes with "We've been friends since kindergarten. You know how it is."

I smile, being sure to keep my lips closed, just in case he hasn't noticed my jaw. "Like, you learned to burp the alphabet together and now you're bonded for life."

Noah looks puzzled, but he smiles, and I notice that his teeth are perfectly straight and definitely *not* covered in braces. "Yeah. Pretty much. Switch 'learned to burp the alphabet' to 'chased me around on the playground threatening to wipe his boogers on me' and you've basically got our friendship."

We both glance toward Toby, who is laughing maniacally while trying to physically pick Peter up. Peter, for his part, looks resigned to his fate.

"It's nice that some people never change," I say. "Gives you something to depend on."

"BRO!" Toby shouts to Noah as Peter scampers toward Mrs. Mulaney's table. "You ready to roll?"

Noah gives me an apologetic glance. "I have to go."

"So I've heard."

"But I'm glad it's me and you. In the musical, I mean."

I push my lips together to keep myself from grinning. "Yeah. Me too."

With another smile, Noah turns to follow Toby, who jumped off the stage, out of the auditorium.

I allow myself five seconds of elation, five seconds of feeling satisfied, five seconds of imagining a hot and heavy make-out sesh with Noah in the supply closet. Anything more than five seconds and I might start to question what I'm about to do, which is drop out of the musical.

"Mrs. Mulaney?" I walk up to her as she shoves a script into her messenger bag. "Could I talk to you?"

"Prudie!" Mrs. Mulaney says with a smile.

For a second, I think Mrs. Mulaney has forgotten my name before I remember that it's the name of my character. I think about telling her that I'm not doing some sort of method-acting thing like Jared Leto or whatever, but then I remember that I'm not even going to be in the musical anyway, so the explanation is kind of useless.

"Hi," I say. "Could we talk for a minute?"

Mrs. Mulaney stops packing her bag and raises her eyebrows. "Let's sit down."

We sit beside each other in the front row, and before I can open my mouth to speak, Mrs. Mulaney says, "You want to quit."

I blink a few times. "How did you know . . . ?"

Mrs. Mulaney smiles gently. "You have that 'What have I done?' look in your eyes. I know it well."

I can't help myself—I smile, too. Mrs. Mulaney is good at making me feel comfortable. It's too bad I won't be able to hang out with her more.

"Well, yeah," I say. "You see, this was all an accident."

"You mean you accidentally walked onto the stage and performed a scene?" Mrs. Mulaney folds her hands in her lap.

"Well, no. Not exactly. But I thought I was just trying out for a background part, not the lead. I've never acted before—I can't even sing! I don't even like being in front of people. In fact, I hate it."

Now that everyone's left the auditorium, it's strangely quiet in here, and I feel like Mrs. Mulaney can hear my nervous breathing.

"This wasn't an accident, Jolie," Mrs. Mulaney says.

"No," I say uncertainly. "I'm pretty sure it was."

"You and Prudie? You're meant to be. This was the part you're supposed to play, and it's not an accident that it found you. It's not an accident that you walked onto that stage unprepared to sing. It's not an accident that I picked you to be the lead."

I swallow hard. "It's not?"

Mrs. Mulaney shakes her head. "Sometimes we get chances— opportunities—that we're meant to take. And if you take the leap, things will open up and change. And if you take a step back instead? Okay. That's your decision. But you'll never know what you were supposed to find out. And I think Prudie will help you find out a lot."

I press my lips together. Mrs. Mulaney's making this all sound like it's about a whole lot more than just kissing some cute guy (even though he is *really* cute . . . like, put-a-picture-in-your-locker-and-kiss-it-every-morning cute). She's making this sound like it's about my whole life, like this could actually change something.

And, well, if I really do die when I'm on the operating table? Maybe this is an experience I need. Maybe it's one I'm supposed to have.

"I can't make you do this," Mrs. Mulaney continues. "And if you don't want to, I'll cast someone else. But I won't be happy about it. And I really hope you'll decide—"

"Okay."

Mrs. Mulaney smiles, then looks serious. "Okay? Really?"

I nod quickly. "I'm in."

She smiles wider and reaches out to shake my hand. "All right, Prudie. This is going to be a very big month for you."

I don't know what I just agreed to, and I'm mostly (like ninety-five percent) sure I'm going to faint or puke or spontaneously combust when I'm onstage and everyone's looking at me. But that other five percent is just as excited as Mrs. Mulaney, wondering what this month is going to bring.

Chapter Eleven

Mom and Dad have been infuriatingly respectful about Abbi's wishes not to talk about the father of her baby. Just once, when we were watching TV, my mom paused a commercial to say, "I know you said you don't want to talk about it. But the baby's father . . . is he going to be involved? Financially, I mean? It's important to have those things sorted out."

Abbi just pursed her lips and stared at the paused Swiffer commercial. "No. No, he is not."

Mom nodded and pressed play. But that's just how she is—all "Abbi can talk about things in her own time," and "We need to create a loving and supportive environment," and "Jolie, don't pressure your sister to talk about her experience before she's ready."

Frankly, I don't understand how you could *not* be curious about something like that. It's just weird to let Abbi walk around with a growing belly and not know where it came from. I mean, if she was wearing a new shirt, I would ask her where she got it and she would be like, "I ordered it from J.Crew" and then we would all go on with our lives. But I'm not allowed to ask her where the HUMAN GROWING INSIDE HER BODY came from?

It's all seriously screwed up.

It's not like I haven't tried to weasel some information out of her. I've tried subtle questions and little hints, but Abbi is impervious to all my detective attempts. It doesn't help that our sister bond means she usually knows what I'm thinking before I do.

But I've seen a lot of British detective shows on Netflix, and I've learned that people often give themselves away with small details. Abbi may not be a murder suspect, but I know that eventually she'll let something slip.

On Saturday Mom, Abbi, and I go out shopping for a crib to put in the nursery, which is just our old guest room. This isn't really an outing that demanded my presence, but any trip with Abbi typically involves at least two stops at fast-food drive-throughs, and I could really use a Frosty.

First we hit up Buy Buy Baby, where Mom mutters something about capitalism before she totally fawns over the baby-animal mobiles. That's basically my mom in a nutshell: Yes, she has a Le Tigre T-shirt, but damn if she isn't excited about a Bath & Body Works candle sale.

I stick close to Mom as she checks out a bunch of cribs that all look pretty much the same to me. Abbi is off somewhere doing who knows what—maybe falling asleep in a rocking chair. Every time a salesclerk approaches us, I suck in my stomach, afraid they'll think I'm the pregnant one.

"I'm just not sure which of these will look better with our dresser," Mom says, looking back and forth between two cribs that seem to be exactly the same other than a $100 price difference.

"This one," I say, pointing to the cheaper one. "Understated, yet classic. Sophisticated, yet playful. Elegant, yet—"

"Okay, okay." Mom waves her hands. "I get that you don't care about this. But this is your sister's baby, and it needs somewhere to sleep."

"You mean we can't just pull out a dresser drawer?" I ask.

Abbi appears from behind a rack of diaper bags and dumps an armful of onesies into the cart.

"How is it so expensive to dress such a tiny person?" she asks.

"These prices are highway robbery," Mom says, "and . . . oh! This giraffe print is adorable!"

"Oh geez," Abbi says. "I have to pee."

"Again?" I ask.

"In case you didn't notice, there's a baby pressing into my bladder." She thrusts her purse at me. "Hold this. I'll be right back."

I pull her purse over my shoulder and wander away from Mom so she can't ask me any more questions about cribs. But as it turns out, there isn't a whole lot to interest me in Buy Buy Baby since they don't exactly have a juniors' section.

I'm walking aimlessly through a labyrinth of crib mobiles when Abbi's phone buzzes. I ignore it. It's probably one of the endless notifications she gets from whatever baby app she uses. *Alert! Your baby is the size of a grapefruit. Alert! Your baby is the size of a butternut squash. Alert! Why do we compare babies to food? That's, like, super weird, right?*

I'm fending off an offer of help from yet another Buy Buy

Baby employee who surely wonders what a nonpregnant teen-age girl is doing in the store when Abbi's phone buzzes again. And again. And again.

I dig through her purse. It must be Mom trying to find out where I am, since she knows I have Abbi's bag.

But when I look at the screen, I don't see texts from Mom. I see several texts from someone named John.

Please just answer me.

I want to know you and the baby are okay.

I'm sorry.

I toss the phone back into Abbi's purse like I'm playing a particularly revealing and not-fun game of Hot Potato.

I've never met John. I've never even heard her mention any-one named John. But clearly he knows Abbi pretty well—enough to know about her and the baby. And, if he's asking about the baby, I can probably assume he had a hand in creating the baby, as well.

I didn't even have to go full detective and I already found out something pretty big about the father of Abbi's baby. But I don't feel triumphant—I just feel freaked out.

"Hey."

I spin around. "I didn't see anything!"

I come face-to-face with yet another Buy Buy Baby employee. (Seriously, how many people work here? How is our country in a perpetual employment crisis when this one location of Buy Buy Baby is employing upwards of six hundred people?) She widens her eyes.

"You didn't see . . . what? Are you looking for anything specific?" she asks, gesturing toward the mobiles.

I let out a breath. "I'm just browsing. I know I look really sketchy right now but I promise I'm not stealing anything."

She looks even more confused as her eyes dart back and forth between my face and Abbi's purse, which thankfully is too small to hold even a single mobile. "That's . . . good?"

"Okay, bye!" I shout, and power walk back to find my mom. Abbi's back from the restroom and inspecting a crib like it contains the secrets of the universe. I hand her the purse without saying anything, and she doesn't even look at me when she says, "Thanks."

I'm glad, because one look at me and I know she'd see every question in my mind written across my face. Questions like: *Who the hell is John?*

"Explain why you want to do this again?"

I look up at Derek from my perch on our front porch stairs, where I'm tying the pair of sneakers I only bust out for gym class. "Because I want to prove that I can."

"Okay," Derek says slowly. "But you have a pretty serious history of inactivity. Legendary, in fact. Remember that time we tried to go hiking and you just sat down in that cave and said you were making a new life there?"

"In my defense," I say, standing up and lifting my chin, "it was a very nice cave. Spacious."

"Right. Well, running is a lot harder than a leisurely half-mile walk through the woods."

I shrug. "Tomato, to-mah-to."

Derek winces. "Okay, I'll try one more time to talk you out of this . . . Are you sure you don't want to start more slowly? Like, walk for a few minutes, then run for a minute?"

I shake my head vigorously. "Derek! I don't have time to build up endurance! I could be—"

I'm about to mention my possibly impending death when I

remember that I'm not supposed to talk about this around Derek. But of course he knows what I was about to say.

He stretches his legs and says firmly, "Yeah, okay, but you're not going to die. You're just going to get surgery, eat smoothies for six weeks, and then be able to chew better."

And turn into a completely different person, I add silently.

"Whatever. Let's go. I'm ready to run!"

Derek bounces on the balls of his feet. "Just try to keep up with me, all right? I'll take it slowly."

"Don't patronize me," I say. "You're not Usain Bolt. I'm pretty sure I can handle this."

"It's not really about speed," Derek says. "It's more about endurance—"

"Ugh, stop explaining! Let's just go!"

And we're off, running side by side down the sidewalk. It's hard to explain to Derek why, exactly, I want to do this, because I don't entirely know myself. I guess part of it is that I always thought I would become a runner. Like there was this ideal athletic version of myself inside, just waiting to lace up her sneakers and show herself. Never mind that I almost passed out when we ran the mile in gym class. Never mind that I wrinkled my nose in disgust every time pre-pregnancy Abbi attempted to get me to go to spinning class with her. Never mind that my favorite form of exercise up until now has been channel surfing.

I just know that there's a perfect me out there, the one that wakes up with the sun and hits the pavement, coming home sweaty but refreshed, saying something like, *Wow, it's a hot one out there.* And perfect me is also a make-out master, is brave enough to jump off cliffs, has read all the classics in the English canon, and feels comfortable when people look at her.

I don't necessarily have all the time in the world to complete my goals. I think about when Derek's dad died and his mom had to get rid of his stuff. Derek didn't talk about it much, but I was over a lot so I saw how it went down. They wanted to keep everything, but it's not like they could keep a closet full of his clothes or his bottle of contact solution. But the most heartbreaking part for me was all the reminders that he wasn't finished. He had left a half-finished crossword puzzle sitting on the coffee table. There was an open container of yogurt in the fridge. When he went to work that day, he thought he'd be coming back to figure out twelve across and eat some Chobani. He didn't think that hospital's hallway would be the last thing he'd ever see.

I blink back tears as I pump my arms and feel the sidewalk under my feet. I just don't want to have unfinished business before I go into surgery. You never know, do you? Maybe I'll become beautiful and be able to achieve my perfect final form . . . but either way, I want to make sure I don't leave behind any half-finished crossword puzzles. And I wish I could explain all of this to Derek, but I know he would just change the subject and start talking about climate change or whatever his latest podcast episode is on.

"Doing okay?"

I give Derek a probably not-all-that-convincing thumbs-up. My depressing reverie distracted me from running for a few blocks, but now that I realize what we're doing . . . well, it kind of sucks. Actually, it *really* sucks. My lungs are burning, and I'm convinced my insides might be trying to make a break for it. My stomach is cramping, and I'm really regretting having eaten an entire plate full of Dad's Sunday-morning blueberry pancakes. And my knees are on fire . . . are your knees supposed to hurt when you're sixteen?

"Great!" I wheeze.

"Because we can slow down, walk, take a break . . ."

"No breaks!" I try to shout, but it comes out a little less persuasive. I pick up the pace. The faster I can do this, the faster we'll be done, and the faster I can check this bad idea off my list.

I look at Derek through my labored breathing. He's doing this easily—duh, he does cross-country, so a mile is like crossing the street for him. He's staring straight ahead, his brows knitted in concentration, and I wonder what he's thinking about. Derek and I are more about jokes than we are about having deep heart-to-hearts, so I've never spent all that much time thinking about what actually goes on inside his head while he runs.

So I ask him.

"What do you think about when you run?" I try to ask it casually, but it comes out as more of a gasp.

I expect him to think about it a little, but instead he immediately says, "SAT flash cards."

I huff. "What?"

"I go over SAT vocab words in my head," he says easily. "Aberration: a state that differs from the norm!"

"Are you serious?" I wheeze. "You're even studying when you run?"

"Demagogue: a leader who seeks support by appealing to passions rather than logic! Expunge: remove! Munificent: generous!"

"Oh my God! You're the world's biggest nerd!"

"Fractious: easily annoyed!"

"I feel particularly fractious right now," I say.

He turns his head slightly and smiles at me. My heart, acting of its own accord, skips. And not even because I have almost certainly overexerted myself and I'm going to be paying for it later.

No, this was the sort of skip my heart does when it sees a hot guy, I realize with shock.

Which is understandable, I remind myself. Derek is hot now. It's fine to admit that, to admit that his eyes are a very comforting shade of brown, that the firmness of his chest is not *terrible*, that his facial features aren't *unattractive*. It doesn't mean anything if I objectively deduce that my best friend is a good-looking guy. In fact, it would be weirder if I didn't admit it.

"Your face is alarmingly red," he says, not even struggling to catch his breath.

I don't say anything back. Mostly because I physically can't, but also because I'm afraid of what will come out of my mouth. I mean, what am I going to say? *When did you get so cute?*

But I don't get the chance to wonder about it anymore because, while I'm distracted, the toe of my shoe catches on a crack on the sidewalk. My body launches itself into the air and hits the sidewalk, hard.

"Urrrrgggh," I groan, slowly rolling over and sitting up.

"Jolie!" Derek skids to a stop and kneels beside me. "Are you okay?"

"Never better." I wince. "What, does this look like it hurts?"

My knee is all bloody and I'm pretty sure there's gravel stuck in it. Derek gently touches my leg, checking out the wound, and I feel an electric shock go through my body. Which is ridiculous . . . Derek and I have touched a million times before. Punches on the arm, hugs for pictures, my feet on his lap during movie night. A million little touches that add up to nothing but one lifelong friendship.

But there's something about this. I watch his face as he looks at my knee. We're so close I can feel his breath on my leg.

Stop it, Jolie, I tell myself. *Derek would never like you anyway,*

even if this was some sort of alternate universe where it made sense for
you to have a crush on your best friend. He wouldn't ever like you and
then you'd ruin your friendship right before your death and he'd have
to give a really awkward eulogy, knowing you went to the grave having
unrequited feelings for him. Is that what you want?

No, I decide.

Derek's phone buzzes, and he pulls it out of his pocket. In the second before he picks up, I see Melody's face pop up on-screen. I've seen the picture before and I've never really paid attention, but now it hits me: She's pretty. Beautiful. Curly hair that cascades to her shoulders, flawless skin, a perfect smile. There's nothing wrong with her. She's certainly not having surgery to fix her face.

Derek answers, taking his hand off my knee and stepping away from me. "Hey," he says with a softness in his voice. And, I hate to admit it, but I'm annoyed. Annoyed that phone calls from Melody, who I've never even met, are always interrupting us. And, okay, I'm also a little annoyed that he's over there leaning against a tree talking to her all quietly about who knows what, and that there's a whole side of Derek that I don't get to see.

I push myself up off the sidewalk and try to hold in my groan. I certainly don't want perfect Melody to hear the tortured screams of the girl who couldn't run a mile without injuring herself.

But it doesn't matter. Derek's walked a few steps away from me and is talking in a low voice, so I can't even hear what he's saying. He hangs up and walks back toward me.

"So, I hate to say I told you so . . . ," he starts.

"This has nothing to do with my athleticism," I say. "This was a freak accident. It could've happened to anyone."

"That sidewalk had it out for you," he says with a smirk.

"Exactly." I brush some dirt off myself. "So I feel fine, but I thought you might need a break, so let's walk back home."

"Yeah," Derek says, "I am exhausted from taking a leisurely stroll for not even a mile. I'd better walk back. Wouldn't want to hurt myself."

"Glad we agree."

"Maybe we could even call Evelyn to pick us up," he says. "I'm not sure I can make it."

"Shut up." I push him off the sidewalk, and it feels totally normal to touch him again. *The electric shock was just a momentary lapse*, I tell myself. *A temporary delusion caused by physical exertion. It won't happen again.*

Chapter Twelve

The musical is May 13 and it's already April 17, which means we have less than a month to make this happen. Rehearsal is fast and furious and pretty much constant, and I'm so overwhelmed by the thought of learning my lines that I even forget to panic about everyone staring at me. Well, for a little while, anyway.

I walk into today's practice feeling at least slightly more confident. After all, if Mrs. Mulaney thinks I can do this, who am I to say otherwise? Even Peter apologized for doubting me. I'm not saying I'm going to take Broadway by storm, but at the very least I should be able to handle a low-budget, hastily produced high school musical, right?

We're all milling around on the stage, except Toby, who is showing a crowd of girls how he can do parkour by leaping off the auditorium seats. Noah is sitting by himself looking over the script, Marla is casting a cool glare at me from across the stage, and Peter is talking my ear off about . . . well, I'm not sure. I'm not one hundred percent listening. In other words, it's the normal I'm slowly getting used to.

When Mrs. Mulaney walks into the auditorium, she claps her hands to get our attention. But we all stop talking as soon as we see who is following her—a twenty-something skinny guy wearing a backward baseball cap.

"Do you think that's her husband?" Peter whispers.

I turn to look at him slowly. "Peter, she's in her fifties and that guy's, like, barely older than us."

Peter shrugs. "The heart wants what the heart wants."

"We have a very special guest with us today!" Mrs. Mulaney says with a smile. "Johnny McElroy, BHS graduate and the playwright of *To the Moon and Back!*"

We all clap politely. So this is the guy behind Bobby and Prudie—in a way, he's sort of the architect of my first kiss.

"Would you like to say a few words?" Mrs. Mulaney asks, but before she's even finished the question, Johnny hops onto the stage and starts pacing back and forth.

"I'll admit, when I wrote *To the Moon and Back*, I saw it being performed on Broadway. Maybe as a touring production, or a film adaptation starring a young Meryl Streep as Prudie."

I laugh out loud, certain he's joking. But no one else laughs, and his confused look lets me know he's serious. "Sorry," I mutter, eager for everyone to stop looking at me. "Something in my throat."

"But after I sent the script to Carol for feedback—" he continues.

"That's Mrs. Mulaney," Peter whispers. I'm so glad she and Peter are on a first-name basis.

"—and she suggested putting it on as a high school production, I began to see the value in that. Why not work out the kinks with unskilled actors before it makes its way to some more prestigious stage?"

Uh, rude. I mean, I'm aware that I'm not a young Meryl Streep for a lot of reasons, the biggest one being that I don't have a time machine, but still. This feels particularly insulting coming from someone who wrote a song that has a chorus of pigs singing about rockets.

"So I'm eager to see a beginner's interpretation," he says, smiling charitably. "And I'll be here as often as I can to make sure that my vision is carried out. But, please, pretend I'm not here. I'm but a fly on the wall observing your artistic choices."

And with that, he hops off the stage, bows with a flourish, and sits down. We all clap, and I feel like I'm looking at the Ghost of Peter Future.

"Thank you, Johnny," Mrs. Mulaney says, standing up, and I can't tell if I'm simply imagining the look of chagrin on her face. "So let's go ahead and get started. I'd like you to have your lines more or less memorized by next week, but for now feel free to read from your scripts. Toby, Noah, and Jolie, you're all in the first scene, so please stay on the stage. Everyone else, take a seat."

As the rest of our cast files down the steps and sits down on the creaky auditorium seats, I gulp. I guess I didn't realize things were going to be quite so . . . performance-y . . . so soon. Every set of eyeballs in the room is looking at me, and my shoulders start to hunch on their own.

Toby plays an omniscient narrator who's sort of like a carnival barker. This is a perfect part for him because he's extremely loud and, for reasons that don't make any sense, almost childishly charming.

Toby goes through his spiel introducing the musical and the characters through rhyming couplets. I watch Johnny, in the front row, mouthing all the words, his hands tented under his chin.

And then Toby jumps offstage (Mrs. Mulaney: "Toby, next time would you mind using the stairs? The audience may find your leap distracting.") and it's just us, me and Noah, with everyone watching us. The spotlights aren't on, but the regular auditorium lights feel hot on my skin. My mouth goes dry, and I anxiously lick my lips. I can hear the auditorium chairs creak, and someone sneezes.

"Sure is a beautiful day out here on the farm," Noah says, adopting a drawl.

"Sometimes I think I could live here forever and never get tired of this view," I mumble.

"Jolie?"

I look down at Mrs. Mulaney.

"Try tilting your body more toward the audience. And lift your head a bit. That will help you project more easily."

I can tell Mrs. Mulaney is trying her best not to make me feel uncomfortable, but it's too late. There's no way I'll ever feel comfortable up here. And tilting my body toward the audience? I have to fight the urge to say, *But then people will see me!*

I guess that's kind of the point.

I clear my throat, turning myself toward the audience and trying to lift my chin, which feels magnetically drawn toward my chest. "Sometimes I think I could live here forever and never get tired of this view."

Mrs. Mulaney doesn't interrupt, so I assume I did if not great, at least okay. I find her face and she gives me an encouraging smile.

But before Noah can launch into his monologue about the simplicity of farm life, Johnny stands up.

"If I may," he asks, hopping onto the stage. He leans toward me and in what I think is supposed to be a whisper but is definitely loud enough to be heard by everyone, says, "Do you really think that's the best accent to go with?"

"I—I wasn't using an accent," I say. My eyes dart back and forth between him and Mrs. Mulaney. "Should I?"

Johnny shakes his head in frustration, like I'm willfully misunderstanding some great point he's making. "No, I mean the lisp. Is that a deliberate choice? Because that's not really how I saw Prudie."

"You know what, Johnny?" Mrs. Mulaney calls loudly from the front row. "Why don't we just let them get through the scene, then we can give our notes later."

He nods at her. "Good idea. Carry on."

He hops off the stage, and Noah restarts his monologue, but I feel like all the wind has been knocked out of me. Because I wasn't doing an accent—I just have a lisp. It's because of the way my teeth don't meet in the front, and the whole situation is only made worse by my braces. Honestly, by this point in my life I'd pretty much forgotten about the lisp—it's kind of the least of my problems, you know? And given that I avoid putting myself in the spotlight and talking to other people whenever I can, it rarely comes up.

But now, all of the self-consciousness I usually reserve for my appearance transfers itself to my voice. I remember how I was so embarrassed about my lisp in the sixth grade that for the entire year, I tried to avoid saying the letter "s" at all (which was, unsurprisingly, pretty difficult). I remember the shame I felt when kids would snicker at me when I had to read out loud from the textbook in science class. All of those terrible memories come flooding back, and I remember that I don't just *look* weird—*everything* about me is weird.

Noah's done talking, and the last thing I want is for Mrs. Mulaney to have to prod me to say my line so that even more attention is drawn to me, so I hurry through what I have to say. I would do some on-the-spot rewriting to avoid the letter "s," but I know Johnny has this thing memorized and he definitely wouldn't appreciate the improvisation. I feel my shoulders up near my ears again and I know I'm talking to my shoes, but Mrs. Mulaney doesn't say anything.

We move on to the next scene, one that I'm not in. I take a seat in the auditorium and pretend to watch several farmers sing about crop rotation, but my heart's not in it. All I'm thinking is: *I can't do this.* Of course I can't do this. I've built my whole life around blending in, not standing out, so what made me think I could handle being on a stage and under a spotlight? I already told Mrs. Mulaney I'm in, but so what? I'm sure plenty of other girls would happily take my place. I glance across the auditorium and see Noah studiously watching the scene on stage. Now there's someone who's meant to be looked at. And sure, dropping out now will basically kill my chances of kissing him, but no guy is worth this. I'm ready to go into hibernation until my surgery.

And then everyone's standing up, and I realize that today's practice is over. I'm walking toward the stage, where I deposited my backpack and jacket earlier, when I'm almost knocked over.

"Whoops," says Marla as she keeps on walking.

She just shoulder-checked me? Seriously? I rub my shoulder and shake my head in disbelief. She probably already has Prudie's part memorized, so I might as well tell her it's hers.

I can feel tears pooling at the corners of my eyes and the

last thing I want to do is cry in front of the entire cast right before I quit, so I book it toward the exit. But I'm not fast enough—Mrs. Mulaney steps in front of me.

"Don't quit," she says sternly.

"Why not? I'm not exactly a young Meryl Streep," I attempt to say breezily, but the catch in my voice gives me away.

"Even Meryl Streep isn't young Meryl Streep anymore. And who cares? There's already a Meryl Streep and the world doesn't need another one. What it needs is you."

I frown. The world probably could use another Meryl Streep, to be honest—at least we'd be able to divide all those awards between more than one person. But I guess that's not what Mrs. Mulaney is trying to say.

"The world *in general* might need me," I admit. "But this musical definitely does not."

"Well, you can't quit," Mrs. Mulaney says. "If you do, I'll make sure you're in my speech class next year and I'll fail you, and it will ruin your perfect transcript."

My mouth falls open in shock as Mrs. Mulaney smiles.

"But you can't do that," I say when I recover. "It's against the rules."

"Maybe I'm not *supposed* to," she says. "But do you really want to find out?"

And then she walks away and starts talking to Peter.

Okay, so I'm like ninety-five percent sure that Mrs. Mulaney would never actually fail me and she's just kidding, but still. I'm so in shock as I walk through the auditorium doors and across the cafeteria toward the front doors that I barely notice when Noah falls into step beside me.

He smiles widely and I'm sure he's about to tell me how he so admires Johnny McElroy and his insights, or assure me that I really should just drop out and give the part to Marla and her impressive shoulder-checking ability. But instead he says something that truly surprises me.

"Johnny McElroy's kind of a d-bag, right?"

A tiny giggle escapes my lips, but I'm sure Johnny McElroy is hiding behind the vending machines, waiting to hear what we have to say about him, so I don't want to say anything too mean. So instead I just nod. "Total d-bag."

"Glad we agree," Noah says, rolling up his script and sticking it in the back pocket of his black jeans. "Today was fun. See you at practice tomorrow."

And then he's off to wherever Noah Reed goes after school—weekly meetings for the Very Handsome Boys' Club?—and I'm left standing in the middle of the cafeteria, feeling totally worn out and totally exhilarated at the same time.

I guess I'm still the star of this musical.

Chapter Thirteen

A couple of nights later, Mom and Dad take Abbi and me out to dinner to celebrate my role. I think they're feeling guilty that we spend so much time talking about Abbi and preparing for the baby, and they're worried that I feel left out. Little do they know that flying under the radar is kind of my jam. Jolie Peterson: the incredible invisible girl!

Either way, I'm not about to turn down a dinner out, especially because we're driving a whole thirty minutes away to Campton, a town slightly bigger than Brentley that has a few more restaurants. I mean, the choices are still pretty slim—a buffet our entire family got food poisoning at on Abbi's tenth birthday, an Olive Garden that made the news because some waiter was putting breadsticks down his pants and then serving them to customers, and a Burger King that always smells like weed. It's not exactly a culinary haven, is what I'm saying. But there is this one little Italian place with red-and-white-checked table-cloths where we love to go when we're celebrating things. It doesn't smell like weed, it hasn't made any of us sick, and to the best of my knowledge, none of the bread has ever been in somebody's pants. What more could you ask for in a restaurant?

Typically, our few-and-far-between dinners out are some of our best family moments. But as the four of us load into the Subaru and Mom backs out of the driveway, I can detect palpable tension radiating off Abbi. She drums her fingers against the door and looks out the window, silent even though Dad's in charge of the music, and we normally love to make fun of his awful selections (a lot of hair metal).

"Are you okay?" I ask her as Mom drives and Dad fiddles with the radio.

"Can't we go somewhere else?" Abbi says to the front seat, totally ignoring me. "Why do we always have to go to Gionino's? How many times do we have to eat the same lasagna, you know?"

"Um, a million times, because it's the best lasagna in the world?" I shoot her a look of betrayal.

"Well, we're sure as hell not going to that Olive Garden," Dad says over the dulcet tones of Poison.

Abbi shakes her head. "Why do we have to go to Campton, anyway? Let's mix it up! Let's go to Marty's!"

"Marty's *Diner*?!" I screech. "When we were celebrating you getting into college we didn't go to Marty's and make you eat a meat loaf sandwich or burnt onion rings."

"Jolie's right," Mom says over the wailing of me and the guitars. "We're celebrating her today, so she gets to pick."

"And I pick Gionino's." I cross my arms. "Lasagna, here I come."

Abbi sighs and looks out the window again.

"What's your deal?" I whisper. "Are you pissed that we're spending one day paying attention to me?"

Abbi whips her head toward me. "No," she hisses. "Not everything is about you, okay?"

"Well, stop being so hormonal."

"Not everything is about my hormones, either. I just don't want to drive all the way to Campton."

"You go there every day for school. What's the big deal?"

Abbi shakes her head at me. "You could not possibly understand." She rests her hands on her belly and stares out the window again.

After an awkward car ride and a few too many Bon Jovi songs, we finally pull into the Gionino's parking lot. Just the sight of that small, nondescript building with the neon sign fills me with joy, and I practically skip across the parking lot.

Inside, Gionino's is totally different from its bland exterior. There are black-and-white family photos covering the walls, loud Frank Sinatra is playing, and there's the wonderfully overpowering scent of garlic and tomatoes. We don't go to church, so I don't have much of an idea about what heaven's like, but I'm pretty sure it's just Gionino's.

We sit down, and I open my menu, then swing it shut again. It's not like I need to figure out what I'm getting.

The waiter brings our drinks and takes our orders. "Cheers to Jolie," Mom says, raising her glass of wine. Dad does the same, and Abbi and I raise our glasses of iced tea. I'm beaming, but I can't help but notice that Abbi's eyes are darting around the restaurant like she's in a Worst-Case Scenario Television reenactment of a woman being stalked by her psychotic ex-husband.

Which, honestly, kind of sucks. Can't Abbi let me have one day where we celebrate my accomplishments? When I actually have something cool (I mean, relatively speaking) going on, can't she pretend to be excited for me?

But I'm not going to let these negative feelings influence my night at Gionino's. It wouldn't be fair to the lasagna.

Our waiter arrives with a huge tray bearing four steaming-hot plates of pasta. Even though I know there have been happier moments of my life, I'm having a tough time remembering them right now because I'm overwhelmed by the smells wafting my way. When he sits my plate in front of me, I snap a quick pic to send to Evelyn and Derek with the caption "Wish you were here. Haha no I don't, more for me."

Mom frowns. "Put your phone away. This is family time."

I don't bother to point out that Abbi is barely mentally present right now. "Fine, fine, fine," I say, tossing my phone back in my tote bag.

"I just want to say," Mom says with a sniffle, tears forming in her eyes, "that we are very, very proud of you. You've always been a star to us, but now everyone else will get to see what a star you are, too."

Oh no. Mom's officially gone off the red-wine deep end. She's typically pretty even-keeled—a requirement for being a school counselor—but get half a glass of wine in her and all of a sudden she's hugging everyone and professing her love for strangers.

"Thanks, Mom," I say, looking to Dad to make sure he realizes what's happening.

He puts an arm around my mom, but I notice that his eyes are also wet. Dad, unlike Mom, gets emotional at the drop of a hat. You might think a woodworking, flannel-wearing tough guy wouldn't cry much, but he subverts stereotypes like that. In fact, just last week I found him crying while watching a Hallmark movie about a woman who moves back to her small town and falls in love again with her childhood sweetheart with the assistance of a helpful angel.

Obviously, we're a family that likes our television.

"You guys, please don't cry!" I say. "Not in front of the food!"

Mom laughs a little self-consciously and wipes her eyes. "You're just growing into such an amazing young woman. So smart and talented . . ."

This is nice. Really. And it's not like I don't appreciate all of this—the dinner, my family, that my parents aren't afraid to express emotion even if it's super embarrassing—but I also notice what they're not saying. They don't say anything about how I look.

And it shouldn't be important. I get that. I shouldn't care if I'm pretty, because my mind is more important, or whatever. But I do care, and the fact that I can't even remember getting a compliment about how I look? It hurts, especially because I feel like everyone's constantly admiring Abbi's beauty.

I glance at Abbi to see if she's rolling her eyes at this, but she's absentmindedly moving her fork around her plate, turning to look every time the front door swings open.

"What are you doing?" I ask, poking her with my butter knife. "You're not even eating."

"These breadsticks aren't health hazards, which is more than we can say for some Italian restaurants in the neighborhood," Dad says, taking a hearty bite of one. "Or at least if they are, it hasn't made the news."

Mom gives him a disgusted look and puts her breadstick down before turning to Abbi. "Are you feeling sick, Abs?"

Abbi throws her napkin onto her plate. "Actually, yeah. I'm gonna run to the bathroom."

She scoots her chair back hard and books it across the restaurant.

"What's her deal?" I ask through a mouthful of food.

"I was sick all through both of my pregnancies, too," Mom says with a dismissive wave. "Anything I ate, I'd just throw it back up."

"Gross," I say.

"Don't act all high-and-mighty with me," Mom says, glancing back and forth between me and Dad. "You guys are the ones talking about the breadsticks."

We all keep eating, and I wonder when Abbi's coming back. As I stare at her empty chair, I start to feel a little bad. I mean, she's my sister, and she's sick. I think about the time when I was in third grade and I came down with a nasty case of the flu, and Abbi sat in bed with me and read the entirety of *Harry Potter and the Goblet of Fire*. And then when I got so scared of the Death Eaters that I couldn't sleep, she switched to *Junie B. Jones*.

She always tries to help me. The least I can do is repay the favor.

I sigh, standing up. "I'm gonna go check on Abbi."

Mom beams. "Didn't we raise such a considerate daughter?"

"Considerate and hungry," I say, pointing at both of them. "If either of you touches my food, there will be hell to pay when I come back."

I head across the dimly lit restaurant, past tables of old couples and young people on dates and families with kids who are getting spaghetti everywhere. Gionino's is packed, as always, and I wonder if Abbi is just waiting in line for the bathroom.

When I round the corner to the small hallway that leads to the restrooms, I immediately see her. I'm about to call her name and ask her what she's doing when I notice she's not alone. She's talking to some dude, and she looks pissed. I can only see a little bit of his face, but he looks older than her. He's wearing glasses and a maroon sweater with a plaid shirt underneath. In other words, he looks like someone who is trying to be cast in the part of "middle-aged nerd."

He reaches out to touch her arm in a way that looks reassuring (if he looked at all menacing, I would have jumped him by now), but she swats his hand away and says loudly enough that I can hear, "You don't get to touch me, okay? Not anymore."

I back out of the hallway and into the dining room as quietly as possible. Abbi clearly doesn't want us to know about this, and if I can just make it out of here without her seeing me—

"Watch out!"

I spin around to see a waiter with a tray full of food falling toward me. I try to jump out of the way, but it's too late. Plates clatter and crash to the floor as I'm drenched in sweet, warm Gionino's red sauce, plus a little Alfredo sauce and red wine for good measure.

Abbi comes running out of the back hallway (alone) and stops in her tracks when she sees me. "Jolie?"

"I was coming to find you," I say. "But I . . . I . . ."

I can't finish my sentence because I realize that everyone in the very crowded restaurant is staring at me. And why wouldn't they be? There's a girl covered from head to toe in marinara sauce—I'd stare, too.

"Sorry," I whisper to the waiter, who just glares at me as he bends over to start cleaning things up.

Abbi shakes her head.

I try to avoid stepping on broken glass as I walk back to the table, feeling ricotta cheese squishing in my shoes. Mom and Dad are staring at me, as is our waiter.

I pull a spaghetti noodle out of my hair. "I guess we can box up my lasagna."

Abbi's still looking nervous, and now I have at least sort of an inkling why. "Can we just go, please?" she asks.

The waiter hands me my box of lasagna. "Gladly," I say. Being stared at for being covered in food is, as it turns out, even less pleasant than being stared at in musical practice.

"We're gonna have to hose you down in the parking lot." Dad shakes his head as we walk out.

Later that night, after Mom makes me shampoo the backseat of the Subaru because she says we'll never be able to trade it in if it looks like a crime scene, I'm reheating my lasagna in the kitchen when Abbi walks in.

"You'd think you would have lost your appetite for Italian after wearing it," she says.

"Funny," I say as the microwave beeps. "But you clearly underestimate my love for Gionino's."

I watch her rummaging through the fridge. "Feeling better?"

"What?" she asks, holding a container of Greek yogurt.

"You were sick? Earlier?"

Abbi gives me a blank look, then widens her eyes "Oh! I am. Feeling better, that is. I was totally sick before. Couldn't stop barfing."

"But now you can't wait to eat some yogurt," I say, taking a bite of my lasagna. "The preferred food of queasy people everywhere."

"Exactly," Abbi says, looking right at me. It's almost like she's daring me to bring up what happened. Does she want to talk about it? Is this, like, a sisterly moment for us?

I've just opened my mouth when she says, "Can you please just not?"

"What?" I ask.

"I know what you were about to say. You saw us. But I really, really don't want to talk about it, okay?"

I know I should let it go. I should let her walk out of the room to eat her yogurt in peace. But I don't want to—I want to know.

"Just tell me—was it him?"

She slams the refrigerator door. "What part of 'I don't want to talk about it' do you not get? This. Isn't. Your. Business."

She stalks out of the room, and a few seconds later I hear the TV turn on. I glance at the clock—it's time for *Untold Stories of the ER*. I sigh. Okay, so she's engaging in a little comfort viewing—maybe I can give her a break. What she's going through is clearly hard, even if she won't talk about it with me.

I walk into the living room and sit down on the couch beside her. "So, what's this one about?"

She eyes me warily, like she's trying to figure out if I have an ulterior motive. "Some guy's eyeball pops out of his head, and the doctor has to figure out how to push it back in."

I cringe. "I hope this doesn't happen to me during surgery."

"Jolie," Abbi says, turning to me. "You're getting your jaw operated on. How is one of your eyeballs going to pop out?"

I shrug, focusing on the lasagna that I brought in with me. "Stranger things have happened."

"Here." Abbi hands me the remote. "Pick something else."

I flip through the channels until I find one that's showing old reruns of *The Office*. "Is this okay?" I ask.

"I mean," Abbi says, giving me the tiniest of smiles, "I'm fairly certain no one's eyeballs are going to pop out, but I can manage."

I settle in, and we watch a few episodes. So, maybe Abbi won't be honest with me, but she's still my sister. That still means something.

Chapter Fourteen

*J*ohnny McElroy isn't at our next practice, thank God, so there's no one to point out the fact that I'm not Meryl Streep. When Mrs. Mulaney sees me walk in, she gives me a wink before going back to talking to Peter.

So, I guess I'm doing this for real.

And now that I've sort of become used to the idea that I'm going to be in the musical, I have to face the fact that I'll be kissing Noah in front of everyone.

Okay, so it's not a *real* kiss. Not a passionate, steamy, private kiss. No, this will be the most public kiss ever, because it's in the script.

I quickly decide that this doesn't count. A kiss isn't a kiss if it's onstage, if it's in front of an audience, and if one of the kissers is wearing a space suit and there's a live cow on the stage (oh yeah, have I mentioned that there's a live cow?).

No, kissing Noah onstage doesn't count as fulfilling my goal. My first real kiss has to be unscripted. However, that doesn't change the fact that I'm going to have to figure out how to press my face against his under the harsh glare of the lights without passing out from shock.

Evelyn's here working on costume stuff, and I'd love to ask her what the big kiss was like in last year's musical, but she's running around trying to get everyone's measurements. Talking to Evelyn when she's in the zone is basically pointless, and I don't want to come between her and her tape measure. I decide to ask Peter because, well, desperate times call for desperate measures.

Once Peter is finished talking to Mrs. Mulaney, I get his attention.

"Yes, m'lady?" he asks.

"We're not doing a Shakespeare play, Peter," I say. "Also, you're not even acting."

"I may not be in the musical," Peter corrects me, "but a true actor is always performing."

I shake my head. "Okay. Listen, I need to ask you something. That kiss on the last page, between Bobby and Prudie?"

Peter holds up his hands. "I know what you're asking."

"You do?" Is it possible that Peter actually understands my feelings? Have I been too hard on him this entire time?

"I will not help you practice, as much as I would love to. I fear it would be crossing too many important theater boundaries."

My shoulders slump as I let out a sigh. "That's not what I was—never mind. I just wondered what stage kisses are like. I mean, are they . . . real kisses?"

Peter furrows his brow. "I'm not sure I understand what you're asking me."

I frown and start again. "I mean . . . like, do Noah and I actually kiss, or do we just make it look like we kiss? And if we do kiss, how realistic are we supposed to get? Am I supposed to use tongue? Put my hands on him? Don't you have some sort of insight from Mrs. Mulaney?"

"Mrs. Mulaney and I haven't yet discussed kissing techniques in depth," Peter says, "but I'll ask her."

He looks over his shoulder and shouts, "Mrs. Mulaney!"

The full realization of what's happening dawns on me. "Peter, no!" I hiss, ducking to the floor as if that will shield me from everyone's view.

Mrs. Mulaney is way on the other side of the stage talking to one of the crew members. She looks up.

"JOLIE WANTS TO KNOW MORE ABOUT THE SCENE WHERE SHE KISSES NOAH!" he shouts.

Now I'm certain that everyone onstage is looking at us. There are a few scattered giggles. My eyes frantically scan the crowd, hoping Noah picked this exact moment to go to the bathroom and he missed this entire scene. But no, there he is, talking to—Marla. Of course. She gives me a smug smile, and I look at my shoes. I can't even bring myself to look at Noah's face.

Mrs. Mulaney, at least, understands that this is majorly embarrassing. "We'll talk about it later, Peter," she says before going back to her conversation.

"Daaaaaamn, Jolie," Toby says from behind me. "Lookin' to get a little lip friction. Ready for some tongue wrestling. Jonesing for some—"

"Shut *up*, Toby," I growl.

"Well, I tried," Peter says to me with a shrug.

"Yeah, okay, I'm gonna go curl up under a rock somewhere," I say, heading backstage.

"The set designers haven't made the fake rocks yet!" Peter calls, but I ignore him and keep walking.

I find a closet and slip inside, where I sit down on the floor next to some art supplies. It's nothing like my fantasy where Noah Reed and I make out in here. For one thing, I didn't imagine that the smell of paint fumes would be overwhelming. Plus, Noah would actually, you know, be here, instead of onstage wondering why I'm some hormonally crazed weirdo.

There's a knock on the door and, startled, I look up. Noah pokes his head in. "Can I come in?" he asks.

"Uh—yeah—sure," I stammer, quickly adjusting my bangs. "How did you find me back here?"

Noah sits down beside me, leaning up against the shelf. "Toby told me you came in here. Actually, he was like, 'Jolie looked hella upset and she bounced.'"

I fight the urge to cry at how embarrassing this entire situation is. Here I am in the supply closet with Noah, and I can't even appreciate it because all we're talking about is how even Toby thinks I'm pathetic.

"It's not a big deal, you know," Noah says. "The kiss."

I meet his eyes. "It's not?"

He shakes his head. "I had to do one with Marla last year. We didn't even actually kiss. I put my hands on her face, and the audience is so far away that they couldn't tell I was just kissing my thumb."

He puts his hand on my face to demonstrate and I think I might actually faint, and not even because of the paint fumes.

"Just like that," he says, pulling his hand back.

I nod, knowing that I should be saying something but not able to form words. "That sounds . . . okay," I say.

Noah smiles, and I can't help but notice how kind his eyes are. He has the eyes of someone who helps old ladies cross the street, who spends Thanksgiving morning serving food at a soup kitchen, who walks shelter dogs in his spare time.

"I peed my pants once onstage," he says, and my head jerks up at this non sequitur.

"Yep." He nods, taking in my shocked expression. "I mean, it was when I was ten years old, so . . . not exactly last week or anything. But do you remember when we did that Disney medley concert in elementary school?"

I nod. "I was a mop."

"And I'm sure you were the best mop Brentley has ever seen. I was one of the dwarves from *Snow White and the Seven Dwarfs*; I don't even remember which one. Anyway, I was so excited about singing 'Heigh-Ho' that I sang it constantly for weeks. But then when I got up in front of everyone . . . I blanked. I just freaked out. And then—"

"You peed," I say slowly. "Wait, I kind of remember this. But I didn't know that was you!"

"Well, since then I've managed to stop peeing on stage. Hold your applause," he says with a smile. "But my parents were recording the whole show, and they thought it was so funny that they make us all watch it every year at Christmas."

"Oh, geez," I say, trying not to laugh.

"Yeah, I need a new family. But that's not the point. All I'm saying is, you've got this. I know you're nervous, but no matter what you do, it can't possibly be as bad as peeing onstage while dressed as one of Snow White's dwarfs."

I laugh. "No promises. Johnny McElroy might do some rewrites."

"We'll handle the kiss, and it won't be weird," he says, standing up. "Or maybe it'll be a little weird. It's always sort of strange kissing someone when you don't really want to kiss them, but we'll make it as bearable as possible."

Wait. He thinks I'm so upset because I don't want to kiss him? That couldn't be further from the truth. But I can't exactly tell him that—what would I say? *I'm actually so concerned because I want to kiss you for real, in private, not onstage. Maybe somewhere like in this supply closet.*

Instead I just say, "Thanks, Noah," with a closed-lips smile as he leaves.

I lean my head back against the shelf. Ugh. Honestly, it was sweet of Noah to tell me that story about peeing onstage (now there's a sentence I never thought I'd say), but it wasn't exactly the precursor to a steamy make-out. I mean, my knowledge of these things *is* limited, but I'm assuming most kisses don't begin with discussions about bodily functions.

The door creaks open, and I look up eagerly, thinking Noah might have come back. Maybe he was like, *Whoa, that sexual tension was through the roof. . . . I definitely need to go back in there and kiss her right now.*

Instead, Derek steps in.

"I'm not hiding!" I say quickly.

He jumps back, nearly knocking over a shelf. "Good God, Jolie! What are you doing in here?"

"Taking a breather."

"I just came in here to get some paint. Wait." Derek points at me, like he's accusing me of something. "Did I just see Noah Reed walk out of here?"

I nod, then realize what he's saying. "No! I mean, yes, he was in here. But no, we weren't making out, if that's what you're asking me."

"Good," Derek says, pushing some paint cans around on the shelf.

"Why is that good?" I ask, watching him.

"Because I'd be pissed if you accomplished your goal and didn't even tell me," he says, grabbing what he needs.

Right. Because Derek doesn't care who I kiss. Why would he? He has perfect Melody.

"I promise to tell you when I kiss Noah Reed," I say sarcastically.

"That's all I ask," Derek says. "He's not so bad, you know."

I pause. "Wait, could you repeat that?"

Derek turns around and sighs. "You heard me. Noah. He's . . . not awful."

I smile. "What brought this on?"

He shrugs. "I know he's been helping you out, and . . . well, he seems nice. Ish. I guess I kind of get why you want to kiss him."

"So, I guess I was right," I say as my smile gets bigger. "And you were wrong. You finally get the Noah Reed appeal."

"I wasn't wrong." Derek groans. "I was just . . . looking out for you. And anyway, aren't you supposed to be onstage?"

"I'm getting into character."

Derek reaches toward me and puts a hand on the side of my face. This is so like what Noah just did, the way he told me that stage kisses happen, that I instinctively lean toward him.

"You have paint in your hair," Derek says softly, his fingers brushing my scalp.

"Oh," I say, and swallow hard. "I was leaning against the shelf, and I guess there was paint on it, and it was wet?" I clamp my mouth shut to stop babbling. Since when do I have this problem around Derek?

"Well, get back out there," he says. "Knock 'em dead."

I give him a thumbs-up and watch him leave. Then I lean against the shelf in—what? Relief? Despair? Confusion? My feelings right now are like the knotted pile of necklaces in my jewelry box. I could spend all afternoon trying to untangle them, but I'd just end up more frustrated.

I can't totally ignore the way my heart was just racing. Derek said he was looking out for me, which sounds like something a brother would say. And that's fine, because that's exactly what he's like to me. A brother.

I feel something wet on my back and leap forward. I reach my hand around and realize that I just leaned on more paint and now my black cardigan is streaked with blue. I groan loudly as the door squeaks open again.

"Hey, are you running some sort of kissing booth?" Evelyn asks. "There's a steady stream of dudes coming out of here, and Peter keeps telling everyone you're freaking out over your lack of, and I quote, 'onstage amorous experience.'"

I cover my face with my hands. "Can you just go tell him to shut up, please?"

"Gladly," Evelyn says with a smile as she shuts the door.

Great. I embarrassed myself in front of the entire cast and crew, Noah Reed thinks I don't want to kiss him, I'm covered in paint, and Peter is telling everyone I'm an inexperienced kisser. Could this day get any worse?

Chapter Fifteen

*P*ro tip: Never, ever ask yourself if your day could get any worse, because it always could. Because maybe you'll get home and realize your pregnant sister expects you to go with her to her breastfeeding class.

"I thought I only had to go with you to the first class," I whine as we pull out of the driveway. "How am I supposed to help you with breastfeeding? I barely have breasts, and I'm certainly not using mine to feed any babies."

"You don't have to *learn how* to breastfeed," Abbi says. "You're just moral support. My partner. So that way, all those women and their husbands won't look at me and say, 'Oh, poor lady, here all by herself with no one to help her.'"

"Now they'll say, 'Oh, poor lady, clearly here with her teenage sister who doesn't even know how to change a diaper.'"

"News flash: I don't know how to change a diaper, either," Abbi says. "But there's no entrance exam for getting pregnant."

"I just don't get why one of your friends couldn't have come with you."

"If you were the one learning how to breastfeed, would you ask Derek to come with you?"

I think about it for a moment. "Maybe."

"You and Derek have a weird, unhealthily close relationship, so I'm not surprised. But who else was I supposed to ask? Dad? He'd be like, 'Well, Abbi, breastfeeding is just like designing a birdhouse.'"

It's true. Dad does have an annoying habit of using wood-working analogies for everything.

I'm a slow driver, much to Abbi's chagrin, so when we get to the hospital she practically rolls out of the car before I've parked.

"Like it's not bad enough that I'm the only one there without a husband," she huffs, speed walking through the entrance and down the hallway. "Now I also have to walk in late."

"So sorry I didn't want to drive through any red lights," I say, my shoes squeaking on the tile floor as I jog to keep up with her. Seriously, how is she so fast?

We burst through the door and into the darkness of the conference room, where a giant nipple on the screen greets us.

"Whoa," I say, and everyone's heads swivel around to stare at us.

"Thanks, Jolie," Abbi mutters as we sit down.

"I'm sorry, I was startled by a nipple bigger than my head," I whisper, then sit back and cross my arms.

The video's supposed to be showing us what breastfeeding looks like, but I'm too distracted by the woman's tan lines to really pay attention. Also, I think about what it must be like to be the woman who was filmed for this—as she drifts off to sleep at night, does she ever think, *I wonder how many classrooms full of people watched me breastfeed my infant today?*

I don't even bother telling Abbi these observations, because she has her notebook out again and she's diligently taking notes.

After we watch the baby on-screen (who's probably about thirty years old by now) successfully being breastfed for a while, Kathy shuts the video off.

"Okay, so now that you've seen what breastfeeding looks like, let's practice some of the most common positions." She pulls a box out from under the table and starts pulling dolls out of it. She hands one to each couple. Abbi takes the baby gingerly, and I can't help but notice that its face is contorted into a scream.

"Why did they have to make the baby look so angry?" I twist my head around to check out everyone else's baby. "Seriously, did they all get a happy baby? Do we have the only one that looks like a devil child?"

"That's not the point," Abbi reminds me, and I guess she's right.

Kathy's demonstrating the proper way to hold the baby at the breast (I'm not paying super close attention because, as much as I want to help Abbi, it's pretty clear that I won't be helping her with this particular part) and walking from couple to couple and adjusting their holds.

When she gets to Abbi and me, she reaches out and moves Abbi's arm. "Just a little bit higher, and . . ."

But when Abbi moves her arm, the doll slides out and clatters to the floor.

The woman next to us gasps. We all stare at the baby on the floor.

"Well, good thing it's not a real baby!" Kathy says, quickly picking it up and shoving it back into Abbi's arms, where it looks just as upset as it did before.

Kathy moves on to the next couple, but Abbi keeps staring at the baby in her arms.

"It's just a toy, Abbi," I remind her. "A weird-looking toy."

"Yeah," Abbi says slowly, not looking at me.

Kathy claps to get everyone's attention. "Let's take a quick break to get snacks and use the restroom, okay? See you all back here in five."

"I'll be right back," Abbi says, and shoves the baby into my arms.

I watch her leave, then put the baby on the table. I sit there enjoying the free granola bars and bottled water (I deserve some sort of perk for going through this) until our five-minute break is over. All the other women have come back into the room, and Kathy is pretending like she's shuffling through her papers while she's really watching the door for Abbi.

I've had just about enough of everyone repeatedly glancing at me, then at the clock, then at the door, so finally I say, "I'm gonna go check on her."

Kathy nods enthusiastically. "Hurry back!"

Right, because I definitely don't want to miss any of this extremely-relevant-to-my-current-life info.

I practically stomp down the hallway toward the restroom.

"Abs?" I call as I walk into the bathroom. Silence.

I bend down and look for feet in the stalls. And there, in the last one, are Abbi's gray boots.

"Abs?" I call again. "I know you're in there. Or it's someone else with your boots, in which case . . . sorry for making this weird."

I hear the click of the stall door unlocking, so I gently push it open. Abbi looks up at me, her face blotchy with tears, and sniffles.

"What's wrong?" I ask, starting to panic. "Are you in pain? Do you feel sick? Is—"

"I dropped the baby."

I pause for a second. "What?"

Abbi looks at her hands. "The fake baby. I dropped it on the floor. If that was a real baby, someone would've called child services."

"But it wasn't a real baby," I say. "It was made of plastic and it looked like the devil's spawn. I would've dropped it, too."

Abbi lowers her head into her hands. "I can't even handle a fake baby, Jolie! How the hell am I supposed to handle a real one?"

Oh. So that's what this is about.

"Hey," I say, kneeling in front of her (and fighting the urge to remind her that she's sitting on a toilet like it's a normal chair and that's disgusting). "It wasn't real, okay?"

"How am I supposed to do this for real if I can't even do it for pretend?" she says, giving me a defeated look. "All the moms in there have someone to help them if they screw up. I'm alone, Jolie. It's just me taking care of this baby."

I purse my lips, unsure what to say. I guess I never thought Abbi was all that worried about having the baby, mostly because she never expressed any uncertainty. She just came home one day, said she was pregnant, and started preparing for it. It's not that I thought being so beautiful meant Abbi didn't have any self-doubt, but . . . Well, okay, yeah, I did sort of think that. I thought I was the only Peterson who worried about how screwed up her own life was.

I don't think I have the ability to take away her uncertainty completely—after all, I don't know anything about kids—but there's one thing I can offer.

"You're not alone," I say. "Maybe you don't have some guy with you, but who cares? Look at those dudes in there. One of them laughs whenever the instructor says the word 'nipple.' How much help do you think he'll actually be?"

Abbi lets out a snot-filled laugh.

"But you have us—me, and Mom, and Dad. I don't know how to change a diaper or hold a baby, but I'll try to help you. And Mom and Dad did this two times, so they're basically pros. We'll all be there to make sure you don't drop the baby."

Abbi nods. "I know. It's just hard to compare the way things should be to the way they are."

"Yeah," I say. "I know." And I do, because I want things to be perfect, too.

"I don't want to go back in there," Abbi says. "And not because I'm embarrassed or upset. I mean, I am, but honestly . . . I just keep thinking that if I prepare enough, if I learn enough, if I do everything right, then everything will turn out okay. But maybe all I have to do is do it, you know? This baby's coming out whether or not I keep taking these classes."

"And also I don't really want to see those devil babies anymore," I say.

"Seriously. Couldn't they give them happier faces?"

I hold out a hand and help Abbi up. "I can't believe you've been sitting on a toilet this entire time."

She shrugs as we walk out of the bathroom and toward the exit. "It was the only place to sit down and my feet hurt. You up for a Frosty?"

"Literally always," I say.

Chapter Sixteen

*A*nother week of musical practice goes by, and I keep feeling weird about it, but I'll admit: It's getting easier to be in front of everyone. To have everyone staring at me. I start to think of the musical as a refuge from my real life, a way to take a break from feeling like Jolie: The Girl with the Jaw. I'm not Mandibular Prognathism Girl when I'm onstage, I'm Prudie, the love of Bobby's life, temporary resident of the moon, and the owner of a whole lot of singing pigs.

What's not getting easier is waiting for my surgery to happen. It's almost exactly one month away, and I can't believe that the moment that will change my life (presuming I don't die, of course) is so soon. Every morning I look at myself in the mirror, zero in on my jaw like usual, and think, *This isn't permanent.* It seems too good to be true.

I have to skip practice one afternoon to go to yet another

appointment with Dr. Kelley so she can check my braces and make sure everything's lining up in the right place for my surgery. Mom comes with me again, even though (as usual) I tell her she doesn't have to. I wouldn't be surprised if she tries to put on a surgical mask and sneak into the operating room, too.

Dr. Kelley is her typical brisk and efficient self, checking out what's going on with my jaw and pronouncing everything "beautiful" as she snaps the gloves off. *That might be an overstatement*, I think.

"I almost forgot," she says, grabbing a pamphlet and handing it to me. "This has more information about what happens during your surgery. Of course, you'll be asleep, but some people feel more comfortable knowing exactly what's going to be happening."

I eagerly grab the pamphlet.

Mom asks Dr. Kelley something about how long the surgery will take, and I zone out as I flip through the pamphlet. There are cartoon drawings of women before and after underbites, technical terms explaining what's going to happen, lists of the possible side effects (aka Numb Lip, Unintended Corn Syndrome). But there's one paragraph that mentions something I haven't heard Dr. Kelley talk about before. I read the small print under a before-and-after drawing of a woman's profile.

"Some patients choose to have rhinoplasty while having their jaw placement corrected. This surgery can further enhance facial symmetry."

A nose job? I self-consciously touch my nose, which I've never really thought about before unless I have a cold or a particularly prominent zit on it. But maybe there's something wrong with my nose and I've never known it; maybe my face is horrifyingly asymmetrical, like a Picasso painting, and I've just been living in a state of blissful ignorance and assuming my jaw is my only problem.

Mom and I drive home, her phone shuffling through music from badass female rock stars who've spent years fighting the patriarchy and sticking it to the man. These are the women my mom's always held up as heroes—Kathleen Hanna, Carrie Brownstein, Kate Bush. I start to feel a little bit weird about my surgery—am I betraying some sort of feminist ideal by wanting to change my face? Is there something wrong with changing how I look?

"Is it a bad idea to get surgery?" I ask.

Mom turns down the music. "Are you still worried that you're going to die? Because, honey, Dr. Kelley told you that's not likely."

I shake my head, not exactly ready to explain to Mom that I've created an entire plan around the assumption that I'm going to die during surgery. It's not the time. "I mean . . . am I, like, conforming to society's pressure by getting my jaw fixed? Am I basically getting a nose job?"

Mom glances at me before looking back at the road. "I'm not sure how this relates to getting a nose job, but you know what Dr. Kelley says: If you don't get the surgery, you'll have to deal with more jaw pain later on, and you'll keep getting headaches. You might even end up having speech difficulty. And our insurance wouldn't agree to cover a surgery that's just cosmetic."

"Sure."

"But," Mom says, turning onto our street, "if you don't want to get the surgery . . . you don't have to. This is one hundred percent your choice, and I don't want you to feel like you're being pressured into it."

"I don't feel like you're pressuring me," I say, and I'm not lying. Mom and Dad have never made me feel like I need the surgery. But I'm more concerned about what *I* think, and I'm not sure why I actually want to have this surgery. Am I excited about being able to chew better, about not having lasting jaw pain? Duh. But do I also want my face to look different? Well, yeah. And is that a bad thing? I'm not sure.

I'm still mulling all this over when we pull into the driveway and I see Evelyn sitting on our front porch steps.

"Did we have plans?" I ask as I step out of the car, already feeling crappy about forgetting.

"No," Evelyn says with a wry smile. "This is a surprise visit. A little 'my mom blew up and says that if I don't pass my next history quiz she's going to make me drop out of the musical' social call."

I gasp. "Seriously?"

Evelyn nods, then looks at my mom. In a voice that sounds smaller than usual, she says, "Sorry to show up unannounced."

Mom unlocks the door, and I can tell she's trying to be easy-breezy even though she shoots me a concerned look. "You know you're always welcome here, Evelyn. Wanna stay for dinner? It's taco night."

Evelyn looks at me, and I nod eagerly.

"Rebecca, you're a doll," Evelyn says with a bit more bravado.

I pull Evelyn upstairs to my room after giving Mom strict instructions to let us know when dinner's ready. I've barely shut the door behind me when I explode.

"Seriously?! She wants to make you drop out? But then who will make our costumes?"

Evelyn sighs and flops back on my bed. "Listen, no offense, but I'm less concerned about your costumes and more concerned about the state of my college applications if I can't list being in charge of costume design. Like, there are only so many opportunities to stand out in Brentley, you know? And I don't think Parsons is going to be all that impressed by my mood-board Tumblr."

I slide down the wall and sit on the floor. "So . . . you just need to pass your next quiz."

Evelyn lets out the world's most sarcastic snort-laugh. "*Just.* Easy for you to say, genius. I'm not like you and Derek. I can't just look over my notes in the five minutes before class and still ace every test."

"I study!" I say defensively, but Evelyn has a point. The truth is, Derek and I definitely study, but it's not like school is a struggle for us. I spend most of my free time watching TV, and Derek is always researching lemurs or whatever.

"Everything is so easy for you," Evelyn mutters into my pillow.

I bristle, unsure where Evelyn got this idea. Everything is easy for me? Has she forgotten about the little problem known as my rapidly expanding jaw?

I don't want to get into an argument, so instead I change the subject. "Do you think I'm a bad feminist?"

Evelyn lifts her head and squints at me in confusion. "What?"

"I mean," I continue, leaning my head against the wall, "I'm a feminist. Voting! Equality! Beyoncé! Down with slut-shaming! I'm here for it all!"

"Right?"

"But what does it say about me that I might die soon and the main thing I care about is smashing my lips into Noah Reed's perfect mouth?"

"May I ask what brought this up? Did Abbi cancel her subscription to *InStyle* and start getting *Bitch*?"

I fill her in on what happened at the doctor's office and the pamphlet.

"Shouldn't I be spending my limited time on earth, like, doing something? Protesting something? Helping people? Marching? What are people marching for in Brentley? Where can I march?!" I ask, growing increasingly frantic.

"I think the citizens of Brentley are mainly concerned about getting McDonald's to carry the McRib year-round," Evelyn says.

"At least that benefits other people."

"Debatable. Do you know what's in a McRib?"

"But my goals are all about me. Kissing a boy, for God's sake. Making my face look pretty. That doesn't feel very feminist."

"Isn't your surgery going to make it possible for you to chew normally?" Evelyn asks, propping herself up on her elbows.

"Well, yeah," I say.

"There are reasons why you need this surgery that have nothing to do with how you look. But if you do care about how you look? That's okay. It doesn't make you a bad person or a bad feminist or whatever. No one's saying you can't care about social justice or even McRib permanency and also want to be pretty on your own terms."

I realize that she's right. Literally no one—not Dr. Kelley, not my mom, not anyone—has tried to make me feel bad about getting my surgery. That's something I did all on my own.

"Maybe you should incorporate all this wisdom into your English essays," I say. "You would definitely get an A."

"I'm not sure your surgery relates to *Our Town*, but sure." Evelyn sighs, then gives me a serious look. "Listen, I hate to say this, but . . . I think I need your help with history."

"Of course!" I say. "We'll spend the rest of the night making flash cards! I'll quiz you during dinner! I'll—"

"Whoa!" Evelyn holds up her hands and laughs. "I'm gonna take a pee break first, then I'll come back to nerd out with you and hopefully save my musical-costuming career, okay?"

While Evelyn's in the bathroom, I stand up and walk over to the mirror above my dresser. I look at my face from the left, then from the right. I smile and look at my braces, my teeth, the way my jaw juts out.

Maybe she's right. Maybe there's nothing wrong with caring about how I look, or with wanting to change it.

I flare my nostrils. I'll probably still skip the nose job, though.

Chapter Seventeen

*H*ere's something that surprises me: I'm good at singing. I mean, I'm not Beyoncé singing the national anthem or anything, but I'm, like, a local person you might get to sing the national anthem at a Minor League Baseball game. The weirdest part is that I actually *enjoy* singing. Noah and I have a duet about how much we miss each other while I'm on the farm and he's in a spaceship, and I manage to find surprising emotional depth in a chorus that's mostly about space ice cream. After a lifetime spent making sure no one sees or hears me, it's weird to realize that maybe I do actually deserve to be heard after all. As long as I can focus on the song, the lines, and the musical itself (and Noah's grounding presence), I can sort of forget that everyone's staring at me.

One day after practice, I'm about to leave through the auditorium's double doors when Marla stops me.

"Hey, Jolie, wait up," she says. It's not a question, but a command.

"Actually, I—I . . . ," I stammer, trying to think of any excuse to get away from her. "I have food to eat."

She looks at me quizzically. "That's what you came up with? 'Food to eat'? You're ranked number eight in our class—you should be better at coming up with excuses."

I recoil. "How do you know my rank? *I* don't even know my rank."

She waves a hand. "I know everyone's rank. I'm number one and I intend to stay that way because I'm going to Harvard."

I raise my eyebrows. "Okay. That's . . . impressive."

She exhales impatiently. "Who cares? That's not what I want to talk about."

I take my hand off the door handle and move out of the way of some cast members who are leaving. "Could you, um . . . tell me where this conversation is going, Marla?" I ask, hoping I don't sound too rude.

"I just wanted to say . . . I'm sorry."

Whoa.

When I don't say anything, Marla leans toward me. "Did you hear me?"

"Um, yeah. But what are you sorry for?"

"For, you know . . . being mean. Or whatever." She shifts her feet, clearly uncomfortable. "I thought you didn't deserve the lead, but you do. You're actually good."

I feel a little bit of pride at hearing her say that, but I can't stop myself from saying, "You know, compliments lose a lot of their power when you preface them with 'actually.'"

She nods. "Good point. In that case, you're good. Full stop."

"Um, thanks. That means a lot, coming from you. I'm sorry you didn't get to be the lead this year."

She bristles. "The pigs are actually one of the most important parts of the musical."

"Right."

"Anyway, I don't even like acting. Or singing. I wanted to pad my transcript for scholarship purposes, but instead I just started a Brentley chapter of Habitat for Humanity. Did you know we didn't have one?"

"Uh . . . no." Only Marla would "just" start a local chapter of a national charity.

"Well, anyway . . . break a leg." She shrugs and walks away, her ponytail swinging. She bumps into Peter's backpack as he rushes down the aisle and barks, "Watch where you're going, Turturro!"

I shake my head, unsure of what just happened. I'm not saying Marla is nice, but she might not be entirely mean.

And I might—maybe—be sort of talented.

Derek's house is kind of my second home. I don't spend a ton of time at Evelyn's house, since she's usually over at mine. Her house pretty much reeks with her mom's general disinterest in Evelyn's chosen career, which doesn't exactly put out "relaxing, comforting, come over for meat loaf" vibes. Which Derek's house definitely does, although his mom is more likely to make grilled salmon than meat loaf since she's always talking about cholesterol and vitamins now.

Derek was originally going to be an only child, but then his mom got surprise-pregnant with the twins, and now no one can imagine life without Jayson and Justin. While my house is, if comfortable, still pretty quiet and chill, their house is constantly loud and full of Legos and Nerf darts—which is nice, because it makes it a little bit easier to forget that his dad isn't here.

After Marla's aggressive apology on Friday, I head over to

Derek's, give a courtesy knock, and walk in (his mom, Dr. Jones, told me a long time ago that they'd never hear me if I rang the doorbell and I'd be waiting on the steps forever, but I still feel weird unless I at least symbolically announce my presence), where Jayson greets me wearing a surgical mask and holding a lightsaber.

"Hi." I give him a wave.

"There's a zombie outbreak," he says, handing me a mask. "Wear one of these if you don't want to get zombied."

"I thought zombies had to bite you," I say, but I put on my mask anyway. Better safe than sorry, and anyway I haven't finished *World War Z*, so who knows, maybe zombie germs are also airborne?

"What's the lightsaber for?" I ask, but before Jayson can answer, Derek bolts around the corner, grabs me, and lunges for my neck.

"He's a zombie!" screeches Jayson, running away and leaving me to my fate.

"I thought zombies were slow!" I yell, panting from the shock.

"I'm the fast kind," Derek says. "Like in *28 Days Later*. Didn't you listen to my episode of *Deep Dive* on the different interpretations of the zombie myth in popular culture?"

"Of course I listened, but I'm assuming the twins didn't."

"No, but that's the cool thing about having little brothers. They'll believe literally anything you tell them. Anyway, you're a zombie now, so you might as well take off the mask."

"A lot of good it did me," I say.

He's still holding on to my shoulders when Dr. Jones peeks around the corner. "Jolie!" she says pleasantly. "I thought I heard you come in. We're having walnut-crusted tilapia for dinner— would you like to stay?"

"Actually, Jolie and I are going out tonight," Derek says, pushing me by my shoulders into the living room.

"We are?" I ask once we're out of Dr. Jones's earshot. "I thought it was Terrible Movie Night."

We're planning on watching *Troll 2*. It's a movie so bad that they made a movie all about how bad it is—truly an achievement worthy of Terrible Movie Night. We already have our snacks picked out: microwave popcorn with extra butter for me, and microwave kettle corn for Derek because he's a weirdo.

"How about a change of plans?" Derek asks.

I sit down on the extremely comfortable and juice-stained couch. "Wait, Derek Jones? Going out somewhere? Leaving the confines of his living room? But I already tried all the Applebee's appetizers."

Derek laughs. "Maybe we could actually try going somewhere other than a chain restaurant for once? Like, maybe Happy Endings."

I stare at him with my mouth open. "Seriously? You'll go?"

Derek sighs, but he's smiling. "I'm still morally opposed to the name."

"Me too," I say.

"But, for you? Okay. Let's go to Happy Endings. Maybe I'll meet a beautiful forty-year-old divorcée and leave Melody for her."

"Who knows where the night will take us?" I say, pulling out my phone and dashing off a quick text to ask Evelyn if she wants to come with us.

No thank you very much, she responds. *My mom hangs out at Happy Endings, and anyway I have tons of costume work to do.*

"She's busy," I tell Derek, sliding my phone back into my pocket. "Unrelated: Have you ever had any interest in dating Evelyn's mom? Because it's starting to look like a real possibility."

Derek frowns at me. "Don't make me change my mind."

We stop by my house so I can change into something a little less "sweatpants" and a little more "leaving the house." It's hardly flashy—a plaid shirtdress, tights, and boots—but when I come downstairs Derek wolf whistles sarcastically. I think it's sarcastic, anyway.

"Don't you clean up nice," he says.

This all feels a little patronizing, like when someone praises a little kid for coloring inside the lines, but I don't get a lot of compliments on my appearance and I start blushing in spite of myself.

"Let's go," I say, grabbing the tote bag that serves as my purse.

The passenger seat of Derek's truck is one of the most familiar places on earth for me. Although Derek's mom could afford to buy him a nice car, she's all into teaching her kids not to be entitled or whatever. Even though she drives a super expensive sports car, he has to make do with a rusty truck from his uncle that doesn't have AC. Derek doesn't even complain about it, which I would totally do if my parents were cruising around town in sports cars and I was on a payment plan with my uncle. But I guess Derek's mom's plan is working.

"Are we going to be able to get in?" I finally think to ask as we're driving toward the sad strip of buildings (Marty's Diner, an antique store, a salon, the post office, another antique store, and Happy Endings) that constitute Brentley's downtown.

Derek fiddles with the radio. "Happy Endings is only twenty-one-and-over on Saturday nights. Otherwise they'd never get enough business."

"I'm low-key afraid we're going to see one of our teachers here," I say. "Why can't Brentley have an actual cool place to hang out? Like someplace where bands could play, or any restaurant other than Applebee's or Marty's Diner? All due respect to Marty, but Mom literally got food poisoning from his pancakes. I don't even know how that's possible."

"Because," Derek says, pulling into a parking spot on the street. "If it was hip, it wouldn't be Brentley."

"Are you ready to have an 'APP ENDI'?" Derek asks as we cross the street and he gestures toward the half-burned-out "Happy Endings" sign.

"What a promising sign for the quality of our evening!" I say, stepping quickly to catch up with Derek's long, easy strides. I'm trying to be all "whatever" about this, but the truth is, Derek and I don't usually do this kind of thing together. Yeah, we hang out basically 24/7, but usually Evie's there or we're just on my sofa watching TV. This whole leaving-the-house thing? It's not us. And it's *definitely* not Derek—I can't even remember the last time he wanted to do something other than watch movies or work on his podcast.

Just as Derek promised, there's no one at the door checking IDs. As we walk in, I can hear the music coming from the back of the bar before I can see it. As my eyes adjust, I see that there's a live band playing. I'd be impressed, except this band is playing what sounds suspiciously like a very bad Maroon 5 cover.

Derek and I take a seat at a high-top table and he asks what I'd like to drink.

"The hard stuff," I say. "Root beer."

While he's at the bar, I inspect my surroundings. The walls are decorated (well, "decorated" might be a charitable term) with seemingly random stuff. Some class pictures from Brentley High in the '90s. A big, faded advertisement for the Kevin James movie *Paul Blart: Mall Cop*. Strangely, a few hats. It all works together to create a very specific feeling of not trying at all and still somehow failing.

By the time Derek hands me my root beer and sits down, the band has moved on to a cover of Justin Bieber's "Sorry," which sounds much more depressing when it's sung by a group of fifty-five-year-olds who only sort of know how to play their instruments.

"I think the drummer's falling asleep," Derek observes as we watch him move his sticks more and more slowly.

"I'm almost put to sleep by this lovely lullaby myself," I say, swirling my straw around in my soda.

It's uncomfortably hot in here, and I can feel the back of my neck starting to sweat.

"Have you considered the possibility that we've descended into the depths of hell?" I lean over to ask Derek.

"Hell has a better soundtrack," he says, pulling off his red hoodie and hanging it over the back of his chair.

Happy Endings may lack any amount of ambiance, but something about the dim light from the neon signs bouncing off the white T-shirt that clings to Derek's body, well . . . I guess the realization I had when we were running wasn't just an exercise-induced hallucination. The music and conversation around us fade into the background as I stare at Derek watching the band. He absentmindedly bites his lip as he bobs his head to the off-tempo beat, and my heartbeat quickens.

To everyone else at this bar, we must look like we're on a date, the two of us sharing a table. I wonder what they think—that guy in the American flag T-shirt, the woman in the polka dot top with a plunging neckline—if they wonder why this frankly gorgeous guy is on a date with this weird-looking girl. Do they think it's a pity date? I self-consciously push my bangs into place, as if perfect bangs can save me.

Then Derek glances at me and his eyes widen. "Why are you

staring at me like that? Did I grab a T-shirt that Justin barfed on again?" He starts wiping his shirt, lifting it up so the tiniest flash of his stomach shows, and my eyes dart there of their own accord.

"No!" I whisper-shout, leaning across the table so quickly that I almost fall off my chair. I yank down his shirt so I'm no longer staring at his abs, because this. Is. Inappropriate. He grabs my shoulders to steady me so I won't fall off my chair, and I land against his chest.

"Jolie?" Derek asks, looking down at me with his brown eyes full of concern. "Are you sure you're okay?"

I'm pressed against him, his chest both solid and warm, and I can feel his steady heartbeat. I stay there for one too many beats before I sit up and give myself a little shake. "Sorry. I'm just . . . in a musical trance," I say, not meeting his eyes.

"Right," he says slowly. I concentrate as hard as I can on the band, but I can feel Derek's eyes on me. As I watch the lead singer warble his way through what I think might be an original composition that features that phrase "make love" way, way too much, one thought runs through my head:

Uh-oh.

This is Derek, I remind myself forcefully. My friend. Who cares if he's suddenly and inexplicably hot? He is never, ever going to have any sort of feelings for me, because if he did, he would have had them by now. Obviously. We've only known each other since forever. And he has a girlfriend—one who's perfect and pretty and mysterious and very much *not me*.

Plus, a guy who looks like that just doesn't go for a girl who looks like me. Ever. I'm banking on Noah Reed falling for my stunning personality, but either way, I only need him to *kiss* me. Then we can both move on with our lives. But Derek couldn't ever be just a kiss, because I see him every day. You can't just shove your tongue in your best friend's mouth and then be like, *Hey, do you want to watch* Troll 2?

But this will be okay, I tell myself. Clearly I'm just under the romantic spell of Happy Endings—Flag T-Shirt and Polka Dot Top are totally making out over there in the corner, so there must be something in the air here (besides the overpowering scent of air freshener that's covering up the scent of God knows what). June 2 and my possible impending death are just a few weeks away, and fear makes people do and feel crazy things, like form romantic attachments to whoever happens to be around them at the time. I think that's, like, biology or something. But I have a plan and I'm going to stick to it: Noah and I are going to kiss, Derek and I are going to be friends, and that's that.

I deliver this entire silent monologue to myself very convincingly (perhaps musical practice really is making me a better actor), but when I turn to Derek, he's still staring at me.

"Do you want to leave?" he asks just as the lead singer of the band rips his shirt off.

"Yes," I say quickly. I hop down off the chair and grab my tote bag, but before I can make my way toward the exit, a guy grabs my arm.

"Hey," he slurs, pulling me toward him. "I haven't seen you here before."

"I'm actually just leaving," I attempt to say politely, but he grabs my waist and pulls me closer to him. He's broad-shouldered and his receding hairline makes him look like he might be in his thirties, aka way too old to be hitting on me. His boozy breath hits my face, and I wince.

"Don't you want to dance?" he asks as I try to wriggle away from him. But he's strong, and I'm small, and I can feel my throat constricting. I try to remember what Evelyn told me she learned in her self-defense class—am I supposed to knee him in the balls or poke him in the eyes? In a panic, I look toward where Derek was sitting, but he's already beside me, wrenching me away from the guy.

"What the hell, man?" Derek shouts, holding me against him with a protective arm.

"Whoa, sorry." The guy holds up his hands. "Didn't know you had a boyfriend."

My breath comes quickly, and I want to say a million things, but I can't. Things like, *I never want to feel your gross, drunk hands on me ever again.* But the words get caught in my throat.

"It doesn't have anything to do with whether she has a boyfriend," Derek says. "You shouldn't grab random girls. Ever."

The guy shrugs and starts to walk away. "Your girl's hot," he says, as if this explains everything.

Derek seems to gain several inches of height in an instant as he takes a step toward the guy. "You have anything else to say, bro?"

"Derek!" I grab his arm and pull him toward the door. "He is so, so not worth it. Come on."

Derek lets me lead him out of the bar, but he keeps his eyes on the guy the whole time. I've never seen him like this before—protecting me, like I'm not just his best friend in his living room, but a girl out in public.

Once we're safely on the sidewalk, I turn to him. "That was terrifying."

Derek isn't looking at me. He's watching the door. "I wish I could end that guy. I'd do it. I'd—"

"Dude!" I shout, and he looks at me. "What are you going to do? Punch that rando? Get arrested for defending my honor against some drunk, desperate sleazebag?"

Derek laughs, but it doesn't sound happy. "Yeah. Maybe."

I rub my arms to try to warm up. Now that the sun's down, it's actually a little chilly. "Why did you come out tonight, anyway? You never want to go anywhere."

He shrugs and looks around us. "Because you wanted to. I just . . . thought you would enjoy it. And look what happened."

"Were you really going to hit that guy?" I ask, half-horrified and half in awe.

"In the moment, could I have? Yeah."

"But why?" I ask.

"Because I'm looking out for you, Jolie," he says, and my heart skips a beat. "Because we're friends."

My heart goes back to its previously scheduled rhythm. Right. We're friends. Derek was reacting as a *friend*, not anything else.

I shudder at the memory of that guy's hands around my waist, at the way I struggled but couldn't move, at the panic that prevented me from fighting back. "That's not you—hitting random douches at bars. That's not the kind of guy you are."

"Oh yeah?" Derek asks. "And what kind of guy am I?"

He meets my eyes and I realize that I don't know what to say. Or maybe I do, and I'm just too scared to say it.

But I'm distracted because out of the corner of my eye, I see two people come out of Marty's Diner, both of them laughing. One of them is tall with long, brown, shiny hair. The other one has gray hair. Wait a second. Is that . . . ?

"Evelyn and Marla?" Derek asks.

I pull him behind a mailbox. "Duck!"

"Why are we hiding?" Derek asks.

"Because they clearly don't want to be seen!" I hiss. "Evelyn told me she was working tonight . . . and she's literally never mentioned hanging out with Marla, ever. I didn't even know they were friends."

The gears turn in my head. Why the hell is Evelyn secretly hanging out with my mortal enemy? Well, maybe "enemy" is a strong word; after all, she did apologize to me. But still, why is Evelyn hanging out with someone who actively hated me until recently?

"Something's up," I whisper as we watch them get into Evelyn's car.

"Yeah, you're a maniac is what's up," Derek says, pulling me up from my crouch. "Evelyn can hang out with whoever she wants. Come on, Peterson. Let's bounce. If we hurry up, we'll still have time to watch *Troll 2*."

He puts his arm around me as we walk toward his truck and this, in itself, isn't unusual. Derek is a full head taller than me, so I'm basically nestled into his armpit and normally I would make a comment about how he smells bad, but this time I don't. I lean against him as we walk, and I let myself relax a little bit. I wonder: What if he wasn't Derek, and I wasn't me, and we were just two people who were on a date? What would that be like?

"I can't believe we were almost involved in a bar fight," Derek says with a laugh, and I can feel the words rumble through his chest and vibrate into my skull. "This night kind of got out of hand, right?"

"Yeah," I say, swallowing hard. "It kind of did."

Chapter Eighteen

I get home on the latish side, but Abbi's sleep schedule is so erratic (she tends to fall asleep on the couch at seven p.m., then complain about being unable to sleep at midnight) that I don't feel bad about knocking on her bedroom door. She grunts, which I assume is Abbi for *Please come in.*

She's lying on her side with her back to the door and she rolls over to face me, groaning. In her hand is her constant companion, a dog-eared copy of *What to Expect When You're Expecting.* "Are you here because you've magically found a cure for constant heartburn? Because otherwise I don't want to see anyone right now. I want to sit around, alone, and think about how uncomfortable I am while this stupid book scares the hell out of me."

I gesture to myself. "Do I look like Larry the Cable Guy in a Prilosec commercial? I'm here for advice."

Abbi narrows her eyes and rests the book on her stomach. "About what?"

"About kissing."

Abbi sits upright faster than I've seen her move in months and the book tumbles to the floor. "Who are you kissing?" she shouts.

"Keep it down!" I whisper.

She rolls her eyes. "Please. No one else here cares that much what you do with your lips. Unless you learn how to operate a miter saw with your mouth, Dad isn't paying attention."

I sit down beside her on the fluffy floral comforter she's had since we were little, back when I used to climb into her bed when I got nightmares after watching particularly scary episodes of *Scooby-Doo*.

"I just want to know what it feels like," I say. "My one and only kiss was in kindergarten, and I don't remember much."

Abbi perks up. "Who are you planning on kissing? Derek?"

"No!" I practically shout, then lower my voice. "Of course not. Why would you think that?"

"Too bad." She sighs. "He is much better-looking than he was when he used to ask me if I liked seafood and then open his mouth and say, 'See? Food!'"

"Yeah, he rarely does that anymore," I say, eager to change the subject. "So. Kissing. Locking lips. What's it like?"

"First," Abbi says, "tell me about this kindergarten kiss. How have we never talked about this?"

I sigh. "No."

Abbi crosses her arms over her protruding belly. "Well then, sorry, I'm not spilling any of my kissing secrets."

"Fine." I scowl. "But you can't tell anyone."

"My lips are sealed. And so are hers," Abbi says, pointing to her belly.

"It was . . . Derek."

She squeals. "I knew it! I knew you had the hots for him!"

"This was in kindergarten!" I whisper-shout. "We were getting married under that big oak tree on the playground and we had one chaste, playground-appropriate peck on the lips. I don't think that really counts."

"Still, though." Abbi looks vindicated. "Don't you want to return to the scene of the crime?"

"No, I do not," I say forcefully. "Derek is my *best friend*, and he always will be, the end. What I want is to kiss Noah Reed, and I want to be prepared. Teach me your ways."

Abbi sighs. "I can't just tell you what kissing is like."

"Why not?" I ask, throwing my arms up in exasperation. "Google told me plenty, but things started getting pornographic, and I was afraid Mom and Dad would look at my search history, so I had to stop."

"Please tell me you didn't google 'what does kissing feel like.'"

I stare at the framed photo on Abbi's desk of her being crowned Miss Brentley and let my silence speak for itself.

"Ugh, okay, but only because you're so 'Are You There, God? It's Me, Jolie' and it's bumming me out."

"Fine. I'll take your pity."

Abbi scrunches up her face and looks at the ceiling, as if the right words are written there. "It's hard to explain in words. It's more of a feeling. Like . . . like the finale of the Brentley Fourth of July fireworks show. Or like the bubbles in a fountain Coke. Or like riding a bike down a hill, when your hair lifts up off your back and you're half-exhilarated, half-terrified. I mean, that's what it feels like when you're kissing the *right* person."

She sighs and leans back on the bed and I sit there, shocked.

Who knew Abbi was sort of a poet? I guess all I had to do was get her to talk about making out.

"And you *feel* it," Abbi says.

I nod. "See, that's what I'm worried about, because there's a chance I could end up with some numbness in my lips and I'm worried I won't be able to feel . . ."

"No," Abbi says meaningfully, raising her eyebrows. "You feel it everywhere."

"Oh," I say, and then I feel myself blush. "*Oh*."

"Which brings me to the biggest point: You have to take your birth control every day if you want it to work." She points to her belly again. "Because otherwise this happens."

"I may not know much about kissing, but I do know that it doesn't result in pregnancy. Mom told me that in one of her extensive 'your body is your property' sex-positivity talks."

"All I'm saying is that one thing leads to another." Abbi shrugs.

I shake my head. If I'm freaking out this much over a kiss, I won't be ready for sex until I'm, like, forty-five.

I pull out my notebook and write down what Abbi just told me. *Fireworks. Soda bubbles. Bike riding. Everywhere.*

"Um, what are you doing?" Abbi leans over to look. "Are you taking notes?"

I look up at her. "Yeah?"

"Okay," Abbi says. "I guess that's the most important thing for you to learn, besides the birth-control thing. You can't study for this one. It's not about facts, or preparation, or doing everything right."

I slowly lower my notebook.

"It's sort of like childbirth, or what I think childbirth is going to be like," Abbi says, pointing to *What to Expect When You're Expecting*. "You can read all the books and take all the notes you want, but at some point you just have to do it to find out what it's like."

I absentmindedly chew on my lip as I mull this over. "But I like reading books and taking notes."

"No kidding," Abbi says. "But that's life, dude."

I sigh and let my gaze drift around Abbi's room. The trophies she still has from when she won pageants as a kid. Photos of her and her friends where she looks like a literal model. I walk across the room and pick up her prom queen sash, which has been looped over her closet doorknob ever since she won. Running my fingers over it, I think, *Abbi has never had this problem. She's never had to ask someone else to explain to her what kissing is like, and she's definitely never googled it.*

"Ugh," Abbi says, groaning as she pushes herself off the bed. She shuffles over to me, then grabs the sash out of my hand and chucks it into the garbage can under her desk. "I can't believe that thing was still there."

"You're throwing away your prom queen sash?" I ask, horrified. "But . . . you won it."

She shrugs and, with difficulty, bends over to pick up her book. "Yeah, well, being prom queen isn't my whole life. Thank God."

I leave Abbi to her reading and head back to my room, where I pull my scrapbook out from under my bed and run my fingers over the pasted-in faces and straight, perfect smiles. *Being beautiful didn't solve all of Abbi's problems, or make her life easy*, I think as I stare at a picture of Cara Delevingne until her features start to blur. A sinking feeling hits my stomach as I begin to wonder, *What if getting the surgery doesn't fix everything? What if I wake up on June 3 alive, but still the same old me?*

Chapter Nineteen

*D*espite talking a big game about how she was totally going to come to the Cliff with me, Evelyn backs out on Saturday because she's working on costumes again.

"How many costumes can one musical have?" I whine. "I miss you!"

"Girl, you should see my list. Noah Reed alone has to wear overalls, a suit, a space suit, and multiple wigs. Plus I should probably actually, you know, do some homework." She sighs forlornly. "Wow, I really hate saying that."

Evelyn ended up passing her history quiz, proving yet again that actually doing the assigned reading and studying can lead to improvement. But she's still afraid of facing her mom's wrath if her grade slips again.

I don't ask her if she'll really just be hanging out with Marla because they're now BFFs and she doesn't need me anymore, but the point is, it ends up being just me and Derek going to the Cliff. Even though he initially didn't want to go, I bugged him until he agreed to go as long as I would stop texting him about it.

It would be so much cooler if Brentley had some sort of agreed-upon name for the Cliff, like Dead Man's Drop or Leap of Faith or something. But, because Brentley is the kind of place where we can't even put on a real musical, we just call it the Cliff.

I pull the car into the makeshift parking area, my tires crunching along the gravel. The sun is out and beaming through the freshly green tree branches, but it's not all that warm today.

Derek turns to look at me with his hand on the door handle. "You sure you don't want to do this another day? When it's not borderline cold?"

I shake my head. After talking to Abbi last night, I've been afraid of what will happen if I get my surgery and nothing changes. Maybe I'm going to have to change myself. "I just need to do something. Like, maybe if I can cross another thing off my list I won't feel so hopeless."

"You're not hopeless. Peter Turturro trying to make berets happen at Brentley High? That's hopeless. You? You're a hope machine."

I barely contain my eye roll. "A hope machine?"

"A hope rocket! A hope cannon! A double hope rainbow painted across the sky!"

I open my car door. "Okay, you're right, you're not great at pep talks."

"Ouch."

We walk to the edge of the cliff. Although people are often swimming down below, today there's no one—probably because of the aforementioned slight chill in the air. The water bubbles past us, and a breeze rattles the branches, sending a shiver through my whole body.

"Maybe let's just warm up a bit," I say, taking a few steps back and sitting down in a patch of sunlight. "You know, get our courage up."

"Okay." Derek plops down beside me. "So how's surgery prep going?"

I shrug. "Fine. Do you know I could get a nose job?"

"Finally. I've always said your nose was holding you back."

"That's what I thought." I look at him and give him a small smile. "It's gonna be okay, right?"

"Yeah," he says. "You're gonna be fine."

I lean back and look up at the trees, at the tiny green buds on the branches. We sit in silence for a minute before he says, "You don't actually like Noah, do you?"

I avoid looking at him. "I don't know."

"Come on."

"No, I'm serious. I really don't know. I think he's really cute, and I think he's really nice. But I don't, like, feel some sort of love-at-first-sight spark with him, if that's what you're asking."

"But you want to kiss him," Derek says flatly.

"I've had a crush-from-afar on him for years," I say defensively. "And maybe I don't know yet if it's true love forever, but I want to at least find out."

Derek leans back beside me and doesn't say anything.

"How did you know Melody was the one for you?" I ask.

I can hear him breathing and I realize I'm taking this conversation down a potentially dangerous path. His fingers tap out a rhythm on the dirt.

"I don't actually know that she is the one," he finally says.

"Trouble in paradise?" I ask lightly, but my voice shakes a little bit.

"Uh, for that to be true we'd have to be in paradise instead of where we are, which is literally about a thousand miles from each other." He does an awkward little half laugh, half cough, then picks up a pebble and tosses it over the cliff.

If I were a puppy, my ears would be perking up right now. Derek hardly ever talks about Melody, let alone says anything negative about her. And I try to avoid asking because, well . . . I guess I don't really want to know. If we don't talk about Melody, then it's like she doesn't exist, and if she doesn't exist, then it's still Derek and me in our own little best-friend world.

"It's just . . . we hardly ever really talk anymore. She texts me a lot, and you know how I feel about that . . ."

"Yeah, I'm aware, Grandpa."

"And it's like, we can't make a relationship out of that weird little kissy-face emoji."

"You send each other the kissy-face emoji?" I coo. "Aren't you guys sweet!"

"It's been a one-sided kissy-face emoji lately. And I don't know if I really feel like putting so much effort into a thing with someone who I won't even get to see until the next Academic Challenge meet."

"But . . . you like her, right?" I ask.

"I mean, yeah, I like her. She's smart, and she's funny, and she's nice, but . . ."

"Can you talk to her about your dad?" I ask, feeling bold.

He doesn't say anything.

"Wait." I sit up. "You haven't told her?"

"It hasn't come up," Derek says.

"The most important thing that's ever happened to you hasn't come up? With your girlfriend?" I ask.

"She's not like you, Jolie," Derek says, rubbing his hands over his eyes. "I can't just be like, 'Hey, here's a fact about lemurs. Hey, I'm deeply traumatized by my dad's sudden death.' She would think it was weird."

I feel a strange sense of smugness that I know something about him that Melody doesn't. And then I wonder if I'm breaking some sort of unwritten girl code by feeling the way I feel. I mean, I don't even know Melody, and here I am feeling happy that I have a better relationship with her boyfriend than she does. Not that Derek actually talks to me about his dad, but still. I was there for him.

"Are you telling me that you and Noah talk about your deepest, darkest secrets?" Derek asks.

I think about it. Other than that embarrassing pee story, I don't really know anything about Noah, and I'm not even all that curious. Not the way I am with Derek, where I want to know everything he's thinking and talk about it with him for hours.

"No," I admit. "But he's not my boyfriend. I just think that when you're in a relationship with someone, you should be able to tell them anything and not worry about them thinking you're weird."

"So you're some kind of relationship expert now, huh?" Derek says, but he's smiling as he says it.

"Just call me Steve Harvey," I say. "But with more hair. And fewer suits."

The silence that stretches between us suddenly feels unlike the normal comfortable quiet we usually exist in. It feels heavy, hot, and scary, like one of us is supposed to be doing something. The feelings I have right now are distinctly unfair to Melody, and that terrifies me.

"Jolie—" Derek says.

I stand up so fast that I almost fall down again. "I'm ready to jump."

Derek raises his eyebrows. A few expressions flicker across his face until he settles on confusion. "Now?"

"Now or never!" I shout. I feel a burst of adrenaline, like if I exert enough energy for both of us, maybe I can forget about the tension in the conversation we just had.

Derek stands up and brushes off his pants. "All right. It's go time, I guess."

I stand at the edge of the cliff and peer down at the river below. "That's pretty far," I say.

Derek stands beside me. "Yep."

I meet his eyes. "You ready?"

His face breaks into a smile. "You know if you don't want to do this you don't have to, right? Like, I'll just tell Evie you did it and no one will have to know."

My whole body practically melts with relief. "Seriously?"

He barks out a laugh. "Yes, seriously, Jolie! Good God, you know this is incredibly dangerous, right? Brendan Cooper broke his leg doing this last year, and he was lucky that's all that happened."

I look at him in disbelief. "And you were just going to let me jump?"

"Have I ever been able to stop you from doing something?" Derek holds up his hands. "You tend not to listen to me."

"That's true." I peek over the edge of the cliff once more, observing the water, the rocks, the tree branches. "Yeah, this was a terrible idea. Why does anyone do this?"

"Because they're trying to prove to their friends that they're cool. But you have nothing to prove. I already think you're cool, okay?"

"Yeah, I'm the coolest girl with a deformed jaw in school."
I watch the current carry a stick down the river.

"Why do you say shit like that?" Derek says with a rare note
of annoyance in his voice.

I whip my head around to face him. "Like what?"

"Like that you're weird, or untalented, or ugly. You're just
fishing for compliments. You know none of that's true."

I raise my eyebrows. "You think I'm fishing for compliments?"

He gives me a *no duh* look. "Come on. You know you're
pretty."

I can feel my cheeks getting red. I'm getting so tired of Derek
saying stuff like this because it's ridiculous at this point for him
to tell me I'm pretty or perfect or whatever when we both know
I'm not. Because if he really thought all that about me, then why
would he be dating Melody? It's borderline condescending.

"I think it's time to go home." I turn and start to walk back
to the car.

"Hey," Derek calls from behind me. "Do you want to go
swimming?"

I turn around so fast that my feet slip on the pebbles.

"Now?"

Derek shrugs. "Why not? We're here. I'm wearing swim
trunks. And if you show up at Evie's house covered in muddy
river water, she will definitely believe you jumped."

I wrinkle my nose.

"Come on. Don't make me tell you all the facts I know about
river microbes." Derek turns and starts making his way down
the steep path that snakes down to the river.

I hesitate for a moment.

"I'm gonna start talking about heterotrophic protozoa!" he
shouts.

Rolling my eyes, I hurry after him. I carefully step down the path, grabbing trees and rocks to avoid sliding all the way down. A few crushed beer cans remind me that this is one of the places where Brentley's teenage population goes to get drunk and make out, two activities that I would think would be better done far away from a dangerous cliff. But then again, I have limited (read: nonexistent) make-out experience, so what would I know?

The trail ends at some big rocks that surround what is charmingly known as a "swimming hole," which is deep enough that people are usually able to jump into it without injuring themselves (unless you're Brendan Cooper). The sun glistens off the water, making it look deceptively warm.

"Isn't it sort of cold for this?" I ask, sliding off a flip-flop and dipping one toe into the water.

And then Derek pulls his shirt off, and all of a sudden, every single word in my head evaporates.

He climbs up on a rock and, without giving himself a second to think about it, jumps in.

"Oh, geez," I mutter as I scramble up onto the rock Derek just jumped off.

"Come on, Peterson!" Derek yells as he treads water.

"Is it warm?" I ask, my fingers toying with the bottom of my shirt.

"No way," he says easily. "I think my toes are numb. Wait . . . yes. Definitely numb."

"Well, maybe I . . ." I start backing up.

"Don't you dare!" Derek shouts. "I thought you were trying to accomplish every item on your list! I thought you were valiantly fighting against the scourge of hopelessness! I thought you were Jolie Goddamn Peterson!"

"Okay, okay, fine." Quickly, I pull off my shirt and jeans, then instantly regret it. It's not like I'm wearing something all that revealing—I have one of those high-waisted two-pieces like the one Taylor Swift wore when she was in her Kennedy-dating phase and she looked all retro. My belly button may not be visible, but I still feel exposed, like I'm on a stage in front of an audience of one.

I can't stand it anymore, so I jump.

My feet hit the water and I realize that this was, in fact, a pretty terrible idea. The cold shoots through my body, and I burst back up to the surface, gasping.

"Why didn't you warn me?" I shriek.

"I said it was cold," Derek says, unperturbed.

"You said it was cold, not freezing." I swim toward a patch of sunlight to see if I can get any relief. Nope.

"It's just sort of chilly."

"And Charles Manson was *sort of* a bad guy," I say.

Derek gives me a look. "Kind of weird that you took it to a Manson place, but okay."

"I listened to your *Deep Dive* episode on his music career," I mutter. "Shut up."

"My number one fan," Derek says smugly.

We tread water for a minute, the motion bringing a little bit of feeling back into my limbs. It's beautiful down here, even though it's cold. It reminds me of what I actually like about living in Brentley. Like, yes, it's annoying to live somewhere with no culture and no interesting food and no concert venues except for the New Life Baptist Church auditorium, where Christian bands play sometimes. But there's this, too. The river and the trees and the cliffs.

I look at Derek and he's already looking at me. Is he staring at my probably-smudged mascara? Thinking about what's wrong with my face? Wondering what I'll look like after surgery?

"Jolie," he says. "Why did you ask me about Melody?"

"What do you mean?" I ask, and even though this water is seriously freezing, my entire body gets hot.

"I mean . . . you don't ever ask me about her. In fact, sometimes I think you're just pretending she doesn't exist."

I swallow. "I don't . . . I don't pretend your girlfriend doesn't exist. Why would I do that?"

Derek looks at me and kicks himself slightly closer, so that we're both occupying the same spot in the sun. "I don't know," he says without taking his eyes off me. "Why would you?"

I try to swallow again, but it's like something is stuck in my throat. I need to focus on staying above water—it's been a long time since swimming lessons—but all my focus is going toward Derek, toward his face, toward his eyes that are holding my gaze.

He moves himself even closer, so our faces are practically touching. "Have you ever thought about . . . I mean, do you think we . . ."

"CANNONBALL!"

We both look up to see a tiny body hurtling toward us, rapidly becoming larger.

I scream as Derek grabs me by the shoulders and pulls me roughly out of the way. The jumping person narrowly misses us, hitting the water hard and creating a splash that covers the rocks with river water.

"What the hell was that?" Derek shouts, climbing out of the water and onto the rocks. He grabs my hand and helps me hoist myself out.

As we stare down into the water, a person surfaces and I realize that I recognize that face. "Peter?"

"Oh. Hey, Jolie," he says, as if we're meeting in the hallway at school, not like he just almost killed both of us.

"That was incredibly dangerous," Derek says. "I mean, not just that you almost hit us. But are you here by yourself?"

"Yeah?" Peter says, treading water and sounding totally unconcerned.

"What if something happened to you, dude?" I ask. "What if you hurt yourself?"

"What can I say? I'm a rebel." Peter raises his eyebrows. "Is it my badass nature that you find so attractive?"

"No offense, Peter," I say, wrapping my arms around myself to stop my shivering. "But I don't find you attractive."

"And yet you wanted to kiss me."

"I did not!" I say at the same time Derek says, "What?"

"I mean, I know I barged in on your sexy swim time, but if *he* wasn't in the picture," Peter says, pointing to Derek, "would you be interested?"

"Oh, no," I say too quickly, feeling Derek's eyes on me. "That's not what this is. We're just swimming. Just friends. Nothing sexy."

"I suppose you could say sexy is in the eye of the beholder," Peter says.

"Gross, Peter." Derek picks up his hoodie and tosses it to me without looking at me. "You ready?"

He hops off the rocks and starts climbing up the path without looking back. "Um, yeah," I say, scrambling to grab my clothes. "Peter, don't do that again, okay? It's not safe."

"Whatever you say, m'lady," Peter calls as I climb after Derek, feeling a little awkward about the strange intimacy of wearing his most beloved piece of clothing. I zip it up and can't help inhaling the scent of it. I know high school boys have a reputation for smelling gross, but this just smells like dryer sheets. Like clean. Like Derek.

Derek is already sitting in the passenger seat by the time I catch up to him.

"What was that about?" I ask as I sit down in the driver's seat. "You just left me back there with Peter the Weird."

Derek doesn't say anything as I start the car. He reaches over to fiddle with the radio, then says, "You tried to kiss Peter?"

I snort-laugh. "I most certainly did not."

Derek doesn't say anything.

"I didn't!" I shout. "Seriously, Derek, what the hell? In what world do I want to kiss Peter Turturro? No offense to Peter, I'm sure there's someone out there for him, but it's not me."

"So you're just kissing everyone now, is that it? Not just super dreamy Noah Reed." He waves his arms in the air sarcastically. "But Peter Turturro, too? Who's next? Johnson Bennett with the spit jug?"

"That was a misguided crush and I have since rescinded it!" I yell.

Derek sighs and rubs his hands over his face. "Okay. This isn't my business anyway. Make out with whoever you want."

Before I can respond, he cranks up the volume on the radio even though I know for a fact that he hates Selena Gomez and thinks all Top 40 music is *boring and insipid mass-produced garbage,* or whatever snobby thing he said when he did a *Deep Dive* episode on Svengali music producers.

I back out of the parking spot. I know I didn't imagine that moment between us earlier, when we were inches away from each other and I could barely breathe, but it's gone now. I'm certainly not going to ask Derek to say whatever he was about to before Peter cannonballed his way into our awkward conversation. And maybe that's for the best. This is Derek, sure, but just because he's Derek doesn't mean that the immutable laws of the universe have changed. Guys who look like him don't like girls like me.

They just don't.

Chapter Twenty

*O*ur last week of practice flies by, and suddenly it's one day before the musical, one week until junior year is over, and exactly three weeks until my surgery. That means my freak-out levels are at an all-time high, but I don't even have a second to stress because it's time for our dress rehearsal. It's a relatively low-pressure performance, with an audience of the Brentley sixth-grade class that's been bused over from the middle school. They're too excited about getting out of school to heckle us, and even I'm not enough of a nervous wreck to get freaked out about eleven-year-olds watching me.

It helps that the costumes that Evelyn and the rest of the costume department made are amazing—my dress makes me look like a convincing farmer's wife, and my space suit is surprisingly realistic.

At least I'll look good from a distance, I tell myself. But I can't help it—I'm getting nervous thinking about tomorrow. Performing this afternoon with only an audience of overexcited sixth graders is one thing. But tomorrow night, all of these seats will be full. This is pretty much all Brentley has going on in the spring besides prom, which only seniors are allowed to go to, anyway. My parents will be here. Abbi will be here. Everyone in the entire school will be here. And I'll be onstage, under the spotlights, the Girl with the Incredible Growing Lower Jaw.

"Jolie!"

I turn around to see Peter staring at me.

"What?" I ask.

"Is that really how you're wearing your hair?"

I touch my hair. "Uh, yeah?" I pretty much just have the one way to wear it.

He shakes his head. "It's all wrong for Prudie. She would never have such a cosmopolitan bob."

I start to explain to Peter that my wavy cut would never, ever be described as "cosmopolitan," but he keeps going.

"The entire town of Brentley is going to be here tomorrow night. Do you know that the mayor is coming? And we need every single detail to work together."

I freeze. The mayor? I can't even picture the guy in my head, but this still freaks me out for some reason. *The entire town of Brentley is going to be here* replays in my head in Peter's voice, and frankly, I've never wanted anything Peter has said to replay in my head.

My throat dries out, and my tongue suddenly feels huge. Maybe I'm having an allergic reaction. Like in seventh grade when Darren Thomas accidentally got fish instead of chicken at a buffet after our field trip to the art museum in Columbus, and they had to call the emergency squad, and after that we weren't allowed to stop for food on field trips. Except I'm pretty sure I haven't accidentally eaten any seafood.

Peter's in the middle of a sentence, but I say, "I'll be right back" and walk backstage.

"Where are you going?" he yells after me, but I don't care. I make a beeline for my safe space, the art supply closet, and shut myself in.

I take a deep breath, then start coughing when I realize I've just inhaled a bunch of paint fumes.

A knock on the door. Startled, I run my tongue over my braces and stand up straight. "Uh, come in," I say, like I have any control over who comes into the art supply closet.

It's Noah. "Hey," he says softly, stepping inside and closing the door behind him. "Art supply closet party again?"

I smile weakly, too freaked out to even care how it looks. "Yeah. Didn't you know? This is the place to be."

He's wearing his farmer outfit—overalls, a dirty white shirt, and a cowboy hat. It works for him—but then again, when you look like Noah Reed, a garbage bag with arm holes poked in it would work for you, too.

He leans against the shelf beside me. "Nerves, huh?"

I laugh a little. "Uh, yeah. You could say that. If by 'nerves' you mean 'I'm pretty sure I'm gonna pass out or barf.'"

A month ago, I never would've thought I'd feel comfortable enough to talk about this kind of stuff with Noah Reed. But that's what being in a musical does to you, I guess.

I roll my eyes self-consciously. "This probably seems really silly to you."

He shakes his head. "Nope. I felt the same way when I was in the freshman musical. I sort of feel that way right now."

I raise my eyebrows. "You do?"

He nods. "I think everyone does. You'd have to be super-human to not feel a little bit nervous before you go onstage."

"I bet Marla doesn't."

"Like I said: superhuman."

I laugh. "So . . . what do you do when you feel like this? Like you're gonna hyperventilate or wilt in front of everyone?"

He turns to face me. "Here's what I tell myself: The audience isn't there to make fun of me. They don't want me to fail. They just want to watch a good show. They're rooting for me to do well, because they don't want to watch something that sucks."

I nod slowly.

"Just imagine that the entire audience—"

"Is in their underwear!" I finish, eager to contribute the one piece of theater advice I know.

He shakes his head and winces. "I tried that once. It was extremely distracting, and kind of upsetting because my parents were there. No, just imagine that everyone in the audience is cheering for you. That everyone is hoping you'll do the best job possible. Because they are."

I breathe in and out. "That was actually pretty helpful."

He smiles. "You're gonna be fine, Jolie. You're gonna be better than fine. These sixth graders are gonna love you today, and everyone else is gonna love you tomorrow."

And then he reaches out and pulls me into a hug. I relax into it, feeling . . . well, grateful for us being friends. What I don't feel is anything romantic, surprisingly. Like, I'm pressed up against Noah Reed and I'm not fantasizing about our lips touching. *Maybe*, I think, *this is even better for our kiss*. I'll be able to get it out of the way without developing any messy feelings for him.

"Just don't pee out there, okay?" Noah says into my ear, and I burst out laughing, which is exactly when the door swings open.

"Whoa!"

Derek tries to back out of the closet again, but runs into a shelf, knocking paintbrushes onto the floor. Noah and I break apart.

"Sorry, I—I'm just leaving," Derek says, trying to pick up the paintbrushes and dropping them.

"Do you need help?" Noah says kindly, crossing the floor to help him.

"Nope!" Derek says, pushing all the paintbrushes under a shelf with his foot. "I'll just see you guys later!"

He bumps into the door before scooting out of the closet.

I can't believe this just happened *again*. "I have to go talk to him," I mutter, running after him and leaving Noah behind.

"Hey!" I call when I finally reach Derek, who's doing some touch-up work on a fake rock.

"Uh, yeah?" he says crisply, as if he's deeply engaged in his task and unable to talk.

"We weren't doing anything!" I hiss urgently. "He just gave me a hug because I was nervous."

Derek turns to look at me, his calm eyes a little more frantic than usual. "Why would I care, Jolie?"

I step back as if I've been slapped. "What?"

"You can do whatever you want with whoever you want wherever you want. But actually, maybe stop doing it in the art supply closet because that's where I keep my stuff, and this is getting kind of ridiculous."

I mean, he has a point. "I just . . . didn't want you to think anything was going on."

He shrugs. "Why?"

I balk. "I . . . because . . ."

All the words fly out of my head as I look into Derek's

searching eyes. I don't know what I'm supposed to say—because he's right. Why do I care so much if he thinks something is going on between me and Noah?

But I know why it is—it's because I *do* feel something between Derek and me, something that wasn't there before, and I *do* care what he thinks about me. But he's only started acting like this now that my surgery's coming up, and I'm starting to wonder if he's only doing all this—caring about who I kiss, having prying conversations while we're both wearing swimsuits—because I'm getting fixed soon. Because I'll be pretty enough for him once a doctor breaks my face and moves it all into place. And as much as I have been thinking about what it would be like if we were more than just friends, I don't want him to like me just because I'm going to have a new face.

So instead I just stand there, staring at him, as he looks at me expectantly. And then Peter Turturro calls out, "Places, people!" which I'm sure he's been waiting his entire life to say, and I take the opportunity to run out onto the stage and stop thinking about this.

Evelyn comes over after the rehearsal so she can do some last-minute alterations to my costumes. But I'm not really thinking about my costumes right now—I'm thinking about Derek, and the way he looked at me when we were swimming. I'm thinking about the way it made me feel, like I was just a normal girl and not his friend with the deformed jaw.

As Evelyn pins some fabric under my arm, I get the nerve to say what's on my mind. The question I've wanted to ask someone for basically forever, the one I've been avoiding because I'm terrified to hear the answer.

"I need to ask you something. Am I pretty?"

Evelyn looks up at me and stares for so long that I start to think she didn't hear me. And then I realize she's just trying to come up with a nice way to tell me what I already know—that there's something wrong with me, that I'm not pretty, that I never will be, that there is no way to fix my face, not even with surgery. Because Evelyn is honest, but she's also kind, and I know she'll want to come up with the least hurtful way of telling me the truth.

But instead, she puts down her pins and asks me a question.

"What's 'pretty' to you?"

"Listen, I'm not here to get all existential, 'what's the meaning of life,' okay? I just want an answer."

"That *is* my answer." She crosses her arms and leans back. "What do you think? What's 'pretty'?"

I sigh, frustrated. I'd like to ignore this, but it's always easier to just play along with Evelyn's tangents. "You know what 'pretty' is. We all do. 'Pretty' is Abbi. Symmetrical features. A jaw that's where it's supposed to be. Looking normal. Looking like everyone else."

"Okay." Evelyn nods. "Do I look like Abbi?"

"No," I say, not understanding where she's going with this.

"Of course not. But do you think I'm pretty?"

"Yes!" I say. "But that's not—!"

Evelyn holds up her hands. "Okay, stop. Because that's not the point. With all due respect, you're my best friend, but I don't really care if you think I'm pretty. Because I think I'm pretty." She points to her chest.

"Not to be self-centered, but, uh . . . what does this have to do with me?"

"I'm just saying . . . there's not, like, one universal standard of beauty. Life isn't a Miss America pageant, as much as Abbi would probably love that. Do I think you're pretty? Yeah, but that's a useless question."

"That's really easy for you to say," I grumble. "You know you look good and your face isn't deformed. You've never felt the way I feel."

"Jolie!" Evelyn almost yells. "Listen to yourself. Yes, I am confident. But we live in a world where a lot of jerks equate 'fat' with 'ugly.' I regularly go to clothing stores and can only buy hats because they don't carry my size. There are people everywhere who would love to tell me that the way I look isn't good enough, that I should change, that there's something wrong with me. So don't say I don't get it, because I do."

I drop my hands, properly chastised. "I'm sorry. I just never thought you felt this way, because . . ." I trail off.

"Because I carry myself like I'm worth something," Evelyn says. "You're right, I don't give a single bedazzled shit what anyone else thinks of the way I look, or act, or think, but that doesn't mean I'm not aware of it. You aren't the only one who lives with self-doubt, Jolie."

"You are really pretty, though," I say quietly.

She smiles back at me, then laughs. "I think you're pretty, too, babe. But it's more important that *you* think you're pretty."

When Evelyn finishes the last minor fixes to my dresses, I ask her if she wants to hang around and Netflix something.

"Sorry, can't," she says, giving me an altogether unconvincing pouty face as she packs her sewing supplies into her vintage bowling bag.

I'm disappointed, because I would love to forget about tomorrow's performance for a few episodes of literally anything, but I try to be supportive. "You're right. You should probably study instead."

She looks at me for a moment and purses her lips, then heads toward the door. "Yep. Good point. Try to actually get some sleep tonight, okay?"

After Evelyn leaves, I pull out my scrapbook and page through it. Logically, I know Evelyn's right. But emotionally? Well, that's a different story. I flip past pictures of Karlie Kloss and Zendaya and some girl in a mascara ad. I'm not delusional; I know that when my swelling goes down, I'm not going to magically look like a supermodel. But I'm starting to wonder if, even after my surgery, I'll ever think I'm pretty.

Chapter Twenty-One

The next day, I send Evelyn about one million freak-out texts, most of them including that Kermit gif where he's waving his arms frantically. She repeatedly tells me to chill out about the musical, but that's much easier said than done. When we're all running around backstage doing last-minute makeup and costume fixes, things are a lot more stressful. I fight the urge to peek through the curtains, but I can hear the murmuring of the audience and know it's a full house.

I'm pacing back and forth nervously when Peter steps on my dress.

"No!" I shout as I hear a loud, horrifying rip.

"Emergency!" Peter yells. "Dress emergency!"

"Peter," Mrs. Mulaney says calmly. "We've talked about this. You're not allowed to use the word 'emergency' unless there's blood, okay?"

He points silently at my dress, which is torn right up the side.

"On it!" says Evelyn through the pins in her mouth. She pushes in between us and gets to work.

"Thanks, Evelyn," Mrs. Mulaney says as she walks away, presumably to manage another crisis Peter's started.

"Thank you," I exhale. "I can't believe that happened right before the show starts!"

"I can," Evelyn says, pins still sticking out of her mouth like she's a villain in a horror movie that would be great for Terrible Movie Night. "Something always happens right before stage time. Just be glad it's only a rip; last year, Marla's dress got dog poop on it, and we had to create a completely new one in like half an hour."

"How did she—" I start.

"Don't ask," Evelyn cuts me off. "Strange things happen backstage."

I sigh. "I guess I should consider myself lucky."

Finishing her work, Evelyn pulls the pins out of her mouth and stands up. "Hey, did Derek tell you he broke up with Melody?"

It's like someone reached out and turned down the volume. I can't hear the murmuring of the crowd, Peter's frantic yelling, or the general hubbub of backstage. I can't hear anything except the echoing of Evelyn's words and the roar of my own blood rushing through my body.

"What?" is the only word I can formulate.

"Yeah, I don't know what happened. I just saw him, and he said it happened earlier today."

"He—they—wait—" I stammer.

Evelyn looks at me quizzically. "Are you sure there's nothing going on between you guys?"

I shake my head, but I must not look very convincing,

because she just widens her eyes and says, "Oooookay," sort of sarcastically.

"Places, everyone!" Mrs. Mulaney yells, and the volume is turned back up. Now I can hear everything—the squeak of every shoe, every whispered word, every nervous cough. I clear my throat a few times.

Derek broke up with Melody. I don't know what it means or how to feel, but I can't think about it right now, because Noah's squeezing my hand and we have literally seconds before the curtain opens and I have to be Prudie.

"You ready?" he whispers, catching my eye.

I look at him and feel myself smiling as I squeeze his hand back. No matter what happens tonight, and whether or not I ever end up kissing him in a situation that doesn't involve a stage or his thumb, I'm glad we became friends.

"Yeah." I exhale, pushing out all the stress and worry and doubt. "I am."

When Noah says the last line of the play while staring dramatically off into the distance, the curtain drops, and I hold my breath.

And then, applause.

I can't believe it. It happened. I didn't trip or barf or faint or forget my lines. I sang on key, I delivered a monologue convincingly, I kissed Noah's thumb like it was my job. The musical is over and *I did it.*

Noah grabs my hand and pulls me out onstage to take our bows. The audience, which has been applauding this entire time for the rest of the cast, stands up. My heart beats overtime as I bow, but for once it's not because I'm afraid of people looking at me; this time, it's because I'm actually proud of what I just did.

A standing ovation for me, Jolie Peterson, the girl who's spent basically her entire life hiding from the spotlight. I think about everything I would've missed if I'd backed out of the musical when I got scared: new friendships, a tiny bit of confidence in my own abilities, and *this*. There's an entire room of people staring at me, and I'm shocked to realize that I don't feel like hiding or wilting; in fact, I could stay out here for a few more minutes to take in the adoration, but eventually the curtain goes down for the last time.

Euphoric relief hangs in the air. We're all running around, hugging each other, yelling congratulations. I can't wipe the cheesy, oversized grin off my face, and for once I don't want to.

"I'm so proud of you, Jolie," Noah says as he gives me a huge hug. "Everyone loved you."

I hug him back as I smile, even though I know it means he can see my braces and just how much my lower jaw sticks out.

"You were amazing," I say as I pull back to look at him.

He runs a hand through his hair, and it magically flops back into place. "No barf, no pee, no fainting. That means it's a success, right?"

I laugh and give him a double thumbs-up. He smiles back at me and then turns around to be congratulated by a long line of people. I see Derek across the room, wearing his black stage crew T-shirt. I open my mouth like I'm about to say something, but of course he wouldn't be able to hear me from across the crowd—and anyway, what would I say?

"AMAZING!"

Evelyn grabs me in a hug and spins me around.

I laugh. "Your costumes were amazing!"

I look over to see if Derek's still there—he's not. My heart slumps a little.

"You're going to Toby's, right?"

I nod. "Yeah, of course. Isn't everyone?"

Apparently, after every musical there's an after-party at someone's house. This year, since Toby's parents are spending all weekend getting some sort of lamp appraised on a taping of *Antiques Roadshow* in Cleveland, the party's at his place.

"Anyone who's anyone, darling," Evelyn drawls, before adding, "But yeah, seriously, even the freshmen are invited."

"Do you need a ride?" I ask.

She shakes her head. "Marla's picking me up."

"Oh," I say. "Okay."

I'm slightly fonder of Marla now that she apologized to me, but I still don't get why Evelyn's hanging out with her. But I know that right now, in the crush of excitement, it isn't really the time to have a deep conversation about it.

"Why don't you ask Derek if he needs a ride?" she asks pointedly, her eyebrows raised.

"Will do." I give her a thumbs-up before she spins off to congratulate someone else. But I have no intention of doing that, because I don't want to have this conversation with him right now. If he broke up with Melody, then he's not always-there-yet-always-unavailable Derek. And if he's not unavailable . . . well, I don't want to think about it. Because the last thing in the world I want is for our relationship to change.

"It's Jolie, right?"

I turn around and come face-to-face with Johnny McElroy himself. My smile slides off my face. I'm way too excited to get bummed out by listening to him tell me how I didn't live up to his vision of Prudie.

"What do you want?" I snap, surprising even myself.

He takes a step back.

I sigh, then remind myself that Johnny McElroy has no power over me anymore. The musical's done. What's the worst thing he's going to tell me?

"I get it, okay? You don't think I was good enough. I'm not young Meryl Streep, or old Meryl Streep, or any Meryl Streep. But I'm not ever going to be Meryl Streep because I can only be Jolie Peterson."

I pause to take a breath and realize that Johnny McElroy isn't saying anything.

"I just wanted to tell you," he says when he regains his composure, "that I greatly enjoyed your take on Prudie."

Wait, what?

"And," he continues, "if you're ever in New York, I'm putting on a small production of my next play—"

I hold up my hand to stop him. "No offense, but no thanks, Johnny."

And then I walk away. It feels good.

I head to the bathroom to change out of my costume (as great a job as Evelyn did, I'm not wearing a gingham dress to Toby's party). As I'm fixing my now-faded mascara in the bathroom mirror, ignoring all the girls around me who are shrieking and laughing and full of giddy relief, I take a good look at myself.

I think about what Derek looks like—his lean muscles, those eyes that are deep and kind, the way his *ears* look cute even though I've never noticed another person's ears before. And what do I look like? Not that bad if you focus on my hair, my expertly done eyeliner, my always-completely-covered-up zits, my cute but not flashy outfits. But when you take a good look at me? Well. *That's not a girl who should be with Derek*, I think, staring at myself. I highly doubt that even my surgery is going to magically transform me into a girl who's worthy of him. It hurts a little (or a lot) to think that he only started feeling this way about me when I'm just a few weeks away from being fixed, but I still don't want that to ruin our friendship.

I swipe on some sticky lip gloss that smells like cinnamon rolls. I'm going to avoid him tonight, I decide. If we don't even talk, then we can't have any awkward conversations, and maybe the next time we get together this entire weird vibe between us will have blown over and we can go back to talking about lemurs and watching terrible movies.

Tonight's about celebrating. Tonight's about fun. Tonight's about finally getting that kiss from Noah, getting my surgery in less than three weeks, putting this entire kiss-less life behind me, and starting over.

Chapter Twenty-Two

I drive to Toby's nervously, my hands gripping the steering wheel tightly. It's not like I haven't been to parties before, but I've never gone to one with the express purpose of kissing Noah Reed.

"First time for everything!" I say cheerily as I adjust the radio. Brentley gets, like, three stations, and one of them is conservative talk radio, so I have to be content with listening to a country song about a guy with a broken heart. Surprisingly, it isn't the pump-up jam I'd hoped for.

I'm just going to have to pump myself up. "You can do this, Jolie," I whisper to myself as I park a street away from Toby's so as not to alarm any suspicious neighbors ("I live next to some *seriously* unchill senior citizens," Toby told me). "Carpe diem! Seize the day! Kiss a boy! You can do it!"

I feel a pair of eyes on me and look over at the sidewalk, where Peter is watching me. He waves.

I get out of the car and lock the door. "How long have you been watching me, Peter?"

"This is a terrible parking job," he comments, and holds out his arm. "Would you like to walk into the party as my plus-one?"

"No, I would not," I say politely. "Also, this isn't a wedding. I don't need to be your plus-one—I was invited."

Toby greets me with a hug as soon as I step into the house. "Jolie!" he shouts, and I'll admit, it's nice to be so enthusiastically welcomed. "Let me show you around my humble abode."

"This is the kitchen," he says as we walk into a kitchen, where people are crowded around multiple bowls of potato chips.

"And there's the beer," he says, pointing to a cooler in the corner. Several stage crew guys are crowded around it. "Do you want something to drink?"

"Um . . . ," I say. I should say no. I don't usually drink, both because I think beer tastes disgusting and because I have a pathological fear of being caught.

But I want to take chances tonight. I want to be someone different. I want to be a girl who can drink a beer and not loudly say, "Why does this taste so bad?"

"Sure," I attempt to say breezily.

Toby grabs a can and hands it to me. I crack it open and take a sip as he leads me into the dining room. I hide my grimace behind my hand. Yeah, this is just as awful as I remembered. I scan the room for places I can hide my almost-full can.

I spot Noah across the room, talking to a huge group of people. He looks good, just like he always does. He runs his hand through that hip British-boy-band hair, and I wait to feel my heart flutter.

Nothing. I feel the way I did when we watched *Magic Mike* and Abbi thought the stripping scenes were so hot, and I was just like, "Wait, why would I want some sweaty stranger to pick me up and rub me all over his chest?" Like, I get that there's an appeal for some people, but it's just not working for me. Apparently, fake-kissing Noah killed any last lingering bits of my crush on him.

This is good, though, I tell myself. I can kiss Noah for real and we can keep feelings out of it and not have to worry about anything scary or weird. I can go into my surgery and my possible death without any regrets.

He looks up, sees me staring at him, and waves with a smile. I wave back.

Then I look a few feet to the right and see Derek talking to Evelyn. My heart stops, then comes roaring back to life, beating a million times a second.

He changed out of his stage crew shirt and he looks good—God, he looks good. He's wearing a white T-shirt that looks like it was made especially for him, and I'm stuck wondering how something so basic looks so amazing on him.

I hate that I feel this way about my best friend, because I know the odds. How many people actually stay with someone they dated in high school? Pretty much none, right? And the thought of losing Derek like that . . . well, I can't even think about it. And I know, I just *know*, that he would come to his senses sooner or later and realize that he can do better than me—that if he can date girls like perfect Melody, with her pretty hair and her perfect face, that he doesn't need to mess around with a girl like me. Someone who's laughably far from perfect, someone who wears all of her imperfections on her sleeve (or face, as the case may be). And even if we did date and stay happy together forever, I would have to know in my heart that he only liked me once I changed. He only liked me once he knew I was getting fixed.

Toby's still talking his way through the tour, but I can't focus on his story about the time he "majorly bit it" and fell down the stairs because I need to get out of here. I can't stop myself from imagining what it would be like if Derek and I were more than friends, if we spent Terrible Movie Night with his arm around me instead of my feet in his lap, if we . . .

It would never work, Jolie. It just wouldn't.

"I need some air, okay?" I pivot away from him and walk toward the porch.

It's just slightly chilly, the good kind where you can snuggle up in a jacket and feel comfortable, so there are plenty of people on the porch. But it's still quieter out here than it is inside. I sit down on the front steps and cross my arms over myself. I idly take another sip of beer and then make a face.

"That bad, huh?"

Derek sits down beside me.

"Oh!" I say. I didn't think he'd follow me out here, didn't think he'd even seen me. My eyes dart around as I wonder if I can make a break for it, but running away would probably be even weirder than staying.

"You really bolted out of the auditorium," Derek said.

"Couldn't wait to get to the party! I, um, love partying!" I smile as wide as I can and take another sip, wincing.

"Yeahhhh," Derek says slowly. "You're acting really weird."

"Am I, though?" I give him a *who can say?* look.

"Listen," he says, looking at his hands. I look at them, too. His fingers are intertwined; I think about how my fingers would look tangled up with his.

Stop it, Jolie.

"I'm just gonna say it." He looks up at me. "I broke up with Melody."

"What?" I feign surprise, but apparently I'm not as good an actor in real life as I was in the musical.

"Evelyn already told you?"

"Yes," I admit.

I think that maybe, just maybe, we're going to sidestep all of this and avoid talking about what's been going on. Maybe we're just going to ignore all of the electricity between us, the way the air practically crackles when we touch. But then, he just blurts it out.

"I broke up with her because I can't stop thinking about you."

I drop my can and we both watch the beer flow out onto Toby's mom's decorative walkway.

"Did you hear me?" Derek asks.

I swallow hard. "Yeah."

"Are you . . . going to say anything?"

I don't know what to do. Like, yeah, Right Now Jolie would love to grab Derek's face and smash it into mine. Right Now Jolie would love to get rid of this gross beer taste by finding out what Derek's mouth tastes like. Right Now Jolie would love to inhale his sweet laundry-and-sweat boy scent.

But Future Jolie knows it's a bad idea. Future Jolie knows that eventually, he'd come out of this temporary fog and figure out that he could date someone much hotter.

I try to bite back the question that's threatening to tumble out of my mouth, but finally I let it spill.

"Do you only want me now that I'm going to be fixed?"

I meet his eyes slowly, and he's looking at me with nothing but confusion. "What?" he asks.

I shrug dejectedly, my eyes back on the now empty beer can.

"It wouldn't work, Derek. Okay?" I say, tears in my eyes. "Look at you, and look at me. Doesn't something seem off to you?"

"What are you talking about, Jolie?" he asks, his brows knitted in confusion.

"I mean . . . you're, like, basically some Greek god. You're all perfectly proportioned and your muscles aren't too big or too small and your smile's so shiny and your eyes are like museum paintings that I could stare at all day and still find new things in!" I throw my hands in the air.

"I'm not sure I'm following you, but . . . thanks?"

"I've looked like this my whole life." I point at my face. "I've always known there's something wrong with me. And you've known it, too, because you've looked at me, day in and day out. I know I'm not pretty. You know I'm not pretty. It's common knowledge."

"Jolie," he says softly. Just hearing his mouth say my name physically hurts me, because I'm starting to sense that this isn't going to turn out well and I'm afraid I won't ever hear it again.

I pull my hands up inside my sweater's sleeves. It's getting chilly. "I don't know why you suddenly think you like me, Derek, but this is a phase. Melody was, like, some Academic Challenge supermodel. That's not me. And if you think you like me now because I'm going to be prettier after surgery . . . well, that kind of sucks."

Derek sits back. He opens his mouth and closes it a few times. Finally, he says something I haven't been expecting.

"What the hell, Jolie?"

I open my eyes wide.

"Do you get that you're the only one who thinks these things about yourself? Like, you know that, right? That you complain about the way you look constantly, but there's nothing wrong with you?"

"Oh, there's *nothing wrong with me*. Thanks for the praise," I snort.

"What do you want me to say?" he almost yells. "That I think you're beautiful? Would you even believe that?"

I think about it for a second and then answer, my voice thick. "No."

"How many times have I told you how stupid your weird scrapbook is, or how great you are? And how many times have you listened to me?"

I don't say anything.

"That's what I thought. Look at how great you were in the musical, Jolie. Everyone loved you. You were the lead, for God's sake. When are you going to understand that you're the only one holding you back—"

"You know what?" I turn to face him, suddenly full of anger. "Can you maybe not play armchair psychologist for a second? I don't really need to hear a list of things that are wrong with me from someone who's spent the last four years ignoring reality and hiding in a tiny, windowless room so he can talk to a bunch of people in Denmark instead of his real friends."

Derek doesn't say anything. I hear a bottle break somewhere inside.

"You think I'm ignoring reality?" he says slowly and quietly.

"You used to have friends, Derek. Like, friends besides me and Evie, remember? And then your dad died," I say, holding up my hands, "and I know no one's allowed to talk about it, but you quit soccer and you stopped playing video games with all those guys. Now you only leave your house if it's for school stuff, and you spend the rest of your time holed up in your closet or going down Wikipedia holes."

"Yeah," he says forcefully. "I quit soccer, and I stopped hanging out with those guys. You know why? Because I didn't care about soccer anymore. I didn't care about those guys. They're fine, but we never really had anything to talk about, and after my dad died I didn't want to pretend I had any interest in *Grand Theft Auto*."

I chew on my lip, starting to feel like I've said some very wrong things.

"And honestly, Jolie? I'm not ignoring reality. Reality is there every day, when I wake up and my dad's not there. When I come home and he's not there. When I see the twins and realize they're never going to get to know him the way I did. *That's* my reality. I don't have to talk about it all the time for it to be real."

"Well, maybe you should talk about it *sometimes* instead of making everyone act like it didn't happen," I say.

"I can handle it however I want!" he almost yells. "You can't tell someone else how to deal with their dad dying!"

"And you can't tell someone else how to feel about her own face!" I shout.

He rubs his hands over his face. "You want to know something ridiculous? I thought . . . I thought this conversation was going to go a whole lot differently. Because the whole reason I stopped hanging out with those guys is because after Dad died, I didn't want to spend one single second of my life doing things I didn't want to do. And all I *ever* wanted to do was spend time with you. I've liked you since we were kids, Jolie, okay? Since that playground kiss, I've wanted you to be my girlfriend."

All the air leaves my chest. *Wait, what?* Derek hasn't liked me since we were kids. "That isn't true," I whisper.

He ignores me. "And I never pushed it because you never seemed like you were into it, but lately we've been having these conversations and you keep, like, *staring meaningfully* at me, so I thought maybe there was a chance . . ."

He looks at me and I don't say anything.

"But I must've been imagining that, huh?" he says. "All those things I thought were moments were just . . . nothing?"

I chew on the inside of my cheek. What am I supposed to say? *Maybe I do like you, Derek, but our friendship is one of the only things I can count on, and also I can't—like, mentally can't—even envision a reality in which the things you're saying are true?*

I can't say that, so instead I look at the ground and say, "This is all a mistake, okay? You'll figure it out, and we'll go back to the way things have always been, and it will be fine."

He laughs bitterly as he stands up. "Yeah, sure. I don't think that's going to happen. Have a great night."

He walks off, presumably toward his car, and I'm left alone on the steps. I look behind me to see if anyone on the porch noticed us, but they're all drawn into their own conversations. The Invisible Girl strikes again.

That's it. I need another beer.

Chapter Twenty-Three

J stomp up the steps and into the party. "Toby!" I bellow.

"Yo!" he shouts.

"Beer me!"

"Yes, ma'am!" he says, handing me a can. I drink it as fast as I can, the noxious liquid sliding down my throat. And then, when I'm done, I have another.

I lose track of how much time passes, but eventually I find myself in the kitchen, eating handfuls of potato chips. *That whole thing with Derek did* not *go how I wanted it to*, I think as I lick salt off my fingertips. I can't stop his words from tumbling through my mind, over and over. He's liked me since we were kids? That can't be true. I shove another potato chip in my mouth.

"Jolie."

I spin around and see Evelyn, arms crossed, looking angrier than she did when we were in elementary school and her mom wouldn't let her go to New York to see the Alexander McQueen exhibit at the Met.

"What?" I snap, then take a swig of my beer.

"What are you doing?" Evelyn asks. "Are you drinking? Who gave you that?"

"What's this, twenty-five questions?" I roll my eyes.

"It's twenty-one," Evelyn says flatly. "And you can just answer one: Who?"

"Toby."

"Don't drink something a guy gave you, let alone Toby." Evelyn widens her eyes in alarm.

"Toby's not dangerous," I say, finishing my drink and throwing the can on the floor. "He's just an idiot."

"Hey." Toby comes up behind me with two beers in his hands. I grab one of them. "That's not very nice."

His face does look the slightest bit wounded, but I don't really care.

He sees Evelyn and gestures toward her with the other beer. "You want this?"

"I'm not drinking Natty Light." Evelyn says this as if someone just asked her to wear yoga pants in public.

Toby shrugs, and I grab the other can from him as I drain mine. "Fine. More for me," I say.

"I heard about what you—" Evelyn stops and looks at Toby. "I'm sorry, could you let us talk privately?"

"Hey." I throw an arm around Toby. "Whatever you have to say to me, you can say in front of Toby."

Toby, for his part, doesn't seem at all surprised by my sudden loyalty. He looks at Evelyn expectantly.

"Fine." She sighs, then looks straight at me, avoiding Toby. "I ran into Derek as he was leaving."

"Oh, yeah?" I lift my chin.

"Is Derek your boyfriend?" Toby asks.

"No!" I shout.

"Yeah, that much is clear," Evelyn huffs. "What the hell, Jolie? Why did you treat him like that?"

"What are you talking about?" I take another swig. It's starting to taste better.

"I don't care who you like, or who you date, or who you make out with, but you couldn't at least let him down easy? He's crushed."

A tiny shard of panic and remorse is poking through my drunken haze, so I do my best to push it back down.

"This isn't you, Jolie," Evelyn says, her words swirling toward me. "You're nicer than this."

I crush the beer can in my hand.

"Whoa," Toby says.

"Yeah, well, maybe I'm tired of being the nice one," I say. "Maybe I want to be the fun one, or the weird one, or the slutty one!"

Toby backs away from me.

"What is it, Toby?" I yell. "There's nothing wrong with being slutty! Stop being such a slut shamer!"

Toby shakes his head and whispers, "I don't care how slutty you want to be, dude, it's just that everyone's staring."

He's right, but I can't stop. I don't even care that everyone's looking at me, because I'm confused and I'm scared and I'm starting to think that drinking I-don't-know-how-many beers was a bad idea.

"Maybe I'm just trying to grab life by the ovaries, Evelyn!" I shout, throwing my can on the floor and then grabbing a bottle from a dude walking by.

"Hey!" he says, making a grab for it.

"Do not mess with me right now, hat boy!" I snarl. He touches his hat self-consciously and backs off.

Toby picks my crushed can up off the floor. "You're not being very chill right now."

"Maybe your face isn't being very chill," I mutter to Toby. I can feel myself losing steam.

"Come on." He puts an arm around me again. "Let's go sit down somewhere and get you some water. You're gonna fall and hit your head on my mom's glassware collection, and then we're gonna have to call an ambulance and she's gonna be mad and it's gonna be a whole thing."

"I'm watching you!" Evelyn calls out as Toby asks two girls to move off the sofa ("There are pigs in a blanket in the kitchen and I swear to God they're so dope," he says). I flop onto it and Toby sits down beside me. We're surrounded by people, but they all seem to be pretty caught up in their own conversations. I catch tiny fragments of what everyone's saying and see some guy still wearing his pig costume, but I'm feeling too queasy to focus on anything.

"Here." Toby hands me a plate with some pigs in a blanket and potato chips. "When's the last time you ate something? You're gonna feel hella nauseated soon."

I look up at him, impressed. "You're right. It's nauseated. Not nauseous. Everyone says nauseous."

"Yeah." Toby looks frustrated. "Just because I like to have a good time, everyone thinks I'm not smart. Like, you can call people 'bro' and still be in the top ten percent of your class. It's not inconceivable."

He shrugs, then burps.

"Truer words," I say, toasting him with my bottled water.

"So, are you okay?" he asks, leaning back on the floral sofa.

I'm suddenly touched by how kind he's being, and how good these pigs in a blanket are. "Toby," I say with my mouth full. "I'm sorry I misjudged you. I shouldn't have said you were a shallow bro child."

He furrows his brow. "When did you say that?"

I keep going. "I just want to be honest, Toby. For once in my life, you know? To have a real conversation."

Toby nods enthusiastically.

"It's just . . . I know Derek likes me. But we're friends, you know? Friends don't make out! Do you make out with your friends?"

Toby nibbles on a pretzel. "Not usually."

"Exactly!" I spread my arms, vindicated. "That's all I'm saying! Like, is Derek hot? Yes. Do I want to make out with him? Maybe. Should I? Probably not."

Toby looks at me skeptically. "It kind of sounds like you like Derek."

I shake my head, my hair flying back and forth. "Nope. Nope. Nope."

Toby shrugs. "Okay."

I sigh heavily. "How are you always so happy all the time, Tobes? Can I call you Tobes?"

"I guess." Toby takes a sip from his water bottle. "I'm not, though. Happy all the time, I mean."

I snort. "What are you talking about? We're having a party right now at your amazing house . . ."

"Yeah, but . . . I know I should be happy that my parents are out of town because it meant I could have everyone over, but, like . . . isn't it kind of weird that they skipped town on the one weekend I was starring in the musical?"

"You're not the star," I remind him.

"One of the stars. Still. It's hella uncool."

I pat him on the arm. "I'm sorry, Toby. That's not very nice. But if it's any consolation, your parents might suck but everyone else loves you. Just look at everyone who's in your house right now."

To prove my point, I shout, "Hey! Let's hear it for our man TOBY!"

Everyone around us cheers.

Toby gives a little laugh and starts to look more like regular Toby, not this strange, sad, phantom Toby I've been getting to know.

Toby sighs as we watch someone shove an empty beer can into a potted plant. "This is gonna suck to clean up."

As bad as I feel for Toby and the eventual cleanup he'll have to do, I've got other things on my mind. "Do you know where Noah is?"

Toby shrugs. "He went outside for some air a little bit ago."

"Okay." I stand up. "I'm gonna go kiss him."

Toby narrows his eyes. "Wait, are you guys, like . . . a thing?"

"Not necessarily," I say.

"Because he hasn't mentioned anything," Toby says, still skeptical.

"Okay, well," I say, starting to lose my nerve. "I'm going to kiss him anyway, okay? Stop trying to hold me back!"

"I'm not trying—"

"I get it," I snarl. "You don't think I'm pretty enough or perfect enough. You don't think I could get someone like Noah Freakin' Reed to kiss me."

"Do you want some more water?" Toby asks. "I think you might be dehydrated."

"I'm not dehydrated!" I shout, even though I'm pretty sure Toby's right. I'm getting a combo head/jaw ache from talking, singing, and yelling so much all night, and I'm pretty sure all the alcohol I just drank isn't helping. But I don't have time to focus on hydration right now because I know what I need to do. I turn around and stomp through the party, bumping into some guys still in their black stage crew shirts (all of them impressively solid) and one girl still in her pig makeup.

"Have you seen Noah?" I ask a kid wearing a space helmet and no shirt. He points toward the front door.

I know I'm walking, but I don't even feel like I'm lifting my feet. All I know is that I have to do this now, while I have the nerve. Time's running out. Derek probably hates me, Evelyn's mad at me, I think I might've offended Toby, but who cares? If I really, seriously die on the operating table, do I want to die without having my first real non-playground, unscripted kiss? This is what I wanted, I mean *want*, and I'm going to get it.

I push through the door and onto Toby's porch. I see Noah on the lawn, staring off into the trees that line the property. He's alone.

"Hey," I try to say intriguingly, but it comes out as a shout. My volume control button seems to be broken, or maybe just drowned.

Noah turns and lifts his hand with a smile. A good sign. "Oh, hey, Jolie."

I skip down the steps, past a few people whose faces are just blurs, and cross the lawn toward him. "What are you drinking?"

He lifts his cup in my direction and rolls his eyes. "Orange soda. Alcohol and caffeine dehydrate your vocal cords, you know."

He sniffs the air as I get close to him. "Or, uh, maybe you don't know."

"I just had a little," I say, attempting to stand up straight with a hand on one hip.

Noah smiles and takes a sip. "Right. Was the party too much for you, too?"

"What?" I ask.

He tips his drink toward the porch. "Honestly, I can't stand these things. Why do I want to watch Marcus Brennerman puke into a space helmet, you know? That's why I came out here."

Oh, geez. Noah really is a nice guy. I may have only picked him for my kiss plan because of his looks, but it turns out he's actually kind of great. He's pretty much the cutest guy in school, just like I've always thought. Unless you count Derek, which I don't, because Derek's my friend. Or at least he was, before tonight. Either way, maybe kissing Noah will be all it takes—maybe once we lock lips, the ensuing chemistry will take over and we'll fall in love and everything will be perfect.

A late-spring breeze blows past us, and I hear the leaves rustle. Noah's hair lifts up slightly. We're still just looking at each other, and I don't know how long it's been, ten seconds or ten minutes or ten years. I can't let this moment pass. I push all the other thoughts out of my mind—my confusion, my fear, Evelyn, Derek, Toby—and launch myself toward Noah.

I close my eyes, my hands grabbing his (just as soft as I imagined) hair as I press my lips into his. This is what I've been waiting for. What I wanted when this whole thing started a month ago. I want to be feeling it all right now—fireworks and soda bubbles and full-body tingles and that red convertible speeding down the highway.

But what I feel right now isn't soda bubbles. It's more like a flat, warm Diet Pepsi. And I can't help thinking about all the little moments I've had with Derek over the past month, and how just touching his arm feels more exciting than kissing Noah. I've been so worried about not getting a chance to kiss someone before my mouth possibly goes numb, but it might as well be numb right now.

I pull back quickly and wipe my mouth. "I made a mistake."

"Wow," Noah says, looking away from me. "Uh, Jolie . . ."

"Oh, no. Oh, I'm sorry," I say, covering my face with my hands.

"I didn't know you—I didn't think we—" he stammers.

"That was a bad kiss, wasn't it?" I say from behind my hands.

"I think if you tell the other person it was a mistake, that's a pretty good sign it wasn't a great kiss," Noah says, and I look between my fingers to see him smiling.

"It's just . . . I wanted to kiss you before I even knew you, because you're all cute and tall and you've got that hair, but then it turned out you're nice, too, so I thought you'd be the perfect person for my first kiss because I'm about to have surgery and I'm afraid I'm going to die or have a numb mouth and not know when I have corn on my lips and—"

"Hey." Noah reaches out and grabs my shoulders. "Maybe just take a breath."

I inhale deeply and relax.

"I think," Noah says, looking directly into my eyes, "that you're a great person. But I didn't . . . I didn't even know . . . Well, I thought you and Derek were a thing."

Derek. The name shoots into my heart like a spear. "Oh, no," I groan, because now I get it. I get it that I didn't want to kiss just anyone, not even a very cute anyone with soft and voluminous hair like Noah. I wanted to kiss a very particular *someone.* And the realization pokes through my boozy fog that this may be, in fact, a pretty big problem. Because I don't want my friendship with Derek, one of the few people who actually gets me, to change. But also because I may have already screwed up that friendship or relationship or whatever-ship by openly rejecting him on the steps of Toby's house right before I had what may be the worst kiss in the history of the world.

Suddenly, I remember the last thing Abbi said to me when she was describing how a kiss felt: *That's what it feels like when you're kissing the* right *person.*

"I think . . . I'm going to . . ."

I lean over and puke right on Noah's shoes, then sit down on the ground. I run my fingers through the grass and sigh. "I'll just rest here for a while."

"I'm gonna help you get home," Noah says, picking me up with his hands under my arms. "You're obviously not driving anywhere tonight."

I can't argue with that, so I let him put an arm around me as he helps me toward his car. "Noah," I say sleepily. "I feel a lot better now."

"I'm glad," Noah grunts, straining to drag me along with him.

"Sorry about the puke. But I have to . . . I have to ask you something. What would you do if you thought you might like someone, but you didn't want to mess up your friendship?"

"I don't know," he says. "I don't have romantic feelings for any of my friends."

"No, I'm not talking about you," I say, struggling to piece my thoughts together in coherent sentences. "I'm talking about . . ."

"Hey, Derek!" Noah says, and my eyes snap open.

"Hey," Derek says. I can't fully focus on him. I just see his disappointed eyes. His pursed lips. His keys jangling in his hand.

"I, um . . . I came back. To make sure you were okay. I wanted to make sure you didn't try to drive. But it looks like you managed pretty well on your own."

Oh no. I think about how this looks: Noah's arm around me, my smudgy, too-bright lipstick, Noah's rumpled hair.

"We're not—" I start.

Derek holds up a hand. "Save it, Jolie. I've gotta get home. Have a nice night."

He walks away, and I just watch him go.

"He seemed angry," Noah says slowly. "Did I do something to him?"

"You didn't do anything," I say, leaning against him. "I did."

And then I puke. Again.

Chapter Twenty-Four

Without opening my eyes, I stretch out my arms and feel a warm body. I bolt upright with a shriek, then almost fall back down as my head spins.

"You're awake." Evelyn yawns and rubs her eyes.

"Wait, why are you here?" We're both crammed into my twin bed, and I'm wearing mismatched pajamas. Late morning sunlight is streaming through my white lace curtains as I blink a few times, trying to remember what happened last night. "And how did I get here?"

"After you puked on Noah the second time, we decided you needed some help getting home."

I groan. If someone has to specify which time you barfed, you know it wasn't a good night.

"And I called Abbi to make sure she could help us get inside without waking up your parents. We both tried to get pajamas on you, but you were very floppy."

I look down at my pajama top, on which only two of six buttons are buttoned.

"But I thought you left the party," I say, piecing together what I remember. "Because you were—are—mad at me."

"Hello?" Evelyn looks pissed. "No matter how mad I am at you, I'm not going to leave you drunk and alone with some dude, even if it is Toby. That's, like, Being a Decent Friend 101. Marla and I stayed on the porch and kept an eye on you until we took you home."

I'm suddenly filled with so much warmth for Evelyn that I think I might puke a third time. "You stayed."

She nods.

"So you saw . . ."

"The kiss. The puke. Derek. The return of the puke." She holds up fingers as she lists everything. "Noah's shoes didn't survive, by the way. He threw them in Toby's pond, where the contents of your stomach are probably giving some fish alcohol poisoning."

I want to crawl back under the blankets and stay there for, oh, a few years. And not just because my tongue feels like it's wearing a sweater. It's because a thick layer of shame is coating my entire body.

"I kissed Noah," I say flatly.

"Yaaaay!" Evelyn sings, then when she sees how I'm looking at her, offers up a tentative "I mean . . . booooo?"

"It sucked," I say. "Like, if that's what kissing is like, then I don't know why people do it. Smashing our mouths together? Who invented that?"

Evelyn raises her eyebrows, which are much fainter than usual since she's not wearing makeup. "In my limited experience, it generally feels better than a mouth smash."

"It's just . . . Abbi and Google made it sound like it was

going to be so great, but honestly, it was like my mouth was already numb. I wasn't into it, Noah wasn't into it . . ."

"Please tell me you didn't google what kissing feels like," Evelyn says, putting a hand on my arm.

"Not the point."

"Well," she says, "I think you might have already hit on the point. You weren't into it, Noah wasn't into it . . . In general, if both parties aren't into it, it's going to suck. Do you actually like Noah?"

I swallow. "I think he's really sweet. And nice. And he's cute."

Evelyn stares at me.

I slump. "Fine! I don't *like*-like him, okay? I just couldn't stand the thought of not meeting my goal before my surgery, and there's no one else I could kiss! Maybe Peter, but I'm definitely not interested."

Evelyn stares at me. "Can we please stop acting like you and Derek aren't totally in love with each other?"

"We're not," I say reflexively.

"Oh, really?" Evelyn asks. "Then why are you guys always, like, *staring at each other meaningfully*? Why is it that whenever I talk to you I feel like this is a romantic comedy and I just interrupted you right before you're about to kiss?"

Heat floods my cheeks. "I don't know what's going on, okay? Maybe I like Derek. I mean, probably."

Evelyn raises an eyebrow.

"Okay, I do!" I say, throwing my hands up. "But I tried to never think about it, because I knew there was no way he could ever like me. And even when he was acting like he did, I figured it was just because he knew I was going to get surgery soon and I'd be prettier."

"That doesn't sound like Derek," Evelyn says.

I sigh. "It's not Derek. At Toby's, he told me he's liked me since we were kids."

"I hate to be a know-it-all, but duh."

"But now I don't know what to do. You don't just make out with someone you've known your whole life."

"Why not?"

"Because!" I croak. "Because . . . what if it sucks? What if it ruins everything? What if it doesn't work out? What if it's like the kiss I just had with Noah, and then we can't be friends anymore because I just look at him and think about flat Diet Pepsi?"

Evelyn shakes her head. "I don't really know what you're talking about, but you're ignoring one important thing: What if it's great?"

I shake my head. "The thing with Noah was fine, because I knew that if I kissed him and he wasn't into it, or if he thought I was disgusting or ugly or he pushed me away, it wouldn't matter. Because I don't *know* him, you know? Yeah, sure, he's a great guy, but I haven't known him that long."

Evelyn nods, encouraging me to go on.

"But Derek . . ." I trail off, tracing a pattern on the comforter with my finger. "He actually knows me, all the good parts and the bad parts. And if he . . ." I swallow. "If he changes his mind . . . If he decides I'm not good enough . . . that means something. I don't know if he's temporarily delusional or just desperate or what, but this can't be for real. And I'd rather save my dignity than get humiliated or crushed."

"Jolie," Evelyn says quietly, "he broke up with Melody. For you."

I stare at the comforter.

"The way you see yourself . . . that's not real, do you get that?" She reaches out and puts a hand on my arm. "This is about way,

way more than a guy, however great Derek is. This is about you, and I wish you could see you're worth it. Now and later. Before surgery and after. With an underbite and without."

I sniffle and brush away a tear that escaped from my eye.

"You're a good friend," I say as I blow my nose. "But I'm scared. I wish I wasn't, but I just am. I know you don't get it because you've never been afraid of anything in your life, but that's the truth."

Evelyn laughs. "Do you seriously think I've never been scared of someone not liking me?"

I nod slowly.

"Well." Evelyn takes a deep breath. "I guess this is as good a time as any to tell you . . . I'm dating someone. Like, officially. Like, exchange-letterman-jackets-in-an-old-movie official."

I almost fall off the bed. "What? What's his name?"

Evelyn smirks. "Marla."

One million thoughts run through my head, and those one million thoughts coalesce into one name that makes its way out of my mouth. *"Marla?"*

Evelyn throws her head back and laughs. "Seriously, Jolie, haven't you been wondering why we've been hanging out so much?"

"But I didn't even know you *like* girls."

She shrugs. "Neither did I. But I like Marla. She's not as much of a hard-ass as she seems—or, well, actually she is, and that's what I like about her. She's just as driven to get into Harvard as I am to get into Parsons. It's nice to be around someone who understands staying in on a Friday night to work. And since you and Derek are kind of in a two-person club . . ."

"Is that what you think?"

"It's the truth." She looks down at my comforter, seeming

different from the usually confident Evelyn I know. "I'm glad you guys have each other, but sometimes there's no room for me. So when Marla and I clicked, it just seemed like you guys wouldn't really miss me if I wasn't around that much."

"Oh, Ev," I say.

She holds up a hand to stop me. "I don't want you to feel sorry for me. That's the thing. It's like, whenever we hang out, you're reminding me I should be studying or doing my homework, but I already have a mom, and frankly, sometimes she's too much mom for me to handle."

"I thought you wanted me to help you!"

"I do." She exhales forcefully. "It's just . . . I don't want that to be the entirety of our friendship, you know? You and Derek have your bad-movie club or whatever, and it's not like I even want to come to that, but I do wish we had more of our own things."

"I'm so clueless. I'm a terrible person," I moan. "I'm at number one on the list of terrible people, right above Justin Bieber when he was in his rebellious phase and he abandoned that monkey in Germany."

"That poor monkey," Evelyn murmurs.

"I'm sorry I've been sucking so hard," I say. "We need to make some new friendship traditions. Maybe we need a handshake? Or we can make some bracelets? Or . . . ?"

Evelyn laughs. "Or maybe I can just come over, and we can watch *The Golden Girls* together and not talk about English essays or history tests."

"Deal," I say, holding out my hand and attempting to make up a handshake on the spot.

"I think we need more practice," Evelyn says.

There are three solid knocks on the door. "Everyone decent?"

"Yes!" I say as my dad pokes his head in. "Duh."

"Just letting you girls know I made some pancakes," he says.

"What kind are they?" Evelyn asks. "Do I dare hope?"

"Blueberry," Dad says with a smile.

Evelyn fist-pumps. Dad's blueberry pancakes are legendary.

"Has there ever been a problem that blueberry pancakes couldn't solve?" Evelyn asks. She's mostly right; we used to have Dad's blueberry pancakes after our childhood sleepovers, and they kind of *did* solve all our problems back then.

Evelyn reminds me to brush my teeth and take a quick shower before we head downstairs because I smell, as she puts it, "like roadkill." Luckily, Mom already left for a morning shopping trip, and Dad is too engrossed in his latest paperback to notice my first hangover.

My stomach settles once I have a few pancakes. But as I think about everything that happened last night and a fog of mortification settles over me, I have the sinking feeling that my current problems are gonna require a whole lot more than simple carbohydrates.

Chapter Twenty-Five

I've texted Derek approximately thirty-seven times (but who's counting?) since the Confession, as I've been referring to it in my head. It has a better ring to it than the Night I Ruined a Friendship and Also Puked Twice. He hasn't responded once.

The upside to all of this is that I have a lot of free time on my hands, most of which I spend constantly replaying what I said to Derek, then coming up with all the big dramatic speeches I should've given about my true feelings and how scared I am and how important he is to me.

In my head, there's definitely an instrumental soundtrack behind those words. It's all very stirring.

But I can't exactly give Derek said speech because, of course, he's not talking to me. The worst part is that while we have to see each other constantly during our last week of junior year, he won't even acknowledge my existence. I spend trig class staring at the span of his shoulders and imagining what would happen if I reached out and touched him. Probably nothing good. Either way, he partners up with Sean Morrison, and I'm forced to become partners with Greg Walker, who doesn't know a sine from a cosine.

And then junior year ends with a whimper, and I have nothing to do. I mean, other than worry about my impending surgery, which is scheduled for exactly two weeks after the last day of school. Evelyn and I still hang out, but she's with Marla a lot, which means Netflix and I take our already close relationship to the next level. I easily finish *Jane Eyre* and move on to the film adaptation, but Dad doesn't like making fun of how Michael Fassbender growls all his lines, so the whole experience is just depressing.

My mood is, apparently, pretty obvious to everyone in my family. Abbi asks me what crawled up my butt and died (charming), and even Mom relaxes her hands-off parenting approach to gently chastise me.

"Once you're done familiarizing yourself with the couch," she says one day while I'm sitting on it and mindlessly deciding which prestige television show I should binge next to take my mind off my surgery anxieties, "maybe you could actually go outside and get a little vitamin D."

I scoff and burrow farther into the couch. "It's way too late to turn me into a nature lover. You raised an indoor kid."

"Maybe you can watch videos on your phone while you sit on the porch. I'll take anything at this point, as long as you're not moping in front of the TV."

I look up at Mom, who has her arms crossed over the St. Vincent T-shirt I bought her for her birthday last year. Between the way she dresses and the artfully rumpled non-style of her hair, she could easily pass for twenty-five if it weren't for the wrinkles around her eyes. She's beautiful, just like Abbi, and I find myself wondering once again if she's embarrassed by me.

"Come on," she says, grabbing one of my hands and pulling me up. "We're going out."

"You're not going to make me experience the great outdoors, are you?" I whine.

Fifteen minutes later, we're eating sprinkle cones in the parking lot of the Dairy Queen.

"We haven't done this since I was, like, ten," I say with a mouth full of ice cream. "You used to take me out for ice cream whenever I was upset to get me to talk about my problems and— Hey, wait!"

Mom smiles behind her cone. "Ah, you've discovered my evil plan."

I frown. "This ice cream tastes like deception."

"You don't have to talk about anything if you don't want to," Mom says casually. "But I've noticed you haven't been spending a ton of time with your friends lately."

"Evelyn's busy with her new girlfriend," I say.

"Okay. And Derek?"

"He's . . . um . . ." I try to think of a way to get out of talking about this with my mom, but honestly? I'm tired of being alone with this. "Derek said he liked me, and I yelled at him because he won't talk about his dad, and now we're not speaking."

I take a deep breath. Whew.

Mom nods. "Derek likes you, huh? Well, I can't say I'm surprised. He's always looking at you."

"Lots of people look at other people," I mutter. "That doesn't mean they want to make out with them."

Mom shrugs. "Yeah, but the way he looks at you is different. How do you feel?"

"Oh no," I say, crunching the last bite of my cone in my mouth. "Don't school-counselor me. I'm not falling for this."

Mom puts up her hands in surrender. "I'm speaking as your mom, and as someone who's been on both sides of a one-sided crush many a time. I'm taking off my counselor hat, promise."

I sigh. "I don't know how I feel. There's a lot going on right now. Junior year just ended, my surgery is next week, Abbi's about to have a baby . . . The last thing I need is romantic confusion."

Mom smiles. "Unfortunately, love is pretty much always confusing, and it doesn't ever show up at a convenient time."

"Well, that's stupid," I grumble.

"But why the confusion?" she asks. "What's not to like about Derek? He's a nice-looking young man. He's polite. You seem to like hanging out with him."

I have to hold myself back from rolling my eyes. " 'A nice-looking young man'? Please tell me you don't talk to other high school students like that."

"Not the point."

"It doesn't have anything to do with whether or not I like Derek," I say, ripping the napkin that came with my cone into tiny pieces. "It's just that he only likes me because he knows I'm going to be fixed."

" 'Fixed'?" Mom repeats, raising her eyebrows. "Wait, did he say that?"

I shake my head quickly. "No. He . . . okay, well, he said he's liked me basically the entire time we've been friends. But if that's true, then why didn't he do something about it before now? Why wait until right before I get surgery?"

"If it was that easy for everyone to talk about their feelings, then I wouldn't have a job," Mom says. "But back up. Who told you that you're going to be 'fixed'?"

"No one," I say. "That's just the truth. Next week when I get surgery, Dr. Kelley is going to fix my face so I don't look like this anymore. I'll look like you and Abbi and every other woman in the world who doesn't have an underbite."

Mom's brow furrows. "You think you're getting *fixed*?"

"I mean . . ." I turn in my seat to face her. "Yeah. That's what's happening."

"No," Mom says forcefully. "That's not what's happening. You're getting a surgery to make it easier for you to eat, and talk, and to avoid more pain and inconvenience down the road. You're not getting this surgery because there's something wrong with you."

A ball of emotion starts to well up in my throat, making it hard for me to get the words out. "Um, okay—easy for you to say. Because there's nothing wrong with you. You and Abbi are perfect and pretty and—"

"Wait, is this what you've been thinking this entire time? That you need to get surgery to make yourself *pretty*?" She practically shrieks the last word, and I'm afraid the people inside the Dairy Queen can hear us.

"I just . . . I just want to be pretty for once in my life, okay?" I say. "I'm tired of feeling like the weird one, and I'm tired of being the smart one, and I don't want to be self-conscious anymore! You never, ever tell me I'm pretty, and I just want to hear it once, okay?"

I lean back in my seat, breathing hard.

"Jolie." Mom leans forward to catch my eye. "I don't talk about your appearance with you because I've never wanted you to think that's all you have to offer. You and Abbi are both smart, and kind, and funny, and a whole lot of other things that matter way more than being pretty."

I swallow hard and stare at my lap.

"But if it makes a difference—and it probably doesn't, because I know I'm just your mom—I think you're one of the prettiest girls I've ever seen. Top two, for sure."

I look up and give her a tiny smile. "Thanks, weirdo."

She crumples up the napkin in her hand. "You don't have to do this if you don't want to, you know—your surgery."

"But I've been working toward this for literally years," I say. "The braces, the palate expander, the second round of braces—"

Mom shakes her head. "That doesn't matter. It's your life, and it's your body, and you can call it off at any point, right up until the second they put you under, okay?"

I nod, and watch a family sit down at a table on the Dairy Queen patio. I could back out—I could just stop worrying about dying and pain and everything else and forget about this.

But is that what I want to do? Do I actually want to face a life with not only more pain and difficulty, but a life where I'm afraid to take a chance?

"I'm gonna do it," I say.

Mom raises her eyebrows. "Yeah?"

"I want to," I say firmly. "Really. It's my decision."

"Okay." Mom gives me one resolute nod. "And what you want is what I want."

She backs out of the parking lot and merges onto the road. She turns on the radio, and I assume we're done talking as she quietly sings along, but then she says, "It's okay to be scared, you know."

I look out the window and watch the Brentley spring greenery rush by—the trees and grass and wildflowers that have just started to bloom. "Yeah, I know."

"I was scared to get into a relationship with your dad," she says, her eyes still on the road. "He had to propose to me three times before I said yes."

My head whips toward her. "Wait, what?"

"I was scared about what it would *mean* if I got married," she says, rolling her eyes. "You know, would I be changing who I was if I decided to marry this guy instead of making out with a different person in every city when I was on tour?"

"Mom." I cover my face with my hands. "No part of me wants to know these details."

"But finally, what I realized was . . . I *was* changing. I loved being in the band, but then I just didn't love it anymore. I didn't want to spend every night in a new city or every day traveling in a van full of empty fast-food bags. I wanted to stay in one spot, with one person. I was still me, it's just that what I wanted changed."

"Right," I say slowly. "Wait, are you trying to trick me into thinking about my feelings?"

She laughs, a deep throaty chuckle. "I'm not trying to trick you. But you're my daughter, and I know you've always been a little bit afraid of taking chances."

"Please don't bring up the Great Birthday Tricycle Incident again."

"I won't. You took a big chance in the musical, right? And look what happened; you killed it. I just don't want you to live your whole life being afraid of change when you're already a star."

I don't say anything else, and we finish our drive home. Mom pulls me into a hug when we get out of the car, and I let her. We don't tell Abbi or Dad that we already ate ice cream, and then we order a pizza, and I kind of start to feel sick. Not just because of the one-two punch of sugar and grease, but because I'm thinking about what Mom said about not being afraid, about being okay with changes.

Maybe my surgery isn't the only thing I'm afraid of, and maybe my jaw isn't the only thing that has to change.

Chapter Twenty-Six

The next day, I'm in my room listening to *Deep Dive*, mostly because I miss Derek's voice, but also because he finally posted that lemur episode, and I'm curious. As soon as he ends the episode with his trademark "Stay deep," I tap out a text.

Just listened to the lemur episode. Turns out the toilet claw was pretty much as gross as I imagined.

I scroll through oral surgery Reddit threads that I've already read a million times and tell myself that I'm not waiting for his response. But of course my entire body is tensed, waiting for that text notification that never comes.

I jump when I hear a noise, but it's only the doorbell. I ignore it because (a) Abbi is home, and (b) the only people who ring our doorbell are the very nice but very persistent people who hand out those religious pamphlets featuring lots of drawings of flames, and I'm just not feeling up to that today.

But a couple minutes later, I hear voices. One of those voices is Abbi's, and she sounds angry. I shut my laptop and creep into the hallway. The voices grow louder and, yes, that's definitely Abbi whisper-yelling. And unless she's getting into an argument about those scary pamphlets, this is a weird situation.

I walk down the stairs as quietly as possible, stepping slowly to minimize creaking. I pause at the bottom, where I can just see Abbi's back as she holds the door half-open. She's blocking the doorway, and I can't see who's outside, but I can see that she's shaking.

"I don't want you to come here ever again," she says in a voice that I think is supposed to be quiet.

The person on the other side of the door says, "But I'm in love with you, Abbi."

My mouth drops open. Okay. So this is probably not the religious-pamphlet people (unless they're trying some new recruiting tactics).

"Are you still with her?" Abbi asks, and there's nothing but silence from the other side of the door.

"That's what I thought," Abbi says. "Goodbye."

She starts to shut the door but something—a hand, a foot?—stops it, and she shrieks, "Get out!"

I can't keep hiding back here anymore—if Abbi's dealing with a persistent, romantically inclined pamphlet pusher, I have to help her.

"She said get out!" I shout, and Abbi jumps back from the door, startled. Now that she's no longer in the doorway, I have a good view of who's outside. It's a man who looks like he's in his thirties, wearing a peacoat and a scarf. His glasses have thick frames and his hair is combed back. He looks like every carica-ture I've seen of an Intellectual. I'm not one hundred percent sure because I only saw part of the guy's face before, but I'm pretty sure he's the one from Gionino's. And right now he and Abbi are both staring straight at me.

I swallow. I don't know why Abbi's yelling at this guy who, frankly, seems like he'd be more into solving quadratic equations than being threatening, but whatever. "Didn't you hear her?" I ask. "She doesn't want you here."

Glasses Guy turns to Abbi, as if I'm not even here. "Is this your sister?"

"Jolie," Abbi says quietly, ignoring him. "Please go in the other room."

"But . . . ," I start.

"I've got this," she says, and the look in her eyes is so pleading that I ignore everything else—the weird guy at the door, her huge, vulnerable belly, the way she was just yelling—and walk into the kitchen without another word.

A couple of minutes later, I hear the front door shut. Abbi walks in and hoists herself onto the barstool beside me with a huff. I don't know what I should say or if I'm supposed to say anything, so I just stare at her until she turns to me.

"So that was John."

My eyes widen. "The father?"

Before I saw part of his face at Gionino's, I always assumed John was mysterious and hot. Maybe he was a sexy one-night stand she met at a bar, or a beautiful foreign man she slept with before he had to leave the country, never to return. But I never assumed he was as thoroughly unremarkable as the man on our doorstep. He didn't seem special or sexy. He seemed old. And, even though I only saw him for a moment, weak.

Abbi nods, then looks startled. "Wait, how do you know that?"

Crap. "Um, I maybe . . . saw your phone one day when he was texting you."

Abbi sighs, then thumps her head down on the island. "My life is a mess."

"Do you . . . want to talk about it?" I ask gingerly, and she opens one eye and peers up at me.

"Not particularly," she says, her crossed arms muffling her voice.

Now it's my turn to sigh. "Listen, I know what Mom says. That, like, you can talk about things in your own time. But I'm your sister. If you can't tell me, who can you tell?"

Abbi sits up. "You really want to know?"

I nod slowly, trying to hide my eagerness.

"Okay," she says. "But it's a long, sordid, thoroughly pathetic story, so don't say I didn't warn you."

"Consider me warned," I say.

"John was my sociology professor. I mean, at the time I called him Mr. Thomson, but I stopped calling him that once we started . . . well . . . you know . . ."

"It's okay." I point toward her belly. "Mom told me where babies come from."

She snort-laughs. "So anyway, it didn't start out as anything romantic. Like, I didn't initially go to his office hours to seduce him or anything. I just wanted to talk about a paper, but it turned out we had a lot in common. He was . . . nice. So we started hanging out a lot. And then we started *really* hanging out a lot."

"Abs. I get it."

"Things were going really well for a few weeks. I even thought about inviting him over here to meet you guys." She widens her eyes, like she's astonished she ever considered it. "And that's when I was like, wait, why do we only hang out sporadically, and why doesn't he ever pick up when I call him?"

"I don't like where this is going," I mutter.

"Right? So I asked him about it. You know, the whole, 'what are we, can we define the relationship' conversation that's so fun for everyone. And that's when I found out that he didn't live alone."

"You mean he has a roommate?" I ask.

"Uh, yeah. You could say that. He has a wife."

"What?" I screech.

"That's why I couldn't come over on certain nights. He only invited me there when she was out of town at conferences. So obviously I got super mad, and maybe I kicked in the side of his car, I don't know." She shrugs like it doesn't matter. "And then two weeks later I found out I was pregnant."

"What did he say?"

"He swore he was going to leave her, said he wasn't in love with her anymore, she was more like his mom than his wife. You know, Cheating Guy 101 bullshit, like he was reading off a script from a really predictable movie. And I believed him for a little bit. But then it was like, 'Oh, okay. Literally nothing is going to change. You're going to stay married, and you're going to stay an asshole.'"

I exhale. "Wow. That sucks."

"That's putting it mildly," she says. "Now my life is a complete shitshow, and I'm a pregnant, unmarried college student who lives with her parents, which, surprisingly, is not really where I saw myself ending up."

"We all make mistakes," I say, thinking about my own life.

"Have you ever made a mistake that involved sleeping with a married man and then getting pregnant?" she asks, eyebrows raised.

I can't exactly dispute that. "So why was he here?"

She groans and puts her head back down on the island.

"Because he's back on his 'No, this time, I'm *totally* going to leave my wife' kick. Like, he thinks everything is going to magically work out somehow, but I'm not falling for it."

"Do you . . . want to be with him again?" I ask.

"Honestly? No. I kind of don't want to see him ever again. But I know that's not possible, since I'm, you know, having his child. But until he either tells his wife about this or actually shows me some divorce papers, I'm not talking to him. I'm not making this baby be somebody's secret."

I nod.

"It's just a mess. This situation. My life. Everything."

"So how are you going to tell Mom?" I ask.

"Oh, she already knows," Abbi says with a dismissive wave. "She did the whole 'take you out for ice cream, convince you to spill all your feelings' thing."

I shake my head. "That sneaky woman."

Abbi sighs heavily and stares at the counter, looking the most defeated I've ever seen her. I think about her reading me books when I was sick and trying to make me feel better. "Hey," I say. "I'm halfway through *The Sopranos.* Do you want to watch with me?"

She looks at me with narrowed eyes. "Why are you watching that show? It ended, like, a million years ago."

"I needed something to take my mind off my surgery, so I was like, 'Well, it could always be worse. I could be involved in a life of crime.'"

Abbi sighs and pushes herself off the stool. "You are too weird, you know?" But she's smiling when she says it, so we head to the living room to get lost in someone's Mafia-related problems for a couple of hours.

Chapter Twenty-Seven

The next day, one week before my surgery (not that I'm counting the days or anything), Mom and Dad leave to visit our aunt Jayne in Cleveland, two hours away.

"Call me if you even think you might, maybe, sort of be going into labor," Mom says, giving Abbi a hug.

"Mom!" Abbi says. "I'm not due for weeks."

"And first babies are almost always late," I say. "I learned that in childbirth class."

Mom purses her lips. It's true that Abbi's been having false contractions for a week, but the doctor assured her that these were just her body's way of "practicing" for real labor and they don't necessarily mean that she's going into labor immediately or anything. But I can tell that Mom's still worried about leaving her.

"I'll be here," I remind her. "And I'm practically an expert on childbirth now. I watched the video."

"You might as well be a doctor," Mom says, sounding unconvinced.

"Let's hit the road!" Dad says, holding out Mom's jacket. Like all dads since the beginning of time, he's obsessed with "making good time" on the road.

"All right, all right," Mom says, shrugging into her faux-leather motorcycle jacket before giving us both one more hug.

And then they're gone, and Abbi immediately slumps against the wall in relief. "Holy-moly. I thought I was going to collapse under the weight of being watched so intensely."

"Come on," I say, pushing her toward the living room. "You're under strict orders to relax and not overexert yourself. What's on TV?"

"Oh! A marathon of *Snapped!*" Abbi says as she presses the on button on the remote. *Snapped* is a show all about women who, well, snap and either murder or try to murder someone. We find it very comforting, for reasons that are probably best left unexamined.

"Perfect," I say. Derek still won't answer my texts, so I've given up on bothering him. It still stings to think about him, but thankfully, TV is here to solve all our problems.

After literally hours of watching *Snapped*, Abbi stands up and stretches. "This baby needs ice cream. You want some?"

I shake my head. "No, but I'll pause it. I know you don't want to miss this woman who tries to kill someone with horse tranquilizers."

Abbi heads to the kitchen, and I scroll through my phone, not that there's much to see. I have a nice text from Noah checking in on me to see if I'm ready for surgery and a few texts from Evelyn. Nothing from Derek, of course.

I think about what I would say to him if he ever responded

to me. That I'm sorry I acted like I don't have feelings for him? That I do have a crush on him but it freaks me out? That I just couldn't believe a guy like him would actually want to date a girl like me, and if we try it and it doesn't work out then it might actually kill me even if surgery doesn't? Those just aren't things you can say through text.

After about ten minutes of scrolling through Instagram, I realize Abbi's still not back. "Abs?" I call, getting up from the chair and walking toward the kitchen. "You okay? Did you go into a Chunky Monkey coma?"

But when I step into the kitchen, I see Abbi sitting on the floor, staring straight ahead.

"Abbi!" I kneel beside her, then realize the floor is wet. "Did you spill something?"

She looks up at me, her eyes wide. "You know how Kathy told us my water wouldn't break until we got to the hospital?"

I nod.

"Well, either I just peed all over the kitchen floor or my water broke."

"What?" I leap up. "You mean I'm kneeling in your amniotic fluid?"

"That's the least of our worries right now!" Abbi says, and when she starts crying I realize—duh—that this is a problem. The baby isn't due for weeks. And if Abbi's water broke, then she needs to go to the hospital. Which means that someone needs to take her. And since Mom and Dad are at Aunt Jayne's, that leaves . . .

Me.

Oh no.

"Do you have your bag packed?" I ask, trying to remember anything we learned in class.

"No!" Abbi yells at me. "I thought I had time!"

"Okay, so we need to get an outfit for the baby, your robe . . ."

Abbi lies down, wincing, on our unmopped kitchen floor. "If this is what a contraction is, I don't like it."

"Um. . . . okay. Remember your breathing?" I pick a crumb out of Abbi's hair.

"I don't want to do the breathing!" Abbi says. "I want to wait until my due date!"

"I'm pretty sure we don't have that option."

Abbi pushes herself up off the floor with a groan. "You need to take me to the hospital."

"Let's just call Mom and Dad and see if they can come back . . ."

"I'm not waiting around, Jolie," Abbi says.

"But Mom and Dad are supposed to do this," I say. I'm thinking of all the movies I've seen where a woman goes into labor in a taxi or an elevator. What am I going to do if Abbi gives birth in my Ford Focus? There's not even enough room in there for her to spread out, let alone have a baby. And I just vacuumed those seats.

Plus, I'm just really, totally, not even a little equipped to deal with this.

As if Abbi can read my thoughts, she says, "You went to the classes with me—you know enough to help me. But," she says, her voice cracking, "it's too early. I'm scared."

I press my lips together and summon up determination I'm not sure I actually have. I'm scared, too, but I'm not the one who's about to give birth, so I push it down. I have to be strong for Abbi.

"Let's go," I say, helping her up off the floor.

Abbi sits in the backseat—I figure if she does give birth in the Focus, at least she'll have more space back there—and times her contractions.

"Do the breathing," I suggest.

"I don't remember how to do the breathing!" Abbi yells.

"I thought you took notes!"

"Yeah, well, it turns out notes are useless right now." Then she attempts to do the breathing we learned in class, a loud "HEEEEE" followed by a loud "HOOOOO."

"Is it helping?" I ask.

"Heeeee. I don't know. Hooooooo. I'm not sure it's supposed to be done in a car. Oh God," she groans.

"Does it hurt?" I ask.

"No. I mean, yeah, but it's not that bad. Yet. I'm just freaking out. This wasn't how it was supposed to happen."

"How was it supposed to happen?" I ask, thinking that keeping her talking might stop her from panicking.

"For starters, I was supposed to be married to the love of my life, a gorgeous pediatrician who—HEEEE—loves me and our two black Lab mixes. HOOOOO. I was supposed to live in a house with a turret and know how to make a piecrust. I was supposed to have some great career—HEEEEEE—that I would keep after I had a kid but not because I needed the money, just because—HOOOOOO—I loved it so much that I couldn't imagine not doing it."

I keep my eyes on the road, realizing that Abbi thinks I'm asking how her entire life was supposed to go, not her birth process.

"I'll tell you what wasn't supposed to happen!" she says with sudden passion. "I wasn't supposed to get knocked up by a shit-bag sociology professor who doesn't even have the guts to tell his wife about me!"

I resist reaching up to cover my right ear, the one that Abbi is nearly screaming into. Okay, so conversation wasn't a good idea. I push the radio on and turn up the volume on the oldies station.

"I HATE THIS SONG!" Abbi shouts.

"Okay, okay." I press off as quickly as I can. I wasn't aware that the mellow tunes of James Taylor could upset anyone so much, but I'm determined to give Abbi what she wants right now.

"How slow are you going?" she asks, her voice suddenly low and menacing. I press my foot on the gas. The hospital is only a few miles away, but I'm not sure I'll make it there alive.

Chapter Twenty-Eight

*A*t the hospital, they whisk Abbi away immediately to check
her. I'm not allowed to go with her, which is fine with me.
I don't like to think about her being alone back there, but I also
can't handle any more responsibility right now. There are only
a few other people in the waiting room—an older couple who
look like they're waiting to be grandparents, a woman holding
a pink-and-blue box that must be a baby gift. We all silently
watch the TV mounted in the corner, which is playing an episode of *The Ellen DeGeneres Show,* as if we've made a tacit agree-
ment not to bother each other with conversation.

When Mom and Dad walk into the waiting room, I slump,
instantly relieved. I hadn't realized I was holding my body rigid
with tension, but upon simply seeing them, I'm overcome with
gratitude that I'm not in charge of this situation anymore.

"She's in the delivery room," I say, pointing down the

hallway. My mom takes off for somewhere—to the nurse's station? The delivery room? If anyone can fight her way back there, it's my mom—and my dad sits down beside me.

He hands me a vending-machine coffee and points to the copy of *HGTV Magazine* in my hands. "Getting into decorating?"

I look down at the magazine in my lap. My fingers are anxiously flipping through the pages, but all I've been able to see for the past hour are colors and shapes. My eyes focus on the headlines on the front.

"Well, you know me." I shrug. "Always looking for a way to liven up my outdoor entertaining space."

I toss the magazine on the table and eagerly take a swig of the coffee. It's disgusting, but this is what you do in waiting rooms, according to all the television shows I've seen: You drink coffee and worry.

"Is this bad?" I ask Dad. "I mean, with Abbi. The baby isn't due for a few more weeks."

He shrugs. "I'm a teacher, Jolie," he says. "Not an obstetrician."

I nod.

"Here's what I'll tell you, though," he says. "Sometimes when I start a project, I have all these expectations. I start with a plan for how I'm gonna build whatever it is I'm building—a table, a bookcase, a bed frame. And I look at that plan and think, 'Yes. That's exactly how this whole thing is gonna turn out.'"

I take another sip and wonder where exactly this woodworking lesson is going.

"But you know how often it turns out according to the plan?" he asks, taking a sip of his own coffee. "Almost never. Maybe a board breaks. Maybe the hardware store's out of the wood stain I want. Maybe it was just a bad plan."

My confusion must be written all over my face, because Dad holds up a hand. "I'm getting to the point, I promise. What I'm trying to say is, at the end of the day, no matter how far off-plan I went, I still end up with a table, or a bookcase, or a bed frame. Maybe things look a little bit different than I wanted them to, but it's okay."

I nod, finally getting it. "So, even though Abbi isn't following her plan, everything's still gonna be okay with the baby?"

Dad looks at me, confused. "What are you talking about babies for? I was just talking about a table."

I sigh heavily and he cracks up, spilling some of his coffee on his lap. Once he calms down, he pats me on my knee in the most Dad-like gesture ever. "It's gonna be okay, Jolie. I promise."

I pull my knees up to my chest and try to get comfortable in the hopelessly uncomfortable chair. Of all the ways I could've chosen to spend my day, sitting in a hospital waiting room while my sister is in labor early wouldn't have been one of them, but right now, sitting in companionable silence with my dad while Channing Tatum dances with Ellen on TV, I think I can handle it.

Mom comes out occasionally, relaying details that involve dilation and centimeters and other words I sort of remember from class. All I really pick up on is that everything's going to be okay, eventually, and that Abbi's gonna have a table at the end of this whole thing.

After a few episodes of courtroom TV shows, Dad says he needs to "wander" and walks off toward the courtyard. That's when I see a familiar person walking down the corridor: Dr. Jones.

"Hi!" I say brightly before remembering that her son hates me now. I shrink back a little, but she doesn't make things awkward. Instead, she sits down beside me and pulls me in for a hug. Even though we're in a hospital, she still manages to smell good.

"I stopped in to see Abbi," she says, pulling back. "She's doing great."

I sigh with relief. I know my mom said things were okay, but it feels better to hear that from a doctor. "Oh, good. Because she was really scared."

Dr. Jones lifts a shoulder. "Well, childbirth can be scary. But then again, most things that are worth it are usually a little bit scary."

I nod. "So, did Derek . . ." I gulp, trying to think of a way to phrase it.

Dr. Jones smiles kindly. "I've noticed you haven't been around the house lately. And I've noticed that he's been moping a lot. But if you're asking me if I know all the details of what's going on, no, I don't. This may shock you, but Derek doesn't exactly come to me with his personal problems."

That, at least, makes me smile. "Okay. I just wondered . . ." I don't know where I'm going with this, so I let the thought trail off.

Dr. Jones puts her hand on my knee. "You guys will make up. Real friends can get through anything."

"You're right," I say, and give her a tight smile because I'm not one hundred percent sure she *is* right. Sure, Evelyn and I can fight and make up, but Evelyn and I aren't harboring awkward, potentially friendship-killing romantic feelings for each other. But I'm not about to mention to Dr. Jones that I think I might want to totally make out with her son.

Her name blares over the speakers, and she stands up. "That's my cue. Congratulations, Jolie—you're going to be an aunt!"

I wave as she strides down the hallway, all confidence and capability. I wonder if I'll ever feel that sure of myself.

Dad wanders back into the room holding a cookie and a bottle of Coke.

"Here," he says. "Keep yourself awake with caffeine and sugar."

"Thank God," I say, practically lunging at them.

But I guess the caffeine and sugar are no match for my stress fatigue, because the next thing I know, I'm waking up with a start: I realize I fell asleep on Dad's shoulder.

"Well, hello there, sunshine," Dad says.

"How long have I been out?" I mumble.

"Only about half an hour," he says, flipping past magazine advertisements for cat food and yogurt.

Only half an hour. And yet it feels like we've been in this waiting room for our entire lives. In fact, I'm starting to feel like we'll spend the rest of our lives here, like we'll never leave, like . . .

"She's here!" Mom says, bursting into the room. "The baby's here!"

Dad and I stand up immediately, his magazine falling to the floor.

"Really?" I ask.

Mom nods, a smile overtaking her entire face, and I realize that she's crying. I can't remember many times when I've seen my mom cry without half a glass of wine in her system. Maybe when Sleater-Kinney announced their reunion tour and she got super emotional, but that's about it.

"Is everything okay?" I ask, panicked.

"More than okay. She's perfect. She's beautiful. I mean, you and Abbi were beautiful babies, but she is just next level."

"I'll try not to be insulted by that," I say as Dad and I follow Mom, but I notice that she said I was a beautiful baby.

I can hear other babies crying as we make our way down the corridor. I can't believe this is the moment I'm going to meet my niece. My niece! Even thinking the word feels weird. I'm an aunt—I thought aunts were, like, my aunt Jayne, who lives with her boyfriend and their yorkipoos, not sixteen-year-old girls.

Mom pushes open a door and waves us in. Abbi's sitting with her baby in bed, still in her hospital gown, her hair plastered to her forehead and every trace of makeup rubbed off her face. She looks exhausted.

She also looks happy—maybe the happiest I've ever seen her.

"Meet Margaret," Abbi says.

"Margaret?" I ask. "Like my middle name?"

"Yeah," Abbi says. "Duh, Jolie. Like your middle name. I wanted to name her after my number one birth partner, even if you weren't here for the big moment."

I'm not a big crier. I mean, I managed to make it through *Inside Out* without so much as smudging my eyeliner, and when I stub my toe I just let out a string of profanity. But this? Okay, I'll admit it. A few tears spring to my eyes.

"So, she's . . . okay?" I ask gingerly.

Abbi nods, not taking her eyes off Margaret. "We must've calculated my due date wrong, or maybe she was just ready to meet us a little early."

"Hi, Margaret," I say, reaching out a finger. Her teeny-tiny fingers curl around mine, and I gasp.

"Is she supposed to do that?" I whisper.

Everyone laughs, so I pretend I was joking.

"She's basically the strongest baby in the world," Abbi says, gazing at her. "And smart. And so, so beautiful."

A golf-ball-sized knot wells up in my throat. Abbi's right— Margaret is beautiful. And as Abbi starts talking about how she wants us to go get her pancakes from the hospital cafeteria because she's only had ice chips since she got here, I realize that Margaret's beauty has pretty much nothing to do with what she looks like. She's beautiful just for existing, for being this little perfect miracle that came early and still turned out okay. For having those little fingers that curl around mine, for bringing us all here and making us happy.

I think about all the time I've spent wondering why I couldn't look different, why I couldn't just look normal, pretty, beautiful. Would I want Margaret to ever feel that way about herself? No. It's literally her first day on earth, and I just met her, but I never, ever want her to feel like she's somehow not enough.

I just want everything for her already. Like, I want her to be an athlete or a doctor or an astronaut or a beauty queen or an artist or anything she could ever possibly dream of. I don't want her to be afraid of trying, or afraid of people looking at her, or afraid of failing publicly.

And maybe to actually help Margaret do everything she wants to do, I have to do the things I want to do, too, even if they're scary. Like how I was in the musical. Like how I made nonromantic friends with Noah. Like how I'm going to get surgery because I want to, and it's a risk, but some risks are worth taking. Like how it might be worth jeopardizing a friendship if there's something a whole lot bigger at stake.

"Welcome to the world, Margaret," I say.

Chapter Twenty-Nine

*A*bbi and Margaret get to come home from the hospital a couple of days later, so I spend the few days that are left before my surgery helping Abbi, waking up at three a.m. to find her bleary-eyed on the couch, holding a screaming Margaret to her boob and wailing, "I don't know why she won't eat!" But it gets better, or maybe we all just get used to it. Between the four of us, we can do it, and it makes me happy to see Abbi finally realize that she's not doing this alone.

Also, I'm still listening to *Deep Dive* whenever Derek posts a new episode. I can't decide if it makes things better or worse to hear his voice when I know that he doesn't want to talk to me.

Because the thing is, I miss him. And I like him. And I should've admitted that a long, long time ago, instead of being scared and assuming he couldn't possibly like me. When I think about the way he looked at Happy Endings, or the way he touched my hair in the art supply closet, I get chills. But I can't make him respond to my texts, or my calls, and I'm not exactly going to show up at his door to beg and grovel my way back into his heart. This isn't a television show, and grand gestures tend to be a lot creepier when they're attempted in real life.

Maybe I messed it up for good. Maybe being afraid to take a chance means I lost my best friend. Whatever it is, I'll just have to deal with it.

The night before my birthday—two nights before my surgery—Evelyn comes over to coo at Margaret and bring us a Stouffer's frozen lasagna.

"I tried to make you a casserole," she says, "but I started watching the episode of *Golden Girls* where Dorothy, Rose, and Blanche end up in prison, and it burned and set off the smoke alarm. I guess cooking's not my thing." She shrugs, unperturbed.

"That's okay," I say, preheating the oven. "This is perfect. Anyone who claims they don't love frozen lasagna is a dirty rotten liar."

"Exactly," Evelyn says, grabbing a seat at the kitchen island. "So where is she?"

I smile. "I'm a little offended that you don't care about seeing me, but I get it. She's napping, but you'll hear her when she wakes up. The entire street will hear her. So how's Marla?"

Evelyn smiles. "Just as batshit determined and intense as ever. Which I love. She's building a house with Habitat today, or she would've come over with me."

"Too bad," I say unconvincingly. I get that Evelyn likes her and I'm all for being a supportive friend, but I'm still kind of scared of Marla.

"But my life is boring and drama-free," Evelyn says, putting her hands on the island and leaning forward like she's in a boardroom-meeting scene in a movie about lawyers. "Let's talk about you. Your surgery is in two days! Are you freaking out?"

"Yeah," I say, and then I think about it for a minute. "Actually, no. I think I had, like, some sort of existential epiphany when I saw Margaret for the first time."

Evelyn looks at me skeptically.

"It's like . . . whatever's going to happen is going to happen. I can't not take a chance because I'm scared. I don't want to have severe jaw pain for the rest of my life. I don't want to have a hard time chewing my food. And, yeah, I want my teeth to meet and for my smile to look different. And I can't not do that because I'm scared."

"Wow," Evelyn says, impressed. "Jolie Peterson, dropping wisdom. Maybe you should write a memoir and get it on Oprah's Book Club so you can talk about what you've learned."

"I just wish I'd learned it a little earlier," I say. "You know, before I ruined everything with Derek."

Evelyn purses her lips, opens her mouth and shuts it. Then finally she says, "How long have you liked him?"

I think about it. "I guess . . . I guess I always did. But I never thought he could possibly like me, not the way I am. I just thought we could keep on going the way we were, where he had some might-as-well-be-fake girlfriend in another state, and I didn't have a boyfriend, and it was pretty much like we were together, but with no kissing, or risk, or taking chances."

Evelyn snorts. "But where's the fun in that? Anyway, he'll come around. He's not going to let you go into surgery without saying something. I promise."

"Yeah. You're right."

We hear Margaret's cry come from the nursery, followed by a frustrated groan from Abbi.

"So," Evelyn says, "did you complete everything on your list?"

I almost laugh. My whole list seems so silly now, after everything that's happened over the past two months. Who cares about any of it? But I can think of one thing I really want to do before my surgery.

"Actually . . . do you want to help me with something?" I ask.

Evelyn claps her hands. "Anything."

I run upstairs, reach under my bed, and pull out my scrapbook. I flip through its pages one last time, past the perfect faces of all those girls. Past their straight teeth and their symmetrical smiles. Maybe I'll look like them after my swelling goes down . . . or maybe I won't. I don't care anymore. Because no matter how my jaw looks, I'm still the same Jolie.

I run back downstairs, scrapbook in hand, and wave it at Evelyn. "You want to have a bonfire?"

"Is that your creepy face scrapbook?" Evelyn asks, tilting her head. "Sure."

So we do. I mean, sure, my dad has to come out and help because it turns out neither of us knows how to build a fire. To his credit, he doesn't ask why I'm burning a scrapbook full of cutout magazine pictures of women, even though it probably makes me look like a serial killer. My mom even comes out, and although she doesn't know about my scrapbook, when Evelyn tells her we're having a "feminist bonfire moment," she yells, "DOWN WITH THE PATRIARCHY!" and we have to remind her that we have neighbors.

After the scrapbook is reduced to ashes and the wood my dad found is still burning, Abbi brings out some graham crackers, marshmallows, and Hershey bars. And as I eat s'mores in front of the fire with my family and one of my best friends, I truly couldn't care less how I look.

I'm not allowed to eat after midnight on the night before my surgery—my birthday—so we celebrate by going to a big family dinner at Gionino's that day. We bring Margaret, and even though Abbi's worried she's going to scream, she sleeps through the whole meal. Evelyn brings over cupcakes later and hangs out for a while, but I still miss having Derek around. But I didn't run into any waiters or cover myself in marinara sauce at Gionino's, so the night's a success.

I eat my leftovers as close to midnight as I can because I'm terrified of being hungry when I go into surgery, and then I head to bed to have what will surely be garlic-fueled nightmares.

After a few minutes of tossing and turning, my phone buzzes. It's a notification that there's a new episode of *Deep Dive*, which is weird, because Derek just posted a new one yesterday. Even though he's not on a schedule, per se, he doesn't usually post two episodes so close together.

Since I can't sleep, I hit play right away.

Derek usually starts each episode with a geeky preamble, his explanation of why he's interested in whatever it is that he's talking about. But this time, he launches right into it.

"The night my dad died, I couldn't sleep. Obviously. I mean, who could just fall into a blissful slumber after the worst day of their lives?"

I actually gasp, alone in my room.

"But eventually I did sleep, even if it was only for a couple hours. And when I woke up, at first, everything was fine. There was that moment—just a few seconds—before I remembered what had happened. When I was just a kid whose dad *hadn't* had a heart attack at work the day before. When I was just a kid whose life was the same as it had always been.

"But then—*bam!*—it all hit me, and it was like I was experiencing it all over again. And that's how it was every morning. Waking up happy, and then feeling the worst feeling, losing my dad over and over again."

I exhale shakily. This is by far the most Derek's ever said about his dad, even if it's to an audience of mostly Danish citizens.

"But eventually, that stopped. I woke up already knowing he was gone, and I didn't have to deal with that awful moment of realizing it all over again. You'd think that would make me feel better, right? But it didn't. It made me feel a lot worse. Because I had been living for those few seconds every morning—the only time I felt like my dad was still alive. And when I didn't get those anymore, well, it was then that I realized he was really gone. Waking up without him was normal."

I swallow hard.

"I talk about a lot of things on *Deep Dive*. And those are all really things I'm obsessed with, don't get me wrong—I'm not acting like I'm not a huge nerd about marine life and cave paintings and all the other stuff I talk about every week. But I spend most of my time thinking about my dad, and none of my time talking about him. And I just realized—or I guess someone helped me realize—that I can't just crowd him out of my brain with a bunch of facts about lemurs. That's not gonna make it hurt any less. And maybe if I do at least acknowledge him . . . well, it won't make it better, but it's not gonna make it any worse.

"This has been Derek Jones. Stay deep."

I can feel my heart beating in my throat. So this wasn't him contacting me, it wasn't our usual jokes, it wasn't a pep talk. It wasn't him declaring that he's totally, madly in love with me even though I screwed up.

But it feels like a whole lot more.

I think about what Evelyn asked me earlier, if I completed everything on my list, and I realize that I haven't actually thought about the list since my kiss with Noah.

When Evelyn created the list, she shared it with me on the list app we both have on our phones, so I scroll through it before I fall asleep.

Eat all the appetizers at Applebee's? Check.

Read *Jane Eyre*? Check.

Jump off the Cliff? Sort of check. At least Peter accomplished this one.

Go to a bar? Check.

Run a mile? Ugh, check.

Kiss Noah Reed? Check, check, and check.

Drive a convertible? Well, I guess there's something to save for after surgery. If I make it through.

On the off chance that I do die during surgery tomorrow—and I realize that there's nothing I can do about that one way or the other—I know that I made these two months something really special. But not necessarily because I did everything on my list. It was because of all the things that happened on their own, the things I never could have predicted. I made friends with people I never would've thought I could. I became an aunt. I realized every kiss isn't a good one. I starred in a musical, for Pete's sake! And apparently I helped my best friend realize that he can talk about the worst day of his life.

I start a new list: "Jolie's New and Revised List of Things to Do After Surgery." There are only two items on it:

1. HANG OUT WITH EVELYN MORE.
2. STOP BEING AFRAID.

I share it with Evelyn, and she immediately texts me the kissy-face emoji. I think about grabbing my laptop so I can scroll through my favorite Reddit threads one last time, but I decide against it. Instead, I head to the bathroom to pee, but first I catch my reflection in the mirror.

Tomorrow morning will be the last time my face ever looks like this. I've hated this face, waged war with it, and covered it up as best I could, but for better or worse it's been mine for seventeen years. After tomorrow, I'll see a different face staring back at me from the mirror—at first, a swollen face, but then one with a smaller jaw and a straighter smile. This is what I've been wanting for years, but standing on the edge of all this change, I feel like I want to pause time and remember exactly what it feels like to be here now—in the before.

Once I'm back in bed, I close my eyes and try to settle into sleep. My thoughts are a tornado of anxieties—surgery, pain, recovery, change. But I have a feeling that this situation is a lot like kissing. No amount of worry or preparation or lists will help me; all I can do is put myself in Dr. Kelley's capable hands.

Chapter Thirty

I have to be at the hospital at the ungodly hour of seven a.m., but it's basically impossible to sleep when Margaret's crying, so I wake up at four.

"Hey," I say, walking into the nursery, where Abbi's breast-feeding Margaret in the rocking chair in the corner. There was a time in our lives when it would've been weird for me to see her boobs so much, but that time is definitely not now.

"Go back to bed!" Abbi says. "Don't you have to wake up in like an hour?"

"I can't sleep." I sit on the carpeted floor and enjoy the silence that now occurs only when Margaret is eating.

But I'm glad I'm up. There's a special kind of quiet that happens at four a.m., and while I don't necessarily want to get up this early for the rest of my life, I appreciate it.

"Are you all packed?" Abbi asks. She switches Margaret to the other breast, and Margaret lets out the most dramatic scream for the two seconds she isn't eating, like not having food *right now* is the worst thing that's ever happened to her. I realize that at this point in her life, it basically is.

"Yeah," I say, which is mostly true. I threw a bunch of stuff in a bag. The truth is, I couldn't really focus on what I might need—clothes to wear post-surgery, maybe my Kindle if I want to read—because there's still a part of me that believes there won't even be a post-surgery.

"You're going to be fine," Abbi says, as if she read my mind.

"I know," I say, picking at the carpet. "I'm just scared."

"You're allowed to be scared," Abbi says. "I'm scared every day now. It's just my way of life."

I smile. "Yeah, but you're rocking this whole mom thing."

She looks at me skeptically. "I haven't showered in four days. I don't think I'm rocking anything."

"Maybe you're rocking smelling bad."

"Probably. But just remember: You're going through a big change, but at the end of it, you're still going to be you. A surgery isn't going to change that."

"You're right." I think about going to make some breakfast, but then I remember I can't eat anything. "Ugh, not being able to eat sucks."

Abbi snorts. "Talk to me when you've been in labor all day and you've only eaten ice chips."

We sit there in companionable silence until Margaret finishes eating, at which point my mom pops her head in the door.

"Ready?" she asks.

I'm not sure I am, but I nod anyway.

Getting to the hospital and into the operating room is a blur, but then I'm there, on the table, as a nurse places a mask on my face. This is the moment I've been dreading and dreaming of for years. It feels surreal, but there's no time to think about it.

"Jolie, just count backward from one hundred, okay?" Dr. Kelley says.

"One hundred . . . ninety-nine . . . ninety-eight . . . ," I say shakily as I close my eyes.

I open them and see a nurse. At least I think she's a nurse. What if this is the afterlife, and she's an angel who's about to explain to me what's going on?

She smiles at me. "You're in recovery, Jolie."

I try to say, "Wait, already?" but my mouth is full of gauze and I feel a little bit like my head is surrounded by pillows. So I guess I'm not dead—presumably the afterlife doesn't involve surgery recovery.

"Just relax," she reassures me. "Your family will be in soon."

I close my eyes and when I open them again, Mom and Dad are standing over me. Mom's arms are crossed as she stares at me with concern.

"Oh!" she says with relief. "You're awake!"

"I'm not dead!" I try to say, but it comes out as a mumble.

"Shhhh." Mom puts her hand on my arm. "Just get some rest, okay?"

So I do. The next day passes in a confusing blur. I wake up to see a nurse changing something, my dad watching a soap opera on the television, my mom eating a pudding cup. And then they're telling me I can go home.

I feel groggy as a nurse pushes my wheelchair down the hospital corridor toward the exit, where Mom and Dad are waiting with the car. I'm wearing my clothes again, but I have no idea how they got on my body.

"Are you okay?" Mom asks as she helps me into the front seat.

I grunt my affirmation.

I feel the car door slam like a shock through my body, and then we're in motion.

"Jolie," Mom says from behind me. "You did great in the surgery—everything went even better than expected. But just as a warning, prepare yourself before you look in a mirror. Because you have some pretty major swelling."

"I can handle it," I mumble, and I glance in the passenger-side mirror as the scenery rushes past me in a woozy blur. I let out what can charitably be called a scream as I take in my current look: Right there above the words "Objects in Mirror May Be Closer Than They Appear," there's a person who kind of, sort of looks like me, but with cheeks like a cartoon chipmunk and ice packs secured to the sides of her face with what appears to be a scarf made of gauze.

"What happened to me?" I try to ask, but it comes out as "Mwah mummuh mummuh?"

Luckily, Dad understands me, or at least guesses what I'm trying to say. "Your face looks pretty gnarly right now—"

"Tim!" Mom says.

"—but this is temporary. Dr. Kelley said this amount of swelling is totally normal and nothing to worry about."

But as I look at myself in the mirror again, I'm kind of worried. Telling yourself you'll be swollen and then actually seeing your own swollen face are two different things. Blood-tinged gauze pokes out of my mouth, and I look like I'm starting to get a black eye. This is like that time when Abbi got her wisdom teeth out, but way, way worse.

"Urrrrgh," I gurgle before falling asleep again.

When I wake up, I'm on the sofa at home, and Abbi's looking down at me.

"Do you want some chicken broth?" she asks.

Truth be told, I want pizza or chicken wings or potato chips or, like, anything chewy or crunchy or crispy, but I know that's not an option, so I sit up and take the bowl from her. I'm just glad I didn't have to have my mouth wired shut, which is the case for some people who have underbite surgery—Dr. Kelley thought I could get by with just some screws holding my jaw in place. Of course, I still have my trusty braces—they'll be there for at least the next six months to make sure my teeth don't stage a rebellion and slide out of place.

"Tell me the truth," I say through my gauze, wincing as the pain reminds me that I need another dose of my meds. "How bad is it?"

Abbi looks away from me, then back at my face, then away again.

"That bad?" I ask.

"Well, I wouldn't say you look great," she says delicately. "But this is just temporary, remember?"

"Ugh," I say, then attempt to spoon a little bit of broth into my mouth. It dribbles down my chin.

"Jolie." Abbi leans over and puts her hand on my knee. "It's gonna be a rough few weeks, but it will be okay. It will be better than okay, because you did it. It's done."

I nod, then spill more broth on myself.

Abbi takes the bowl away from me. "We'll try this again later. You want to watch TV?"

"Yes," I say, so Abbi turns on some show that, as best as I can tell, is about serial killers. Or maybe private eyes. Or a hospital. I don't know; I'm on very strong painkillers.

That's what the next couple of weeks are like. I attempt to make use of my free time and catch up on all the shows I've been meaning to see, but I definitely don't have the mental ability to follow any sort of plot right now, so I resort to watching reality television. I fall asleep so often that it all becomes a blur of housewives yelling at each other, Kardashians staging zany stunts, and British people baking elaborate cakes.

I also get tired of soup pretty quickly, so I start using the blender to chop up anything and everything. Like, for example, a piece of leftover steak I found in the refrigerator, and slices of pizza.

One day in mid-June, I'm putting a can of SpaghettiOs into the blender (perhaps not my best idea, but desperate times call for desperate measures) when the doorbell rings. Abbi has just gotten Margaret to sleep, so I run to get the door before whoever it is rings the bell again and risks waking her up. At the last minute, I grab a dish towel to hold over my face—my swelling has gone down some over the past two weeks, but the bottom half of my face is still alarmingly big. I'd rather not field a lot of questions from whatever neighbor or political canvasser is at our door.

When I swing open the door, I couldn't be more shocked to see who's standing on our front porch.

Derek.

Chapter Thirty-One

We stare at each other for a moment, me gripping the doorknob with one hand and holding my dish towel over the bottom half of my face with the other.

"Hey," he says, and then, gesturing at my face, "Is . . . this a bad time?"

I shake my head. "No, just blending some SpaghettiOs. Come in."

He looks confused, but he doesn't question it. He hands me a glass container filled with something orange. "Mom sent over some soup for you. It's butternut squash with coconut milk and it's supposed to be heart-healthy or whatever."

"Tell her thanks for caring about my heart," I say as we walk into the kitchen. I put it in the fridge, and then I feel self-conscious because, well, our hearts have caused a lot of problems lately.

"Yeah, um." Derek looks around the room anxiously. "Can we talk?"

"Okay," I say, a little too high-pitched. "Let's go sit down."

"Do you . . ." Derek gestures toward the blender.

"Oh, no!" I squeak, my dish towel still in place. "The SpaghettiOs can wait."

We sit down on the couch in the living room in our respective Terrible Movie Night spots. I lean against the very comfortable, non-matching throw pillows Mom bought in an attempt to be stylish yet edgy, and Derek turns to face me. I don't put my feet on him, because this seems like a feet-free conversation.

Finally, Derek is here, right in front of me. Now that I'm not flinging text messages into the void, I'm about to launch into one of my much-rehearsed speeches when Derek takes a deep breath and says, "Do you remember the loneliest whale?"

Out of all the things I thought he might say, this wasn't one of them. "What?" I ask.

"You know, the whale I told you about when I was doing *Deep Dive* research. The one who's just roaming around the ocean, making weird whale noises that are unintelligible to other marine life."

"Uh . . . yeah," I say, still unsure where he's going with this.

"I've been thinking a lot about that whale, and not just because it's a ridiculous story and I spent so long researching it. I've been thinking about what you said to me at the party, about how I should talk about my dad sometimes . . ."

"I shouldn't have said that," I mumble from behind my dish towel.

He shakes his head. "No, you were right. Because I'm always thinking about him, even if I'm not saying anything out loud.

And I don't *want* to be the loneliest whale, you know? I don't want to swim around all by myself, with no one understanding anything I'm actually going through."

I smile a little bit, even though he can't see it. "You're not the loneliest whale."

He doesn't look at me. "I talked to my mom about it—for basically the first time ever—and I'm starting therapy next week. I think it'll help."

"That's great!" I say encouragingly.

He shakes his head. "But that's not why I'm here. I feel like such a jerk for what I did. Or the way I did it, I guess. I had a crush on you, so I read into what you were saying and doing."

My mouth drops open in shock, but of course he can't see that behind my dish towel.

"And, honestly, Melody and I had needed to break up for a pretty long time, so I don't regret that. But I *do* regret ambushing you at Toby's party. That was shitty, and I'm sorry about it. It's cool if you don't have feelings for me—or, it's not cool, but it's okay. You're my best friend—you're the person who helped me realize that I can't just never talk about my dad—and I don't want to lose you."

He looks down at his hands. I realize that they're shaking.

I swallow. "You had a crush on me?"

Derek stares at me. "What?"

"Is it past tense? You *had* a crush? Or do you still have it?"

Derek's shoulders slump. "Jolie," he says softly. "Please don't do this to me. I want us to be friends, but we can't if you're gonna make me—"

"Because I have a crush on you," I say. "And I have for, like, forever, even though I didn't really know it. I'm glad you broke up with Melody, and I'm glad you said you liked me. I'm the one who should apologize for being too scared to do anything about it. But I'm not scared anymore."

Derek opens and closes his mouth, looks at the ceiling and then at me. "Then why . . ."

I shrug. "Because what if it doesn't work out? What if we kiss and it totally sucks? Or what if we start hating each other? I've spent my entire life thinking that there's something wrong with me, so I just assumed you thought there was something wrong with me, too. I figured there was no way you could ever possibly like me, and you only wanted me once I was going to be fixed—"

"You didn't need to be fixed," Derek interrupts me, but I hold up a hand to stop him.

"I just never let myself think about what it would be like if you liked me back, because I never thought you *could*. And now that I know you do, well . . . the thought of us trying and it not working and us not being friends anymore makes me want to barf. But the thought of not trying . . . it kind of makes me want to barf, too."

"Barfing is sort of a thing with you," Derek says, a small smile playing across his face.

"I regret bringing up barfing at a time like this," I say.

"I have a question."

My heart skips around in my chest, and I will it to stay in place. "Okay."

"Can I kiss you? Now?"

The unfairness of this moment suddenly feels unbearably heavy. "No."

"I am . . . very confused," Derek says.

"My jaw," I say. "Not only do I not want you to see my swollen face, but I wouldn't even be able to feel a kiss right now. And I want to feel it."

Derek smirks. "Let me see."

I shake my head.

"*Come on,*" he says, drawing out the words like this is a joke. "Rapunzel, Rapunzel, let down your dish towel."

I sigh, then let it drop.

"Jolie," he says, leaning forward and looking straight at me. "I like you, and I think you're beautiful. I would think you were beautiful if you looked like Nicolas Cage, or Nicolas Cage with John Travolta's face in the terrible movie *Face/Off.* And when your cheeks aren't swollen to three times their normal size, I'm going to kiss you, okay?"

I nod, swallowing hard.

He leans forward and my breath catches in my throat. His lips brush softly against my forehead, one of the few places on my head that actually isn't swollen. And even though my lips aren't involved at all, it feels like fireworks. Like soda bubbles. Like a red convertible.

"Ahem."

We look up to see Abbi standing in front of us, holding the baby, giving me a meaningful look.

"This is Margaret," she says to Derek. "Are you staying for dinner?"

Derek looks at me. I nod.

"Yeah," he says. "I'm gonna stay."

Chapter Thirty-Two

*I*n August, a couple of weeks before senior year starts, Abbi has a party to celebrate Margaret's birth. "I wanted to wait until your head wasn't the size of Texas," she says. "And also until I wasn't wearing a robe all day."

I'm definitely still swollen, but my face is emerging from all the puffiness. I still can't chew anything hard, but I have been eating soft things, like scrambled eggs and the occasional Twinkie (listen, I got tired of smoothies).

The most ridiculous thing is that even though I know I look different, I don't *feel* any different. I thought that after my surgery I would look in the mirror and suddenly feel confident. I thought I'd know, deep in my bones, that I was beautiful. But when I look in the mirror, I just see . . . me, with a slightly different jaw. The exact same Jolie: daughter, sister, friend, aunt, Terrible Movie fan, and musical star.

It would be hilarious if it weren't so depressing that I wasted so much time wishing to look different. All the time I spent on that scrapbook, all the time I spent smiling with my lips closed . . . and after all that, I was just fine all along. Who knew? Everyone except me, apparently.

But it feels good that both Abbi and I are officially on the road to recovery. Yes, I'm going to be a little swollen for a while, and yes, she's constantly complaining about her nipples being sore, but still. We're getting there.

Pretty much everyone we know is in our backyard, enjoying the beautiful summer early evening. Abbi is wearing a pink floral dress that, of course, looks great on her, just like literally every article of clothing does. And I stole one of her (pre-pregnancy) dresses, a yellow sundress that I never would've worn before because it's too bright and draws too much attention. But I don't care; I'm not afraid of attention anymore.

Abbi invited some of her friends from school, and they're all standing beside the punch table cooing over Margaret, who's doing a very good job of being cute. My aunt Jayne is here with her yorkipoos, one of whom definitely pooped on the patio already. Mom created a killer all-female playlist that she titled Mothers of Modern Rock in honor of Abbi's new status as a mom, so we're listening to that instead of bro-country like every other backyard in Brentley. Dad's sitting on one of the benches he made just for this party, happily eating a pulled pork sandwich. There are twinkle lights hung above the patio and a few yellow "Welcome, Baby!" balloons bobbing in the gentle breeze.

"She's a great baby," Evelyn says when I find her and Marla holding hands by the food table.

I nod. "Maybe I'm biased, but I think she's the smartest baby in the world."

Evelyn shakes her head. "Nah. That sounds like a perfectly objective opinion."

"This bruschetta is amazing," Marla says, pronouncing it correctly. "Who did your catering?"

"My dad," I say. "Under the guidance of many Food Network stars."

I look at the table and realize our supply of pulled pork sliders has been seriously depleted. "I'm gonna run into the kitchen and grab some more food," I say.

The kitchen hums with pleasant stillness because everyone's outside. I'm about to open the Crock-Pot and assemble more sandwiches when I hear the front door creak open. I assume it's another one of Abbi's friends, but then Derek steps into the kitchen.

"Hey," he says. He's dressed up a little—for Derek, anyway—in a short-sleeved button-down striped with blue, gray, and pink. It's not tight, but it's definitely snug enough to cling to his somehow lean-yet-muscular chest and oh God, I just realized I've been staring at him without saying anything for way too long.

"Hey," I sputter, unable to come up with something less inane. I haven't seen him all week because he's been volunteering at the twins' soccer camp, although he did become a much more frequent texter by constantly sending me pictures of them practicing. Seeing him now feels like everything good—like jumping into a pool on the hottest, sweatiest summer day. Refreshing, exhilarating, a little bit of a free fall.

"Do you want a pulled pork slider?" I offer, my hands shaking so much that I almost drop the Crock-Pot lid. *This is Derek*, I remind myself. *No need to be nervous.* But things are different now—in a good way, I think, although I don't really like this awkwardness.

He shakes his head. "Maybe later. But right now I have something outside I want to show you."

I throw the lid back on the Crock-Pot with a clatter. Who

cares about pulled pork right now? I follow him out onto the front porch, where he points at the street.

"Um," I say, my eyes scanning the front yard. "What am I looking at?"

"Right there," he says, pointing to the curb.

It's a red convertible.

"My uncle let me borrow it," he says. "I figured you didn't check this item off your list before surgery, so why not do it now?"

Maybe it's a little bit of overkill to say that my jaw drops after it's already been broken and surgically moved into place, but that's what happens. I can't say anything. Derek found a red convertible?

As we walk toward it, Derek stops. "Wait, is it rude to leave the party? Do you need to tell them where you're going?"

I shake my head slowly, still staring at the car. "No. Or maybe. But I don't care."

He laughs, then tosses me the keys.

"Wait, are you serious?" I ask. "I'm supposed to drive this?"

"Wasn't that the plan?"

"Well, yeah, but . . ."

Derek hops into the passenger seat. "Take me to the playground."

I just stare at him from the sidewalk.

"I'm waiting, Jolie," he says, and right at that moment his smile is so winning that I would take him literally anywhere he asked. Because this scenario, this fantasy I had of driving a red convertible and having my surgery, it's all real and it feels so much better than I ever thought it would.

I drive slowly, coming to a full stop at every stop sign and looking both ways about fifteen times at each one.

"This is a car," Derek says. "It's not made out of blown glass.

I think the saying is 'Drive it like you stole it,' not 'Drive it like you're a ninety-five-year-old woman with limited vision.'"

"Shut up, I need to concentrate," I say, my hands gripping the wheel. The last thing I want to do is crash Derek's uncle's convertible. That would put a serious dent in my fantasy, as well as, presumably, the car.

We pull into the parking lot of the playground, and now I realize I don't know why we're here. As we get out of the car, the streetlights pop on. There's no one here except for a few kids practicing on the tennis courts, and other than the sounds of the tennis balls hitting their rackets, all I can hear is the hissing of the summer insects. I look at Derek expectantly.

He waves me along, so I follow him.

"Did you bring me here to show off how good you are at the balance beam?" I ask as we walk past the swing set. I run my fingers over the chains. "Because frankly, that's not so impressive at our age."

Derek stops walking, and I realize where we are. By the slide, under the oak tree.

The site of our first kiss.

"Oh," I say.

"Jolie," he says, and his voice cracks. He's nervous. How could Derek, *my* Derek, be nervous about kissing me? I realize he's gearing up for some big speech, like this is a debate he's practiced for (and if I know Derek, he probably did practice for it).

But whatever he's going to say, it doesn't matter, because we're way, way past words now.

"Just shut up," I say, closing the space between us. Our lips meet and move and it's a little awkward, trying to figure out how to do this brand-new thing with someone I've known my whole life. My hands kind of hover over him as I try to figure out where to put them, but then he wraps his arms around me and I instinctively grab his shoulders. He bumps into my teeth and his lips scrape my braces as we laugh, which sort of makes it okay—like we both realize that this is weird, but good, and we can figure it out together.

Abbi was right: This isn't something you can learn from a book, or by taking notes, or by googling. This is one hundred percent trial by fire, something I had to leap into, a risk I had to take. And then suddenly, it's not so awkward anymore and it feels very, very natural to be kissing Derek Jones. I can't believe I wasted time before my surgery not doing this, that we were friends for so long when we could've been . . . well, friends who *kiss*. My hands grip his shoulders a little harder, and even though I've touched him a million times before, this is different. This is better.

I pull back and look at his eyes, those kind brown eyes I've seen almost every day since I was in kindergarten.

"How's your mouth feel?" he asks. "Numb?"

I shake my head slowly and blink a few times, realizing why people say they have stars in their eyes. It's like my head is floating through the cosmos, planets spinning in front of my face. The bottom part of my face is still a little numb and tingly, to be honest, but this is still ten million times better than my previous kissing experience.

I think about the things I spent my whole life avoiding, the time I spent hiding, the moments when I tried to make myself small and invisible. If only I'd known that this was on the other side of my fear, that all I had to do was let people see me. That I could get up in front of people and they would accept me, *all* of me. That I always deserved this, even when I thought I didn't, even when I thought I never could until I was "perfect" or "pretty" or "normal."

"Definitely not," I say. "I'm feeling everything."

Acknowledgments

When I was a kid, I used to read the liner notes of my Mariah Carey CD and dream about thanking everyone in my life on my eventual album. Well, now I get to do that, but luckily for all of us, I wrote a book instead of recording an album.

A huge thanks to my editor, Anna Roberto, for getting this book and Jolie's voice from the very beginning (and for appreciating all of my weird jokes).

Thank you so much to Stephen Barbara, Best Agent Ever. Thank you for answering all of my many (many, many) questions. I'm extraordinarily lucky to have you in my corner.

Thank you to the entire team at Feiwel and Friends, specifically Jean Feiwel, both for creating this marvelous imprint and for coming up with this book's title! Thanks to Kelsey Marrujo for all your hard work and the hundreds of emails you have to answer from me alone. And thanks to April Ward and Victor Bregante for creating such an eye-catching cover.

The biggest thanks possible to Lauren Dlugosz Rochford. Your feedback was essential to this book and I'm so grateful for your friendship! To paraphrase the great Kelly Clarkson, my books would suck without you.

Thank you to Catherine Stoner for being part of most of the moments that indirectly led to this book, and by that I mean making fun of that ABCs of Abstinence pamphlet.

Thank you to Alex Winfrey and Chase Winfrey for watching lots of terrible and not-so-terrible movies and television shows with me, from *Gilmore Girls* to *Magic Mike* to that Liberace biopic. A particular thank you to Alex for reminding me of the scoring system we created when we watched all those dance movies.

Thank you, as always, to my parents. I realize that not everyone has parents who encourage them to be creative. I'm thankful for everything you've done for the boys and me, whether that was paying for creative writing summer camp or building an art studio under the basement stairs. Sorry none of us turned out to be engineers, but you probably should've seen the signs.

Thank you to all of my friends and extended family members who have been so supportive and encouraging.

Thank you to Carly Rae Jepsen for recording the ideal book soundtrack.

Thank you to the independent bookstores that have been so supportive: Gramercy Books and the Book Loft in Columbus, Main Street Books in Mansfield, and Joseph-Beth Booksellers in Cincinnati.

Writing is lonely sometimes, and I'm thankful for the writers I've met who have reassured me that I'm not alone, particularly Jen Maschari and Emily Adrian.

To all the readers and bloggers who've been so kind and supportive: THANK YOU. A special thank you to Jen from Pop! Goes the Reader. Your blog is a beacon of positivity.

Thank you to Hollis for always thinking I'm J. K. Rowling, despite all evidence to the contrary. You believed in me from the very beginning, and I couldn't do this without you.

Biggest thanks to my cowriter/son, Harry. You were with me for this entire novel—literally, because sometimes I wrote while you were asleep on my chest. Mama loves you, little dude.

And lastly, to all the kids with underbites: I wrote this book because I had an underbite in high school. It was such a source of stress and pain for me, but I hope it isn't for you. You're fine the way you are, with surgery or without, and I hope it doesn't take you as long as it took me and Jolie to figure that out.